The five novels of *Cities of the Interior* were first published during the nineteen forties and fifties, and appeared in a complete sequence for the first time in 1959. They are all interconnected and, at the same time, entirely self-contained, appearing here in the order in which they were published. Sharon Spencer says in her Introduction that they 'can be envisioned as a type of moving – truly mobile – modern sculpture, intersecting and interacting as it moves, not only among its own discrete parts, but also with the surrounding context of life'. Together these novels form a rich tapestry whose overall theme Anaïs Nin described as 'woman at war with herself'.

Volume One contains a Preface by Gunther Stuhlmann, editor of the *Journals,* an Introduction by Sharon Spencer and two of the five novels, *Ladder to Fire* and *Children of the Albatross.*

Anaïs Nin, who died in 1977, was a unique literary figure. Her books, in particular the bestselling *Delta of Venus,* have been published to great acclaim in France, Germany, Italy, Holland, Britain and the United States. The international publication of her *Journals,* which began in 1966, has been greeted as one of the major literary works of the twentieth century.

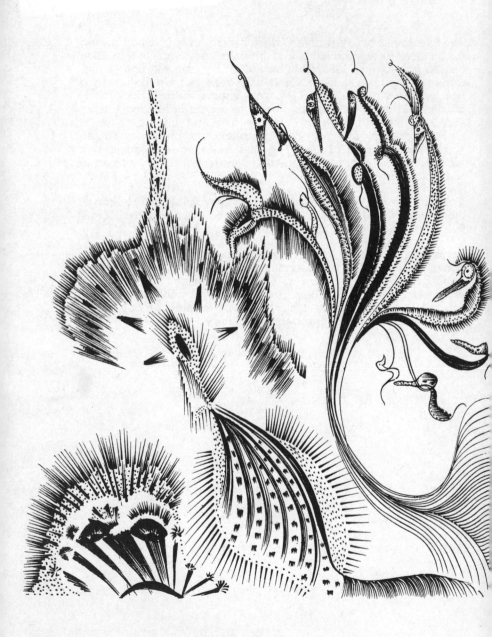

CITIES OF THE INTERIOR

Novels by Anaïs Nin

Volume 1

Introduction by Sharon Spencer

QUARTET BOOKS   *London   Melbourne   New York*

This paperback edition published by
Quartet Books Limited 1979
A member of the Namara Group
27 Goodge Street, London W1P 1FD

First published in Great Britain in one volume by
Peter Owen Limited, London, 1978

Printed in Great Britain by
Redwood Burn Limited, Trowbridge & Esher

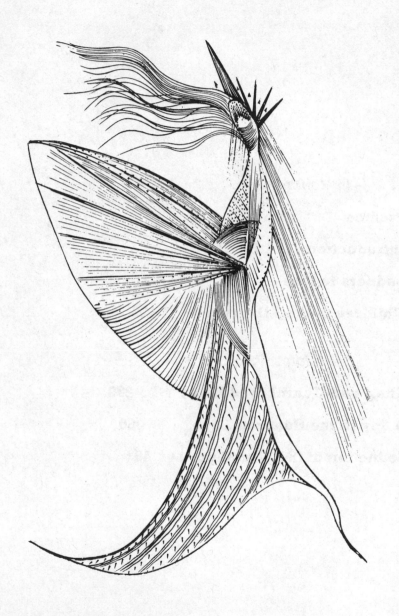

Preface

"The story of *Cities of the Interior* has never been told," Anais Nin wrote in the preface to the American edition of this book, "and it is time to clear up misunderstandings. I have never planned my novels ahead. I have always improvised on a theme. My only preconception was that it was to be a study of women. The first book turned out to be *Ladders to Fire*. All the women I was to write about appeared in it, including Stella, whom I later dropped because she seemed so complete in herself rather than related to the other women."*

When she first explained to her American publisher that *Ladders to Fire* was "part of a larger design, and that other novels would follow and round out the characters," her editors were, as she put it, "aghast", since there would be no readership accustomed to the concept of a *"roman fleuve"* – the public would not buy a novel which threatened to continue somewhere in the future. Thus, the book was published as an independent novel and "nothing was said about development and continuity."

* *Stella*, together with two other novelettes, *Winter of Artifice* and *The Voice*, and the prose poem *House of Incest*, was published in Great Britain in 1974, under the title *Winter of Artifice*.

"I began the next novel, *Children of the Albatross*," Anais Nin explained, "as if it were a new story. I did not develop a method of linking the various narratives. Though the same characters appeared, the theme was altogether different." The second novel appeared a year after the first, and neither the readers nor the reviewers made any attempt to link the two books.

The third novel, *The Four-Chambered Heart*, did not appear for another three years, and once more no effort was made to link this book to the preceding ones. "Unlike Lawrence Durrell's *Quartet*, which was openly described as a unity, my novels (in a much earlier period) appeared without explanation." "Much was lost," Anais Nin felt, "by never stressing the continuity and interrelatedness of the novels." By the time the fourth book, *A Spy in the House of Love*, was published four years later, "the continuity was totally erased."

A Spy in the House of Love was followed by *Solar Barque*, a small book which focused on an episode in Lillian's life. It was published privately, four years after *Spy*, and, at the time, Anais Nin "thought it contained all I wished to say, but like a piece of music which continues to haunt one, the theme continued to develop in my head; and I took it up again and carried it to completion."

Solar Barque eventually became the first part of a new title, *Seduction of the Minotaur*, published by her American publisher, Alan Swallow, in 1961. But once more no explanation of the genesis of this title was given.

By bringing all these books together under the present title, *Cities of the Interior*, the continuity of Anais Nin's novels has been established for the first time. "Now that the links between the novels are made clear," she stated a few years before her death in Los Angeles early in 1977, "I hope the journey through the *Cities of the Interior* will be deeper and less difficult."

GUNTHER STUHLMANN
Becket, Mass., January 1978

Introduction

The Novel as Mobile in Space

T HE FIVE NOVELS OF *Cities of the Interior* were published individually during the 1940s and 1950s, a period that was unreceptive to introspective, lyrical prose. They met with critical misunderstanding and a hostility that has gradually mellowed into a grudging recognition by the U.S. literary establishment of Anaïs Nin's achievement in fiction. This has come about partly because of the publication beginning in 1966 of the volumes of Nin's great *Diary,* whose impact on the public has made people more aware of her other books at the same time that it has obscured them with its own fascinations.

But *Cities of the Interior* is itself a masterpiece. Like other arresting and original syntheses of life in art, this work, a set of five interconnected novels, presents difficulties to the general reader. The assumptions about reality that underlie its conception and the vision for a model of its composition are not those of the main influences on North American culture and, in fact, have been and are still current only among a small but growing group: people who believe that consciousness extends deeper than the data of the senses and far beyond the outlines of things and people.

The beliefs to which I refer go back in recent times to the Symbolist movement of the late nineteenth century, of which so great a poet as W. B. Yeats was a part, and in a much longer expanse of time to eras occurring before the Renaissance and stretching back into centuries and cultures in which the magical, the irrational, that special blend of chemistry and mysticism called alchemy, and the infinite life of the spirit were simply taken for granted. Certainly, as envisioned by men such as Rimbaud, Apollinaire, the German Expressionist painters and poets, Kandinsky, Breton, Aragon, Artaud, and Kurt Seligman (author of the *The Mirror of Magic*), modernism was "new" in its enthusiastic acceptance of the discoveries of modern science, but old—ancient, in fact—in its insistence on the indivisibility of matter and spirit and the power of the unconscious to animate and rejuvenate a life that had become, under the dominance of analytical, empirical science, as mechanical as a clock, its substance as dry as the metal pieces that interlock behind the time-keeper's face.

Cities of the Interior is a modernist work, but it has had the misfortune to be published after the first exciting decades of the movement had passed, repressed in some countries, in others suppressed because of urgent social problems: economic depression, war, and the reaction of the "cold war" period. The individual novels as well as the one-volume edition of *Cities* that was published in 1959 appeared a few years before the rediscovery and return in the 1960s to many of the political and aesthetic beliefs and ideals that characterized modernism. Finally, even though Nin's novel-cycle is a Symbolist and modernist work (not a Surrealist one, as has often been said, or charged), it is a timeless creation. *Cities of the Interior* is the achievement in fiction of the alchemical transformation of ordinary life into art. This is what Nin has always been striving for in writing.

Transformation and animation are ideals that Nin has formulated and expressed in her *Diary* and has struggled to fulfill since she began writing at the age of eleven. In 1952 while admiring a collage that was the gift of Jean (Janko) Varda, whom Nin called a "Merlin," she was transported from depression to ecstasy. She wrote, "It was as if I had stepped out of my life into a region of sand composed of crystals, of transparent women dancing, airy dresses, figures which no obstacle could stop, who could pass through walls being themselves constructed of apertures which allowed the breeze through, the feeling that through these floating figures with openings like windows, life could flow." Sadly, she concluded that Varda succeeded in expressing what she could not express because "his image being visible to the human eye was stronger than the moments I describe and enclose in a book."

Nin's sense of the relative impotence of words (she is a pianist's daughter) explains both why she has developed a poet's style in prose and why her writing has been so strongly influenced by the nonverbal arts. Motion, which she associates with freedom, has always been her great concern. Nin's writing is filled with images of ships, rivers, elevators, geological expeditions, voyages, excavations, labyrinths, tangled streets, prisons, cages, pools, dancing. "There is a way of living," she wrote, "which makes for greater airiness, space, ease, freedom. It is like an airplane's rise above the storms." For Nin the magic process through which psychic liberty is achieved is alchemy (art), the transformation of the ordinary or the base into the substance of highest value: gold. Except for the "charcoal burners," who wanted only money, serious alchemists envisioned the gold itself as symbolic. Their efforts were focused on a four-fold process to attain the gold, which the ancient alchemists regarded as the symbol of illumination and of salvation. For Nin, as for all of us who no longer believe in the power of churches to bestow illumination and salvation, the artist becomes a *voyant,* as Rimbaud said, or a wizard. Ingmar Bergman and Thomas Mann are among the many creators who have explored the theme of the artist as magician, a figure endowed with marvelous power.

With this aspiration and the ambition to explore the psyche of woman more deeply and more honestly than it had ever before been probed in fiction, Nin began in the late 1930s to write *Ladders to Fire,* the first published volume of the five novels. The fifth book is *Seduction of the Minotaur,* published in 1961, a portion of which is included in the one-volume edition of 1959, *Cities of the Interior: A Continuous Novel.* The timeless scope of this work is suggested in an obvious way by the metaphor "cities," which are, of course, ancient as well as modern. Nin set out to excavate the buried cities or psychic worlds of her three main characters: Lillian, Djuna, and Sabina. But the idea of continuity is much more complex. It suggests that the work is "open," like certain modern sculptures, that its creator intends it to extend into the surrounding space or context of life. At the same time that this book is not set off from life or carved out of it, bounded by the conventions of classically written symmetrical fiction with resolved conclusions, *Cities of the Interior* is always "open" to the addition of new parts. The five individual books are entirely self-contained. A reader can enjoy any one of them without moving to the other novels. A volume could be removed or a new one inserted into the cycle without in any way disturbing the overall composition. As Nin uses the word, "continuous" does not at all mean "to be continued." *Cities of the Interior* is not "continuous" in the sense of linear, progressive, or cumulative. There is no fixed starting point or concluding point. The books have been bound—because books, seemingly, *must* be bound —in the order in which they were written.

A reader can begin with any of the five volumes and move to the other four in any order. He will lose no essential connections. He can read one or two if he wishes, or even take up the novels in the reverse order of printing. In short, the five novels of *Cities of the Interior* are interchangeable in position in the total composition, which can be envisioned as a type of movable—truly mobile—modern sculpture, intersecting and interacting as it moves, not only among its own discrete parts, but also with the surrounding context of life. Nin's idea of continuity is circularity or total immersion in the movement of time. There are no beginnings and, as one of Nin's characters in *Collages* remarks, quoting the Koran, "Nothing is ever finished." In *Creative Evolution,* Bergson writes, "If matter appeared to us as a perpetual flowering, we should assign no termination to any of our actions."

To Nin life does, indeed, appear as a "perpetual flowering." In her novel cycle she has selected and expressed significant relationships and states of feeling and soul from the ever-changing, continuous process of the psychic lives of her three women figures. An alchemical motto reads: "Make a circle out of a man and a woman, out of this a square, out of this a triangle, make a circle and you will have the Philosopher's Stone." This geometric figure exactly illustrates the composition of *Cities of the Interior.* Imagine the outer circle as the total work, the five individual books as points on the circumference. Next, visualize inside this circle a triangle whose three points represent the women, each of whom suggests an element: Djuna, air; Sabina, fire; Lillian, earth. The square located within the triangle suggests the four novels which echo the symbolism of elements. In *Ladders* the earth-bound Lillian yearns to ascend to fire—passion—but must first descend the ladder to the fire—hell—of her own being. The design of *Children of the Albatross* is animated by the phosphorescent, airy, "transparent" children. At the end, Djuna's lover sails away to India. In *The Four Chambered Heart,* Djuna's own water voyage is a melancholy one as the houseboat she shares with Rango plies up and down the Seine, moving but not progressing. Finally, there is release, a baptism, as Djuna attempts to sink the boat. *A Spy in the House of Love* presents Sabina in images of fire and motion. At first she is represented as the firebird, but at the novel's close she is grounded, drooping, exhausted by her flight from one man to another. The center both of the inner and of the outer circles, as in the alchemical motto, is woman and man, their relationship in all its many forms. In *Seduction of the Minotaur* earth, air, fire, and water are united as Nin traces Lillian's course through the labyrinth of self.

Seduction of the Minotaur is central not only to an understanding of Nin's aspirations in fiction but also to the cycle of *Cities* and its basis, no doubt unconscious on the author's part, in the process of alchemy. The book is set in Golconda, a place which inspires a passage of lyric improvisation. (When Nin took LSD she envisioned herself as liquid gold.) Lillian works at a club called the Black Pearl (black is connected with one of the four alchemical processes). Her journey to Mexico in time present brings Lillian a series of experiences which are superimposed on selected painful experiences of her childhood. The superimpositions are fused in images, all of which are symbolic: the labyrinth, a prison, a doctor and the process of healing, diving and swimming, excavations, dancing. Polarities are resolved; there are both solar and lunar barques to carry the bodies of the physically dead to realms beyond this terrestrial one; inner and outer merge in Lillian's battle with her own minotaur, the masked woman who is her false self or persona; time present, in which she has no deep relationship with a man but many friendships, restores to her a past love for her estranged husband, Larry.

Mythology suggests that one way of escaping from a labyrinth is by air (today there are remains of five labyrinths in Europe and Egypt). In alchemical emblems the release from suffering and dedication to spiritual striving (symbolized by the condition of gold) is often portrayed by a creature without wings being borne aloft by a winged creature. *Seduction* closes as Lillian leaves Mexico in an airplane; she meditates upon her new understanding of her self and of her past; her meditation promises the rejuvenation of love. In Nin's writing the "dream" is always the miracle of love fulfilled.

Archeologists and anthropologists speculate that terrestrial labyrinths, besides being replicas of the heavenly constellations, were used for rituals to prepare initiates for the experience of death. *Seduction of the Minotaur* includes the only death in Nin's fiction (before *Collages* of 1964). It is that of Dr. Hernandez, the most complex male character in *Cities of the Interior*; he is the healer who plays an important part in Lillian's cure. The murder of Dr. Hernandez brings sorrow to the novel's conclusion, but it is a natural sorrow, an acceptable grief because it is a part of life as essential as self-confrontation, joy, or love.

My own visually symbolic vision of *Cities of the Interior* is a very personal one, and it is intended merely as suggestive. Symbolism, distinct from allegory, is always fluid, particularly now that we have come to recognize the universe itself as open and the nature of reality as a constantly evolving process, an activity so rapid and so complex that we cannot apprehend it except by lifting from it certain still moments, composing these into images and forms which we can contemplate long enough to orient ourselves in the continuous process of time and change. Such instants of arrest or stasis are what artists give us in their compositions. Perhaps this has always been so, but modern artists, certainly Joyce, Proust, Woolf, and Faulkner, to name only a few, were fully aware that this was what they were doing when they composed novels, not representing a copy of reality but making a composition of significant moments selected from an endless process of such moments. Bergson designated these frozen instants as "snapshots."

Nin's writing is not, however, primarily visual. Her style and her structures are intimately related to the nonverbal arts of painting, dance, and music, not only in the obvious sense that she writes about artists, but more deeply, because she has so brilliantly adapted techniques of the other arts to prose. The visual arts appeal to her because of their power to bring images to life, to give them color; her characters often discover truths about themselves when they look at paintings. But Nin's writing is essentially musical, "symphonic," as she herself has said. Its beauty and its evocative power lie in the equally strong development of three modes of symbolism: words, characterizations, and structures. These are individually perfected, then fused by force of imagination into a synthesis that renders psychic states in images that are more rhythmic and auditory than visual. Painting brings to her writing color and solidity of forms outlined; through the music of her prose Nin places her characters within the flow of time, while dance suggests the constant interplay between the human being in motion, interacting as he moves with the space around him. If they are truly to live, Nin's characters are obliged to remain in motion. Although she recognizes that there is meaningless motion, like Sabina's flights from man to man, Nin insists upon ceaseless change as essential to psychic life.

This raises the question of Nin's concept of the self, a concept without which the construct of *Cities of the Interior* would not have been possible. Here an exchange of ideas with the analyst and brilliant thinker Otto Rank is important. His books *Art and Artist* and *Will Therapy and Truth and Reality* are essential to a reader with an interest in the creative personality. For Rank and for Nin, once his patient, the self is not an entity but a process. The self is never fixed, though it is the center of being; it is always forming and re-forming itself through relationships of identification, friendship, or love, and the endless absorption and interpretation of sensations, ideas, and experiences. The self is itself a mobile, a process, as Bergson argued, of constant becoming. At the same time, it is a tool, an instrument which serves to connect dimensions of consciousness and of reality. Nin wrote, "My self is like the self of Proust. It is an instrument to connect life and the myth." She has made many statements about the nature of the self, not so much in essence, as in its relationships with other people. Unequivocally, she wrote, "The quest of the self through the intricate maze of modern confusion is the central theme of my work." "We know," she has observed, "that *we are composites in reality,* collages of our fathers and mothers, of what we read,

of television influences and films, of friends and associates. . . ."
The self, then, is condemned to submit to constant motion, to change; if it is to grow, it is committed to a life of constant transition between its own boundaries, which are never fixed, and the equally fluid territories of other people's psyches. It is precisely through this constant process of change, adjustment, and readjustment that the self discovers and rediscovers itself or, in short, lives. Through knowing others we form ourselves and perceive the world. Nin writes, "I could identify with characters unlike myself, enter their visions of the universe, and *in essence* achieve the truest objectivity of all, *which is to be able to see what the other sees, to feel what the other feels.*"

This act of fusion or of merging with another, however, poses the threat of loss of self. This is both a danger and a challenge. Nin has made this challenge the subject of her fiction. Again and again she probes relationships of fusion. Usually they involve a man and a woman, but sometimes, as in *Ladders to Fire,* she explores the way in which members of the same sex seek to strengthen their sense of self by intense identification with another. In every intense and intimate relationship there is the peril that the self of the weaker may be submerged in that of the stronger, but if it is not, if both persons maintain their authenticity, act and are acted upon, then both will have evolved.

Imagine the self as Jung does, as the center of being, including all dimensions, conscious and unconscious. Then imagine that this center possesses the power of motion. The very center, the self, changes and moves, thus moving the entire circle of the self and affecting each ray that extends toward the circumference. We return to the image of the circle. It is only apparently fixed and immobile. When the center moves, so does the entire form, turning endlessly when growth is constant, holding into meaningful form an ever-evolving pattern of energy. Nin as the author is at the center of *Cities of the Interior.* At different times and under the pressure of various influence, Nin herself evolves into the personages of her characters. Of course, they are, as many have observed, aspects of her self. So are the characters of all novelists. As the author evolves, so do her characters, engaging in relationships with one another and with the secondary characters (often comic glosses on the main figures). The concept of the novel as a continuous creation, a mobile turning in space, is made possible by the concept of the self as a mobile turning in space, the space of experiences and of other people.

I return to the figure of the dance. Partly, it was the power of dance that attracted Nin to the women in Varda's collage. Djuna, the character who most resembles Nin, her persona at any rate, is a dancer, as Nin herself once was. Now we can see fused the ideas of art as alchemy, the perception of continuity as circular, and the meditative, worshipful interpretation of dance as observed in Eastern religions. In their book *Mandala*, José and Miriam Argüelles write: "The amazingly fluid capacity for transformation also describes the law upon which Shiva's dance is based—the dance of the continual turning of the four-spoked cosmic wheel whose hub is eternity, and which transforms everything as it gradually rolls along its course." The most beautiful and the most revealing image in all of Anaïs Nin's writing is the figure of the dancer with which *House of Incest* closes:

> And she danced; she danced with the music and with the rhythm of earth's circles; she turned with the earth turning, like a disk, turning all faces to light and to darkness evenly, dancing towards daylight.

The key to Anaïs Nin's "continuous" creation lies in this image. To enter it means that the reader too must learn to move to a new rhythm and into a deeper way of experiencing a novel.

SHARON SPENCER
New York City, 1974

Ladders to Fire

This Hunger

LILLIAN WAS ALWAYS in a state of fermentation. Her eyes rent the air and left phosphorescent streaks. Her large teeth were lustful. One thought of a negress who had found a secret potion to turn her skin white and her hair red.

As soon as she came into a room she kicked off her shoes. Necklaces and buttons choked her and she loosened them, scarves strangled her and she slackened them. Her hand bag was always bursting full and often spilled over.

She was always in full movement, in the center of a whirlpool of people, letters, and telephones. She was always poised on the pinnacle of a drama, a problem, a conflict. She seemed to trapeze from one climax to another, from one paroxysm of anxiety to another, skipping always the peaceful region in between, the deserts and the pauses. One marvelled that she slept, for this was a suspension of activity. One felt sure that in her sleep she twitched and rolled, and even fell off the bed, or that she slept half sitting up as if caught while still talking. And one felt certain that a great combat had taken place during the night, displacing the covers and pillows.

When she cooked, the entire kitchen was galvanized by the strength she put into it; the dishes, pans, knives, everything bore the brunt of her strength, everything was violently marshalled, challenged, forced to bloom, to cook, to boil. The vegetables were peeled as if the skins were torn from their resisting flesh, as if they were the fur of animals being peeled by the hunters. The fruit was stabbed, assassinated, the lettuce was murdered with a machete. The flavoring was poured like hot lava and one expected the salad to wither, shrivel instantly. The bread was sliced with a vigor which recalled heads falling from the guillotine. The bottles and glasses were knocked hard against each other as in bowling games, so that the wine, beer and water were conquered before they reached the table.

What was concocted in this cuisine reminded one of the sword swallowers at the fair, the fire-eaters and the glass-eaters of the Hindu magic sects. The same chemicals were used in the cooking as were used in the composition of her own being: only those which caused the most violent reaction, contradiction, and teasing, the refusal to answer questions but the love of putting them, and all the strong spices of human relationship which bore a relation to black pepper, paprika, soybean sauce, ketchup and red peppers. In a laboratory she would have caused explosions. In life she caused them and was afterwards aghast at the damage. Then she would hurriedly set about to atone for the havoc, for the miscarried phrase, the fatal honesty, the reckless act, the disrupting scene, the explosive

4

and catastrophic attack. Everywhere, after the storms of her appearance, there was emotional devastation. Contacts were broken, faiths withered, fatal revelations made. Harmony, illusion, equilibrium were annihilated. The next day she herself was amazed to see friendships all askew, like pictures after an earthquake.

The storms of doubt, the quick cloudings of hypersensitivity, the bursts of laughter, the wet furred voice charged with electrical vibrations, the resonant quality of her movements, left many echoes and vibrations in the air. The curtains continued to move after she left. The furniture was warm, the air was whirling, the mirrors were scarred from the exigent way she extracted from them an ever unsatisfactory image of herself.

Her red hair was as unruly as her whole self; no comb could dress it. No dress would cling and mould her, but every inch of it would stand out like ruffled feathers. Tumult in orange, red and yellow and green quarreling with each other. The rose devoured the orange, the green and blue overwhelmed the purple. The sport jacket was irritated to be in company with the silk dress, the tailored coat at war with the embroidery, the everyday shoes at variance with the turquoise bracelet. And if at times she chose a majestic hat, it sailed precariously like a sailboat on a choppy sea.

Did she dream of being the appropriate mate for the Centaur, for the Viking, for the Pioneer, for Attila or Genghis Khan, of being magnificently mated with Conquerors, the Inquisitioners or Emperors?

On the contrary. In the center of this turmoil, she gave birth to the dream of a ghostly lover, a pale, passive, romatic, anaemic figure garbed in grey and timidity. Out of the very volcano of her strength she gave birth to the most evanescent, delicate and unreachable image.

She saw him first of all in a dream, and the second time while under the effects of ether. His pale face appeared, smiled, vanished. He haunted her sleep and her unconscious self.

The third time he appeared in person in the street. Friends

5

introduced them. She felt the shock of familiarity known to lovers.

He stood exactly as in the dream, smiling, passive, static. He had a way of greeting that seemed more like a farewell, an air of being on his way.

She fell in love with an extinct volcano.

Her strength and fire were aroused. Her strength flowed around his stillness, encircled his silence, encompassed his quietness.

She invited him. He consented. Her whirlpool nature eddied around him, agitating the fixed, saturnian orbit.

"Do you want to come . . . do you?"

"I never know what I want," he smiled because of her emphasis on the "want," "I do not go out very much." From the first, into this void created by his not wanting, she was to throw her own desires, but not meet an answer, merely a pliability which was to leave her in doubt forever as to whether she had substituted her desire for his. From the first she was to play the lover alone, giving the questions and the answers too.

When man imposes his will on woman, she knows how to give him the pleasure of assuming his power is greater and his will becomes her pleasure; but when the woman accomplishes this, the man never gives her a feeling of any pleasure, only of guilt for having spoken first and reversed the roles. Very often she was to ask: "Do you want to do this?" And he did not know. She would fill the void, for the sake of filling it, for the sake of advancing, moving, feeling, and then he implied: "You are pushing me."

When he came to see her he was enigmatic. But he was there.

As she felt the obstacle, she also felt the force of her love, its impetus striking the obstacle, the impact of the resistance. This collision seemed to her the reality of passion.

He had been there a few moments and was already preparing for flight, looking at the geography of the room, marking the exits "in case of fire," when the telephone rang.

"It's Serge asking me to go to a concert," said Lillian with the proper feminine inflection of: "I shall do your will, not mine." And this time Gerard, although he was not openly and violently in favor of Lillian, was openly against Serge, whoever he was. He showed hostility. And Lillian interpreted this favorably. She refused the invitation and felt as if Gerard had declared his passion. She laid down the telephone as if marking a drama and sat nearer to the Gerard who had manifested his jealousy.

The moment she sat near him he recaptured his quality of a mirage: paleness, otherworldliness, obliqueness. He appropriated woman's armor and defenses, and she took the man's. Lillian was the lover seduced by obstacle and the dream. Gerard watched her fire with a feminine delectation of all fires caused by seduction.

When they kissed she was struck with ecstasy and he with fear.

Gerard was fascinated and afraid. He was in danger of being possessed. Why in danger? Because he was already possessed by his mother and two possessions meant annihilation.

Lillian could not understand. They were two different loves, and could not interfere with each other.

She saw, however, that Gerard was paralyzed, that the very thought of the two loves confronting each other meant death.

He retreated. The next day he was ill, ill with terror. He sought to explain. "I have to take care of my mother."

"Well," said Lillian, "I will help you."

This did not reassure him. At night he had nightmares. There was a resemblance between the two natures, and to possess Lillian was like possessing the mother, which was taboo. Besides, in the nightmare, there was a battle between the two possessions in which he won nothing but a change of masters. Because both his mother and Lillian (in the nightmare they were confused and indistinguishable), instead of living out their own thoughts, occupying their own hands, playing their own instruments, put all their strength, wishes, desires, their wills on him. He felt that in the nightmare they

7

carved him out like a statue, they talked for him, they acted for him, they fought for him, they never let him alone. He was merely the possessed. He was not free.

Lillian, like his mother, was too strong for him. The battle between the two women would be too strong for him. He could not separate them, free himself and make his choice. He was at a disadvantage. So he feared: he feared his mother and the outcries, the scenes, dramas, and he feared Lillian for the same reason since they were of the same elements: fire and water and aggression. So he feared the new invasion which endangered the pale little flame of his life. In the center of his being there was no strength to answer the double challenge. The only alternative was retreat.

When he was six years old he had asked his mother for the secret of how children were born. His mother answered: "I made you."

"You made me?" Gerard repeated in utter wonder. Then he had stood before a mirror and marvelled: "You made this hair? You made this skin?"

"Yes," said his mother. "I made them."

"How difficult it must have been, and my nose! And my teeth! And you made me walk, too." He was lost in admiration of his mother. He believed her. But after a moment of gazing at the mirror he said: "There is one thing I can't believe. I can't believe that you made my eyes!"

His eyes. Even today when his mother was still making him, directing him, when she cut his hair, fashioned him, carved him, washed his clothes, what was left free in this encirclement of his being were his eyes. He could not act, but he could see.

But his retreat was inarticulate, negative, baffling to Lillian. When she was hurt, baffled, lost, she in turn retreated, then he renewed his pursuit of her. For he loved her strength and would have liked it for himself. When this strength did not threaten him, when the danger was removed, then he gave way to his attraction for this strength. Then he pursued it. He invited and lured it back, he would not surrender it (to Serge or anyone

8

else). And Lillian who suffered from his retreat suffered even more from his mysterious returns, and his pursuits which ceased as soon as she responded to them.

He was playing with his fascination and his fear.

When she turned her back on him, he renewed his charms, enchanted her and won her back. Feminine wiles used against woman's strength like women's ambivalent evasions and returns. Wiles of which Lillian, with her straightforward manly soul, knew nothing.

The obstacle only aroused Lillian's strength (as it aroused the knights of old) but the obstacle discouraged Gerard and killed his desire. The obstacle became his alibi for weakness. The obstacle for Gerard was insurmountable. As soon as Lillian overcame one, Gerard erected another. By all these diversions and perversions of the truth he preserved from her and from himself· the secret of his weakness. The secret was kept. The web of delusion grew around their love. To preserve this fatal secret: you, Lillian, are too strong; you, Gerard, are not strong enough (which would destroy them), Gerard (like a woman) wove false pretexts. The false pretexts did not deceive Lillian. She knew there was a deeper truth but she did not know what it was.

Weary of fighting the false pretexts she turned upon herself, and her own weakness, her self-doubts, suddenly betrayed her. Gerard had awakened the dormant demon doubt. To defend his weakness he had unknowingly struck at her. So Lillian began to think: "I did not arouse his love. I was not beautiful enough." And she began to make a long list of self-accusations. Then the harm was done. She had been the aggressor so she was the more seriously wounded. Self-doubt asserted itself. The seed of doubt was implanted in Lillian to work its havoc with time. The real Gerard receded, faded, vanished, and was reinstated as a dream image. Other Gerards will appear, until . . .

After the disappearance of Gerard, Lillian resumed her defensive attitude towards man, and became again the warrior. It became absolutely essential to her to triumph in the smallest issue of an argument. Because she felt so insecure about her own value it became of vital importance to convince and win over everyone to her assertions. So she could not bear to yield, to be convinced, defeated, persuaded, swerved in the little things.

She was now afraid to yield to passion, and because she could not yield to the larger impulses it became essential also to not yield to the small ones, even if her adversary were in the right. She was living on a plane of war. The bigger resistance to the flow of life became one with the smaller resistance to the will of others, and the smallest issue became equal to the ultimate one. The pleasure of yielding on a level of passion being unknown to her, the pleasure of yielding on other levels became equally impossible. She denied herself all the sources of feminine pleasure: of being invaded, of being conquered. In war, conquest was imperative. No approach from the enemy could be interpreted as anything but a threat. She could not see that the real issue of the war was a defense of her being against the invasion of passion. Her enemy was the lover who might possess her. All her intensity was poured into the small battles; to win in the choice of a restaurant, of a movie, of visitors, in opinions, in analysis of people, to win in all the small rivalries through an evening.

At the same time as this urge to triumph continuously, she felt no appeasement or pleasure from her victories. What she won was not what she really wanted. Deep down, what her nature wanted was to be made to yield.

The more she won (and she won often for no man withstood this guerrilla warfare with any honors—he could not see the great importance that a picture hung to the left rather than to the right might have) the more unhappy and empty she felt.

No great catastrophe threatened her. She was not tragically struck down as others were by the death of a loved one at war.

10

There was no visible enemy, no real tragedy, no hospital, no cemetery, no mortuary, no morgue, no criminal court, no crime, no horror. There was nothing.

She was traversing a street. The automobile did not strike her down. It was not she who was inside of the ambulance being delivered to St. Vincent's Hospital. It was not she whose mother died. It was not she whose brother was killed in the war.

In all the registers of catastrophe her name did not appear. She was not attacked, raped, or mutilated. She was not kidnapped for white slavery.

But as she crossed the street and the wind lifted the dust, just before it touched her face, she felt as if all these horrors had happened to her, she felt the nameless anguish, the shrinking of the heart, the asphyxiation of pain, the horror of torture whose cries no one hears.

Every other sorrow, illness, or pain is understood, pitied, shared with all human beings. Not this one which was mysterious and solitary.

It was ineffectual, inarticulate, unmoving to others as the attempted crying out of the mute.

Everybody understands hunger, illness, poverty, slavery and torture. No one understood that at this moment at which she crossed the street with every privilege granted her, of not being hungry, of not being imprisoned or tortured, all these privileges were a subtler form of torture. They were given to her, the house, the complete family, the food, the loves, like a mirage. Given and denied. They were present to the eyes of others who said: "You are fortunate," and invisible to her. Because the anguish, the mysterious poison, corroded all of them, distorted the relationships, blighted the food, haunted the house, installed war where there was no apparent war, torture where there was no sign of instruments, and enemies where there were no enemies to capture and defeat.

Anguish was a voiceless woman screaming in a nightmare.

She stood waiting for Lillian at the door. And what struck Lillian instantly was the aliveness of Djuna: if only Gerard had been like her! Their meeting was like a joyous encounter of equal forces.

Djuna responded instantly to the quick rhythm, to the intensity. It was a meeting of equal speed, equal fervor, equal strength. It was as if they had been two champion skiers making simultaneous jumps and landing together at the same spot. It was like a meeting of two chemicals exactly balanced, fusing and foaming with the pleasure of achieved proportions.

Lillian knew that Djuna would not sit peacefully or passively in her room awaiting the knock on her door, perhaps not hearing it the first time, or hearing it and walking casually towards it. She knew Djuna would have her door open and would be there when the elevator deposited her. And Djuna knew by the swift approach of Lillian that Lillian would have the answer to her alert curiosity, to her impatience; that she would hasten the elevator trip, quicken the journey, slide over the heavy carpet in time to meet this wave of impatience and enthusiasm.

Just as there are elements which are sensitive to change and climate and rise fast to higher temperatures, there were in Lillian and Djuna rhythms which left them both suspended in utter solitude. It was not in body alone that they arrived on time for their meetings, but they arrived primed for high living, primed for flight, for explosion, for ecstasy, for feeling, for all experience. The slowness of others in starting, their slowness in answering, caused them often to soar alone.

To Djuna Lillian answered almost before she spoke, answered with her bristling hair and fluttering hands, and the tinkle of her jewelry.

"Gerard lost everything when he lost you," said Djuna before Lillian had taken off her coat. "He lost life."

Lillian was trying to recapture an impression she had before seeing Djuna. "Why, Djuna, when I heard your voice over the telephone I thought you were delicate and fragile. And you look fragile but somehow not weak. I came to . . . well, to protect you. I don't know what from."

Djuna laughed. She had enormous fairytale eyes, like two aquamarine lights illumining darkness, eyes of such depth that at first one felt one might fall into them as into a sea, a sea of feeling. And then they ceased to be the pulling, drawing, absorbing sea and they became beacons, with extraordinary intensity of vision, of awareness, of perception. Then one felt one's chaos illumined, transfigured. Where the blue, liquid balls alighted every object acquired significance.

At the same time their vulnerability and sentience made them tremble like delicate candlelight or like the eye of the finest camera lens which at too intense daylight will suddenly shut black. One caught the inner chamber like the photograper's dark room, in which sensitivity to daylight, to crudity and grossness would cause instantaneous annihilation of the image.

They gave the impression of a larger vision of the world. If sensitivity made them retract, contract swiftly, it was not in any self-protective blindness but to turn again to that inner chamber where the metamorphosis took place and in which the pain became not personal, but the pain of the whole world, in which ugliness became not a personal experience of ugliness but the world's experience with all ugliness. By enlarging and situating it in the totality of the dream, the unbearable event became a large, airy understanding of life which gave to her eyes an ultimately triumphant power which people mistook for strength, but which was in reality courage. For the eyes, wounded on the exterior, turned inward, but did not stay there, and returned with the renewed vision. After each encounter with naked unbearable truths, naked unbearable pain, the eyes returned to the mirrors in the inner chambers, to the transformation by understanding and reflection, so that they could emerge and face the naked truth again.

In the inner chambers there was a treasure room. In it dwelt her racial wealth of Byzantine imagery, a treasure room of hierarchic figures, religious symbols. Old men of religion, who had assisted at her birth and blessed her with their wisdom. They appeared in the colors of death, because they had at first endangered her advance into life. Their robes, their caps, were made of the heavily embroidered materials of rituals illumined with the light of eternity. They had willed her their wisdom of life and death, of past and future, and therefore excluded the present. Wisdom was a swifter way of reaching death. Death was postponed by living, by suffering, by risking, by losing, by error. These men of religion had at first endangered her life, for their wisdom had incited her in the past to forego the human test of experience, to forego the error and the confusion which was living. By knowing she would reach all, not by touching, not by way of the body. There had lurked in these secret chambers of her ancestry a subtle threat such as lurked in all the temples, synagogues, churches—the incense of denial, the perfume of the body burnt to sacrificial ashes by religious alchemy, transmuted into guilt and atonement.

In the inner chamber there were also other figures. The mother madonna holding the child and nourishing it. The haunting mother image forever holding a small child.

Then there was the child itself, the child inhabiting a world of peaceful, laughing animals, rich trees, in valleys of festive color. The child in her eyes appeared with its eyes closed. It was dreaming the fertile valleys, the small warm house, the Byzantine flowers, the tender animals and the abundance. It was dreaming and afraid to awaken. It was dreaming the lightness of the sky, the warmth of the earth, the fecundity of the colors.

It was afraid to awaken.

Lillian's vivid presence filled the hotel room. She was so entirely palpable, visible, present. She was not parcelled into a woman who was partly in the past and partly in the future, or one whose spirit was partly at home with her children, and partly elsewhere. She was here, all of her, eyes and ears, and hands and warmth and interest and alertness, with a sympathy which surrounded Djuna—questioned, investigated, absorbed, saw, heard. . . .

"You give me something wonderful, Lillian. A feeling that I have a friend. Let's have dinner here. Let's celebrate."

Voices charged with emotion. Fullness. To be able to talk as one feels. To be able to say all.

"I lost Gerard because I leaped. I expressed my feelings. He was afraid. Why do I love men who are afraid? He was afraid and I had to court him. Djuna, did you ever think how men who court a woman and do not win her are not hurt? And woman gets hurt. If woman plays the Don Juan and does the courting and the man retreats she is mutilated in some way."

"Yes, I have noticed that. I suppose it's a kind of guilt. For a man it is natural to be the aggressor and he takes defeat well. For woman it is a transgression, and she assumes the defeat is caused by the aggression. How long will woman be ashamed of her strength?"

"Djuna, take this."

She handed her a silver medallion she was wearing.

"Well, you didn't win Gerard but you shook him out of his death."

"Why," said Lillian, "aren't men as you are?"

"I was thinking the same thing," said Djuna.

"Perhaps when they are we don't like them or fear them. Perhaps we like the ones who are not strong. . . ."

Lillian found this relation to Djuna palpable and joyous. There was in them a way of asserting its reality, by constant signs, gifts, expressiveness, words, letters, telephones, an exchange of visible affection, palpable responses. They exchanged jewels, clothes, books, they protected each other, they expressed concern, jealousy, possessiveness. They talked. The relationship was the central, essential personage of this dream without pain. This relationship had the aspect of a primitive figure to which both enjoyed presenting proofs of worship and devotion. It was an active, continuous ceremony in which there entered no moments of indifference, fatigue, or misunderstandings or separations, no eclipses, no doubts.

"I wish you were a man," Lillian often said.

"I wish you were."

Outwardly it was Lillian who seemed more capable of this metamorphosis. She had the physical strength, the physical dynamism, the physical appearance of strength. She carried tailored clothes well; her gestures were direct and violent. Masculinity seemed more possible to her, outwardly. Yet inwardly she was in a state of chaos and confusion. Inwardly she was like nature, chaotic and irrational. She had no vision into this chaos: it ruled her and swamped her. It sucked her into miasmas, into hurricanes, into caverns of blind suffering.

Outwardly Djuna was the essence of femininity . . . a curled frilled flower which might have been a starched undulating petticoat or a ruffled ballet skirt moulded into a sea shell. But inwardly the nature was clarified, ordered, understood, dominated. As a child Djuna had looked upon the storms of her own nature—jealousy, anger, resentment—always with the knowledge that they could be dominated, that she refused to be devastated by them, or to destroy others with them. As a child, alone, of her own free will, she had taken on an oriental attitude of dominating her nature by wisdom and understanding. Finally, with the use of every known instrument—art, aesthetic forms, philosophy, psychology—it had been tamed.

But each time she saw it in Lillian, flaring, uncontrolled, wild, blind, destroying itself and others, her compassion and love were aroused. "That will be my gift to her," she thought with warmth, with pity. "I will guide her."

Meanwhile Lillian was exploring this aesthetic, this form,

16

this mystery that was Djuna. She was taking up Djuna's clothes one by one, amazed at their complication, their sheer femininity. "Do you wear this?" she asked, looking at the black lace nightgown. "I thought only prostitutes wore this!"

She investigated the perfumes, the cosmetics, the refined coquetries, the veils, the muffs, the scarves. She was almost like a sincere and simple person before a world of artifice. She was afraid of being deceived by all this artfulness. She could not see it as aesthetic, but as the puritans see it: as deception, as immorality, as belonging with seduction and eroticism.

She insisted on seeing Djuna without make-up, and was then satisfied that make-up was purely an enhancement of the features, not treachery.

Lillian's house was beautiful, lacquered, grown among the trees, and bore the mark of her handiwork all through, yet it did not seem to belong to her. She had painted, decorated, carved, arranged, selected, and most of it was made by her own hands, or refashioned, always touched or handled or improved by her, out of her very own activity and craftsmanship. Yet it did not become her house, and it did not have her face, her atmosphere. She always looked like a stranger in it. With all her handiwork and taste, she had not been able to give it her own character.

It was a home; it suited her husband, Larry, and her children. It was built for peace. The rooms were spacious, clear, brightly windowed. It was warm, glowing, clean, harmonious. It was like other houses.

As soon as Djuna entered it, she felt this. The strength, the fervor, the care Lillian spent in the house, on her husband and children came from some part of her being that was not the deepest Lillian. It was as if every element but her own nature

17

had contributed to create this life. Who had made the marriage? Who had desired the children? She could not remember the first impetus, the first choice, the first desire for these, nor how they came to be. It was as if it had happened in her sleep. Lillian, guided by her background, her mother, her sisters, her habits, her home as a child, her blindness in regard to her own desires, had made all this and then lived in it, but it had not been made out of the deeper elements of her nature, and she was a stranger in it.

Once made—this life, these occupations, the care, the devotion, the family—it never occurred to her that she could rebel against them. There was no provocation for rebellion. Her husband was kind, her children were lovable, her house was harmonious; and Nanny, the old nurse who took care of them all with inexhaustible maternal warmth, was their guardian angel, the guardian angel of the home.

Nanny's devotion to the home was so strong, so predominant, and so constantly manifested that the home and family seemed to belong to her more than to Lillian. The home had a reality for Nanny. Her whole existence was centered on it. She defended its interests, she hovered, reigned, watched, guarded tirelessly. She passed judgments on the visitors. Those who were dangerous to the peace of the home, she served with unappetizing meals, and from one end of the meal to the other, showed her disapproval. The welcome ones were those her instinct told her were good for the family, the home, for their unity. Then she surpassed herself in cooking and service. The unity of the family was her passionate concern: that the children should understand each other and love each other; that the children should love the father, the mother; that the mother and father should be close. For this she was willing to be the receiver of confidences, to be the peacemaker, to re-establish order.

She was willing to show an interest in any of Lillian's activities as long as these ultimately flowed back to the house. She could be interested in concerts if she brought the overflow of the music home to enhance it. She could be interested in painting while the results showed visibly in the house.

When the conversation lagged at the table she supplied diversion. If the children quarrelled she upheld the rights of each one in soothing, wise explanations.

She refused one proposal of marriage.

When Lillian came into the house, and felt lost in it, unable to really enter into, to feel it, to participate, to care, as if it were all not present and warm but actually a family album, as if her son Paul did not come in and really take off his snow-covered boots, but it was a snapshot of Paul taking off his boots, as if her husband's face were a photograph too, and Adele was actually the painting of her above the piano . . . then Lillian rushed to the kitchen, unconsciously seeking Nanny's worries, Nanny's anxieties (Paul is too thin, and Adele lost her best friend in school) to convince herself of the poignant reality of this house and its occupants (her husband had forgotten his rubbers).

If the children had not been growing up (again according to Nanny's tabulations and calculations) Lillian would have thought herself back ten years. Her husband did not change.

Nanny was the only one who had felt the shock the day that Lillian decided to have her own room. And Lillian might not have changed the rooms over if it had not been for a cricket.

Lillian's husband had gone away on a trip. It was summer. Lillian felt deeply alone, and filled with anxiety. She could not understand the anxiety. Her first thought always was: Larry is happy. He is well. He looked very happy when he left. The children are well. Then what can be the matter with me? How can anything be the matter with me if they are well?

There were guests at the house. Among them was one who vaguely resembled Gerard, and the young man in her dreams, and the young man who appeared to her under anaesthetic. Always of the same family. But he was bold as a lover. He courted her swiftly, impetuously.

A cricket had lodged itself in one of the beams of her room.

Perfectly silent until the young man came to visit her, until he caressed her. Then it burst into frenzied cricket song.

They laughed.

He came again the next night, and at the same moment the cricket sang again.

Always at the moment a cricket should sing.

The young man went away. Larry returned. Larry was happy to be with his wife.

But the cricket did not sing. Lillian wept. Lillian moved into a room of her own. Nanny was depressed and cross for a week.

When they sat together, alone, in the evenings, Larry did not appear to see her. When he talked about her he always talked about the Lillian of ten years ago; how she looked then, how she was, what she said. He delighted in reviving scenes out of the past, her behaviour, her high temper and the troubles she got herself into. He often repeated these stories. And Lillian felt that she had known only one Larry, a Larry who had courted her and then remained as she had first known him. When she heard about the Lillian of ten years ago she felt no connection with her. But Larry was living with her, delighting in her presence. He reconstructed her out of his memory and sat her there every evening they had together.

One night they heard a commotion in the otherwise peaceful village. The police car passed and then the ambulance. Then the family doctor stopped his car before the gate. He asked for a drink. "My job is over," he said, "and I need a drink badly." Lillian gave him one, but at first he would not talk.

Later he explained: The man who rented the house next door was a young doctor, not a practicing one. His behavior and way of living had perplexed the neighbors. He received no one, allowed no one into the house. He was somber in mood, and attitude, and he was left alone. But people complained persistently of an unbearable odor. There were investigations. Finally it was discovered that his wife had died six months earlier, in California. He had brought her body back and he was living with it stretched on his bed. The doctor had seen her.

Lillian left the room. The odor of death, the image of death . . . everywhere.

No investigation would be made in her house. No change. Nanny was there.

But Lillian felt trapped without knowing what had trapped her.

Then she found Djuna. With Djuna she was alive. With Djuna her entire being burst into living, flowering cells. She could feel her own existence, the Lillian of today.

She spent much time with Djuna.

Paul felt his mother removed in some way. He noticed that she and his father had little to say to each other. He was anxious. Adele had nightmares that her mother was dying. Larry was concerned. Perhaps Lillian was not well. She ate little. He sent for the doctor. She objected to him violently. Nanny hovered, guarded, as if she scented danger. But nothing changed. Lillian waited. She always went first to the kitchen when she came home, as if it were the hearth itself, to warm herself. And then to each child's room, and then to Larry.

She could do nothing. Djuna's words illuminated her chaos, but changed nothing. What was it Djuna said: that life tended to crystallize into patterns which became traps and webs. That people tended to see each other in their first "state" or "form" and to adopt a rhythm in consequence. That they had greatest difficulty in seeing the transformations of the loved one, in seeing the becoming. If they did finally perceive the new self, they had the greatest difficulty nevertheless in changing the rhythm. The strong one was condemned to perpetual strength, the weak to perpetual weakness. The one who loved you best

21

condemned you to a static role because he had adapted his being to the past self. If you attempted to change, warned Djuna, you would find a subtle, perverse opposition, and perhaps sabotage! Inwardly and outwardly, a pattern was a form which became a prison. And then we had to smash it. Mutation was difficult. Attempts at evasion were frequent, blind evasions, evasions from dead relationships, false relationships, false roles, and sometimes from the deeper self too, because of the great obstacle one encountered in affirming it. All our emotional history was that of the spider and the fly, with the added tragedy that the fly here collaborated in the weaving of the web. Crimes were frequent. People in desperation turned about and destroyed each other. No one could detect the cause or catch the criminal. There was no visible victim. It always had the appearance of suicide.

Lillian sensed the walls and locks. She did not even know she wanted to escape. She did not even know she was in rebellion. She did it with her body. Her body became ill from the friction, lacerations and daily duels with her beloved jailers. Her body became ill from the poisons of internal rebellion, the monotony of her prison, the greyness of its days, the poverty of the nourishment. She was in a fixed relationship and could not move forward.

Anxiety settled upon the house. Paul clung to his mother longer when they separated for short periods. Adele was less gay.

Larry was more silent.

Nanny began to weep noiselessly. Then she had a visitor. The same one she had sent away ten years earlier. The man was growing old. He wanted a home. He wanted Nanny. Nanny was growing old. He talked to her all evening, in the kitchen. Then one day Nanny cried without control. Lillian questioned her. She wanted to get married. But she hated to leave the family. The family! The sacred, united, complete family. In this big house, with so much work. And no one else to be had. And she wanted Lillian to protest, to cling to her—as the children did before, as Larry had done a few years back, each time the suitor had come again for his answer. But Lillian said quietly, "Nanny, it is time that you thought of yourself. You have lived for others all your life. Get married. I believe you should get married. He loves you. He waited for you such a long time. You deserve a home and life and protection and a rest. Get married."

And then Lillian walked into the dining room where the family was eating and she said: "Nanny is going to get married and leave us."

Paul then cried out: "This is the beginning of the end!"

Larry looked up from his meal, for the first time struck with a clearer glimpse of what had been haunting the house.

Through the high building, the wind complained, playing a frenzied flute up and down the elevator shafts.

Lillian and Djuna opened the window and looked at the city covered with a mist. One could see only the lighted eyes of the buildings. One could hear only muffled sounds, the ducks from Central Park lake nagging loudly, the fog horns from the river which sounded at times like the mournful complaints of imprisoned ships not allowed to sail, at others like gay departures.

Lillian was sitting in the dark, speaking of her life, her voice charged with both laughter and tears.

In the dark a new being appears. A new being who has not the courage to face daylight. In the dark people dare to dream everything. And they dare to tell everything. In the dark there appeared a new Lillian.

There was just enough light from the city to show their faces chalk white, with shadows in the place of eyes and mouth, and an occasional gleam of white teeth. At first it was like two children sitting on a see-saw, because Lillian would talk about her life and her marriage and the disintegration of her home, and then Djuna would lean over to embrace her, overflowing with pity. Then Djuna would speak and Lillian would lean over and want to gather her in her arms with maternal compassion.

"I feel," said Lillian, "that I do everything wrong. I feel I do everything to bring about just what I fear. You will turn away from me too."

Lillian's unsatisfied hunger for life had evoked in Djuna another hunger. This hunger still hovered at times over the bright film of her eyes, shading them not with the violet shadows of either illness or sensual excess, of experience or fever, but with the pearl-grey shadow of denial, and Djuna said:

"I was born in the most utter poverty. My mother lying in bed with consumption, four brothers and sisters loudly claiming food and care, and I having to be the mother and nurse of them all. We were so hungry that we ate all the samples of food or medicines which were left at the house. I remember once we ate a whole box of chocolate-coated constipation pills. Father was a taxi driver but he spent the greatest part of what he made on drink along the way. As we lived among people who were all living as we were, without sufficient clothing, or heat or food, we knew no contrast and believed this was natural and general. But with me it was different. I suffered from other kinds of pangs. I was prone to the most excessive dreaming, of such intensity and realism that when I awakened I felt I lost an entire universe of legends, myths, figures and cities of such color that they made our room seem a thousand times more bare, the poverty of the table more acute. The disproportion was immense. And I'm not speaking merely of the banquets which were so obviously compensatory! Nor of the obvious way by which I filled my poor wardrobe. It was more than that. I saw in my dreams houses, forests, entire cities, and such a variety of personages that even today I wonder how a child, who had not even seen pictures, could invent such designs in textures, such colonnades, friezes, fabulous animals, statues, colors, as I did. And the activity! My dreams were so full of activity that at times I felt it was the dreams which exhausted me rather than all the washing, ironing, shopping, mending, sweeping, tending, nursing, dusting that I did. I remember I had to break soap boxes to burn in the fireplace. I used to scratch my hands and bruise my toes. Yet when my mother caressed me and said, you look tired, Djuna, I almost felt like confessing to her that what had tired me was my constant dreaming of a ship which insisted on sailing through a city, or my voyage in a chaise through the snow-covered steppes of Russia. And by the way, there was a lot of confusion of places and methods of travel in my dreams, as there must be in the dreams of the blind. Do you know what I think now? I think what tired me was the intensity of the pleasures I had together with the perfect awareness that such pleasure could not last and would be immediately followed by its opposite. Once out of my dreams, the only certitude I retained from these nocturnal expeditions was that pleasure could not possibly last. This conviction was strengthened by the fact that no matter how small a pleasure I wanted to take during the day it was followed by catastrophe. If I relaxed for one instant the watch over my sick mother to eat an orange all by myself in some abandoned lot, she would have a turn for the worse. Or if I spent some time looking at the pictures outside of the movie house one of my brothers or sisters would cut himself or burn his finger or get into a fight with another child. So I felt then that liberty must be paid for heavily. I learned a most severe accounting which was to consider pleasure as the jewel, a kind of stolen jewel for which one must be willing to pay vast sums in suffering and guilt. Even today, Lillian, when something very marvelous happens to me, when I attain love or ecstasy or a perfect moment, I expect it to be followed by pain."

Then Lillian leaned over and kissed Djuna warmly: "I want to protect you."

"We give each other courage."

The mist came into the room. Djuna thought: She's such a hurt woman. She is one who does not know what she suffers from, or why, or how to overcome it. She is all unconscious, motion, music. She is afraid to see, to analyze her nature. She thinks that nature just is and that nothing can be done about it. She would never have invented ships to conquer the sea, machines to create light where there was darkness. She would never have harnessed water power, electric power. She is like the primitive. She thinks it is all beyond her power. She accepts chaos. She suffers mutely. . . .

"Djuna, tell me all that happened to you. I keep thinking about your hunger. I feel the pangs of it in my own stomach."

"My mother died," continued Djuna. "One of my brothers was hurt in an accident while playing in the street and crippled. Another was taken to the insane asylum. He harmed nobody. When the war started he began to eat flowers stolen from the florists. When he was arrested he said that he was eating flowers to bring peace to the world. That if everybody ate flowers peace would come to the world. My sister and I were put in an orphan asylum. I remember the day we were taken there. The night before I had a dream about a Chinese pagoda all in gold, filled with a marvelous odor. At the tip of the pagoda there was a mechanical bird who sang one little song repeatedly. I kept hearing this song and smelling the odor all the time and that seemed more real to me than the callous hands of the orphan asylum women when they changed me into a uniform. Oh, the greyness of those dresses! And if only the windows had been normal. But they were long and narrow, Lillian. Everything is changed when you look at it through long and narrow windows. It's as if the sky itself were compressed, limited. To me they were like the windows of a prison. The food was dark, and tasteless, like slime. The children were cruel to each other. No one visited us. And then there was the old watchman who made the rounds at night. He often lifted the corners of our bedcovers, and let his eyes rove and sometimes more than his eyes. . . . He became the demon of the night for us little girls."

There was a silence, during which both Lillian and Djuna became children, listening to the watchman of the night become the demon of the night, the tutor of the forbidden, the initiator breaking the sheltered core of the child, breaking the innocence and staining the beds of adolescence.

"The satyr of the asylum," said Djuna, "who became also our jailer because when we grew older and wanted to slip out at night to go out with the boys, it was he who rattled the keys and prevented us. But for him we might have been free at times, but he watched us, and the women looked up to him for his fanaticism in keeping us from the street. The orphan asylum had a system which permitted families to adopt the orphans. But as it was known that the asylum supplied the sum of thirty-five dollars a month towards the feeding of the child, those who responded were most often those in need of the thirty-five dollars. Poor families, already burdened with many children, came forward to 'adopt' new ones. The orphans were allowed to enter these homes in which they found themselves doubly cheated. For at least in the asylum we had no illusion, no hope of love. But we did have illusions about the adoptions. We thought we would find a family. In most cases we did not even imagine that these families had children of their own. We expected to be a much wanted and only child! I was placed in one of them. The first thing that happened was that the other children were jealous of the intruder. And the spectacle of the love lavished on the legitimate children was terribly painful. It made me feel more abandoned, more hungry, more orphaned than ever. Every time a parent embraced his child I suffered so much that finally I ran away back to the asylum. And I was not the only one. And besides this emotional starvation we got even less to eat—the allowance being spent on the whole family. And now I lost my last treasure: the dreaming. For nothing in the dreams took the place of the human warmth I had witnessed. Now I felt utterly poor, because I could not create a human companion."

This hunger which had inhabited her entire being, which had thinned her blood, transpired through her bones, attacked the roots of her hair, given a fragility to her skin which was never to disappear entirely, had been so enormous that it had marked her whole being and her eyes with an indelible mark. Although her life changed and every want was filled later, this appearance of hunger remained. As if nothing could ever quite fill it. Her being had received no sun, no food, no air, no warmth, no love. It retained open pores of yearning and longing, mysterious spongy cells of absorption. The space between actuality, absolute deprivation, and the sumptuosity of her imagination could never be entirely covered. What she had created in the void, in the emptiness, in the bareness continued to shame all that was offered her, and her large, infinitely blue eyes continued to assert the immensity of her hunger.

This hunger of the eyes, skin, of the whole body and spirit, which made others criminals, robbers, rapers, barbarians, which caused wars, invasions, plundering and murder, in Djuna at the age of puberty alchemized into love.

Whatever was missing she became: she became mother, father, cousin, brother, friend, confidant, guide, companion to all.

This power of absorption, this sponge of receptivity which might have fed itself forever to fill the early want, she used to receive all communication of the need of others. The need and hunger became nourishment. Her breasts, which no poverty had been able to wither, were heavy with the milk of lucidity, the milk of devotion.

This hunger . . . became love.

While wearing the costume of utter femininity, the veils and the combs, the gloves and the perfumes, the muffs and the heels of femininity, she nevertheless disguised in herself an active lover of the world, the one who was actively roused by the object of his love, the one who was made strong as man is made strong in the center of his being by the softness of his love.

28

Loving in men and women not their strength but their softness, not their fullness but their hunger, not their plenitude but their needs.

They had made contact then with the deepest aspect of themselves—Djuna with Lillian's emotional violence and her compassion for this force which destroyed her and hurled her against all obstacles, Lillian with Djuna's power of clarification. They needed each other. Djuna experienced deep in herself a pleasure each time Lillian exploded, for she herself kept her gestures, her feeling within an outer form, like an Oriental. When Lillian exploded it seemed to Djuna as if some of her violent feeling, so long contained within the forms, were released. Some of her own lightning, some of her own rebellions, some of her own angers. Djuna contained in herself a Lillian too, to whom she had never given a moment's freedom, and it made her strangely free when Lillian gave vent to her anger or rebellions. But after the havoc, when Lillian had bruised herself, or more seriously mutilated herself (war and explosion had their consequences) then Lillian needed Djuna. For the bitterness, the despair, the chaos submerged Lillian, drowned her. The hurt Lillian wanted to strike back and did so blindly, hurting herself all the more. And then Djuna was there, to remove the arrows implanted in Lillian, to cleanse them of their poison, to open the prison door, to open the trap door, to protect, to give transfusion of blood, and peace to the wounded.

But it was Lillian who was drowning, and it was Djuna who was able always at the last moment to save her, and in her moments of danger, Lillian knew only one thing: that she must possess Djuna.

It was as if someone had proclaimed: I need oxygen, and therefore I will lock some oxygen in my room and live on it.

So Lillian began her courtship.

She brought gifts. She pulled out perfume, and jewelry and clothes. She almost covered the bed with gifts. She wanted Djuna to put all the jewelry on, to smell all the perfumes at once, to wear all her clothes. Djuna was showered with gifts as in a fairytale, but she could not find in them the fairytale pleasure. She felt that to each gift was tied a little invisible cord or demand, of exactingness, of debt, of domination. She felt she could not wear all these things and walk away, freely. She felt that with the gifts, a golden spider wove a golden web of possession. Lillian was not only giving away objects, but golden threads woven out of her very own substance to fix and to hold. They were not the fairytale gifts which Djuna had dreamed of receiving. (She had many dreams of receiving perfume, or receiving fur, or being given blue bottles, lamés, etc.) In the fairytale the giver laid out the presents and then became invisible. In the fairytales and in the dreams there was no debt, and there was no giver.

Lillian did not become invisible. Lillian became more and more present. Lillian became the mother who wanted to dress her child out of her own substance, Lillian became the lover who wanted to slip the shoes and slippers on the beloved's feet so he could contain these feet. The dresses were not chosen as Djuna's dresses, but as Lillian's choice and taste to cover Djuna.

The night of gifts, begun in gaiety and magnificence, began to thicken. Lillian had put too much of herself into the gifts. It was a lovely night, with the gifts scattered through the room like fragments of Miro's circus paintings, flickering and leaping, but not free. Djuna wanted to enjoy and she could not. She loved Lillian's generosity, Lillian's largeness, Lillian's opulence and magnificence, but she felt anxiety. She remembered as a child receiving gifts for Christmas, and among them a closed mysterious box gaily festooned with multicolored ribbons. She remembered that the mystery of this box affected her more than the open, exposed, familiar gifts of tea cups, dolls, etc. She opened the box and out of it jumped a grotesque devil who, propelled by taut springs, almost hit her face.

In these gifts, there is a demon somewhere; a demon who is hurting Lillian, and will hurt me, and I don't know where he is hiding. I haven't seen him yet, but he is here.

She thought of the old legends, of the knights who had to kill monsters before they could enjoy their love.

No demon here, thought Djuna, nothing but a woman drowning, who is clutching at me . . . I love her.

When Lillian dressed up in the evening in vivid colors with her ever tinkling jewelry, her face wildly alive, Djuna said to her, "You're made for a passionate life of some kind."

She looked like a white negress, a body made for rolling in natural undulations of pleasure and desire. Her vivid face, her avid mouth, her provocative, teasing glances proclaimed sensuality. She had rings under her eyes. She looked often as if she had just come from the arms of a lover. An energy smoked from her whole body.

But sensuality was paralyzed in her. When Djuna sought to show Lillian her face in the mirror, she found Lillian paralyzed with fear. She was impaled on a rigid pole of puritanism. One felt it, like a heavy silver chastity belt, around her soft, rounded body.

She bought a black lace gown like Djuna's. Then she wanted to own all the objects which carried Djuna's personality or spirit. She wanted to be clasped at the wrists by Djuna's bracelet watch, dressed in Djuna's kind of clothes.

(Djuna thought of the primitives eating the liver of the strong man of the tribe to acquire his strength, wearing the teeth of the elephant to acquire his durability, donning the lion's head and mane to appropriate his courage, gluing feathers on themselves to become as free as the bird.)

Lillian knew no mystery. Everything was open with her. Even the most ordinary mysteries of women she did not guard. She was open like a man, frank, direct. Her eyes shed lightning but no shadows.

32

One night Djuna and Lillian went to a night club together to watch the cancan. At such a moment Djuna forgot that she was a woman and looked at the women dancing with the eyes of an artist and the eyes of a man. She admired them, revelled in their beauty, in their seductions, in the interplay of black garters and black stockings and the snow-white frills of petticoats.

Lillian's face clouded. The storm gathered in her eyes. The lightning struck. She lashed out in anger: "If I were a man I would murder you."

Djuna was bewildered. Then Lillian's anger dissolved in lamentations: "Oh, the poor people, the poor people who love you. You love these women!"

She began to weep. Djuna put her arms around her and consoled her. The people around them looked baffled, as passers-by look up suddenly at an unexpected, freakish windstorm. Here it was, chaotically upsetting the universe, coming from right and left, great fury and velocity—and why?

Two women were looking at beautiful women dancing. One enjoyed it, and the other made a scene.

Lillian went home and wrote stuttering phrases on the back of a box of writing paper: Djuna, don't abandon me; if you abandon me, I am lost.

When Djuna came the next day, still angry from the inexplicable storm of the night before, she wanted to say: are you the woman I chose for a friend? Are you the egotistical, devouring child, all caprice and confusion who is always crossing my path? She could not say it, not before this chaotic helpless writing on the back of the box, a writing which could not stand alone, but wavered from left to right, from right to left, inclining, falling, spilling, retreating, ascending on the line as if for flight off the edge of the paper as if it were an airfield, or plummeting on the paper like a falling elevator.

If they met a couple along the street who were kissing, Lillian became equally unhinged.

If they talked about her children and Djuna said: I never

33

liked real children, only the child in the grown-up, Lillian answered: you should have had children.

"But I lack the maternal feeling for children, Lillian, though I haven't lacked the maternal experience. There are plenty of children, abandoned children right in the so-called grown-ups. While you, well you are a real mother, you have a real maternal capacity. You are the mother type. I am not. I only like being the mistress. I don't even like being a wife."

Then Lillian's entire universe turned a somersault again, crashed, and Djuna was amazed to see the devastating results of an innocent phrase: "I am not a maternal woman," she said, as if it were an accusation. (Everything was an accusation.)

Then Djuna kissed her and said playfully: "Well, then, you're a *femme fatale!*"

But this was like fanning an already enormous flame. This aroused Lillian to despair: "No, no, I never destroyed or hurt anybody," she protested.

"You know, Lillian, someday I will sit down and write a little dictionary for you, a little Chinese dictionary. In it I will put down all the interpretations of what is said to you, the right interpretation, that is: the one that is not meant to injure, not meant to humiliate or accuse or doubt. And whenever something is said to you, you will look in my little dictionary to make sure, before you get desperate, that you have understood what is said to you."

The idea of the little Chinese dictionary made Lillian laugh. The storm passed.

But if they walked the streets together her obsession was to see who was looking at them or following them. In the shops she was obsessed about her plumpness and considered it not an attribute but a defect. In the movies it was emotionalism and tears. If they sat in a restaurant by a large window and saw the people passing it was denigration and dissection. The universe hinged and turned on her defeated self.

She was aggressive with people who waited on her, and then was hurt by their defensive abandon of her. When they did not

34

wait on her she was personally injured, but could not see the injury she had inflicted by her demanding ways. Her commands bristled everyone's hair, raised obstacles and retaliations. As soon as she appeared she brought dissonance.

But she blamed the others, the world.

She could not bear to see lovers together, absorbed in each other.

She harassed the quiet men and lured them to an argument and she hated the aggressive men who held their own against her.

Her shame. She could not carry off gallantly a run in her stocking. She was overwhelmed by a lost button.

When Djuna was too swamped by other occupations or other people to pay attention to her, Lillian became ill. But she would not be ill at home surrounded by her family. She was ill alone, in a hotel room, so that Djuna ran in and out with medicines, with chicken soup, stayed with her day and night chained to her antics, and then Lillian clapped her hands and confessed: "I'm so happy! Now I've got you all to myself!"

The summer nights were passing outside like gay whores, with tinkles of cheap jewelry, opened and emollient like a vast bed. The summer nights were passing but not Lillian's tension with the world.

She read erotic memoirs avidly, she was obsessed with the lives and loves of others. But she herself could not yield, she was ashamed, she throttled her own nature, and all this desire, lust, became twisted inside of her and churned a poison of envy and jealousy. Whenever sensuality showed its flower head, Lillian would have liked to decapitate it, so it would cease troubling and haunting her.

At the same time she wanted to seduce the world, Djuna, everybody. She would want to be kissed on the lips and more warmly and then violently block herself. She thrived on this hysterical undercurrent without culmination. This throbbing sensual obsession and the blocking of it; this rapacious love without polarity, like a blind womb appetite; delighting in making the temperature rise and then clamping down the lid.

In her drowning she was like one constantly choking those around her, bringing them down with her into darkness.

Djuna felt caught in a sirocco.

She had lived once on a Spanish island and experienced exactly this impression.

The island had been calm, silvery and dormant until one morning when a strange wind began to blow from Africa, blowing in circles. It swept over the island charged with torpid warmth, charged with flower smells, with sandalwood and patchouli and incense, and turning in whirlpools, gathered up the nerves and swinging with them into whirlpools of dry enervating warmth and smells, reached no climax, no explosion. Blowing persistently, continuously, hour after hour, gathering every nerve in every human being, the nerves alone, and tangling them in this fatal waltz; drugging them and pulling them, and whirlpooling them, until the body shook with restlessness—all polarity and sense of gravity lost. Because of this insane waltz of the wind, its emollient warmth, its perfumes, the being lost its guidance, its clarity, its integrity. Hour after hour, all day and all night, the body was subjected to this insidious whirling rhythm, in which polarity was lost, and only the nerves and desires throbbed, tense and weary of movement—all in a void, with no respite, no climax, no great loosening as in other storms. A tension that gathered force but had no release. It abated not once in forty-eight hours, promising, arousing, caressing, destroying sleep, rest, repose, and then vanished without releasing, without culmination. . . .

This violence which Djuna had loved so much! It had become a mere sirocco wind, burning and shrivelling. This violence which Djuna had applauded, enjoyed, because she could not possess it in herself. It was now burning her, and their friendship. Because it was not attached to anything, it was not creating anything, it was a trap of negation.

"You will save me," said Lillian always, clinging.

Lillian was the large foundering ship, yes, and Djuna the

small lifeboat. But now the big ship had been moored to the small lifeboat and was pitching too fast and furiously and the lifeboat was being swamped.

(She wants something of me that only a man can give her. But first of all she wants to become me, so that she can communicate with man. She has lost her ways of communicating with man. She is doing it through me!)

When they walked together, Lillian sometimes asked Djuna: "Walk in front of me, so I can see how you walk. You have such a sway of the hips!"

In front of Lillian walked Lillian's lost femininity, imprisoned in the male Lillian. Lillian's femininity imprisoned in the deepest wells of her being, loving Djuna, and knowing it must reach her own femininity at the bottom of the well by way of Djuna. By wearing Djuna's feminine exterior, swaying her hips, becoming Djuna.

As Djuna enjoyed Lillian's violence, Lillian enjoyed Djuna's feminine capitulations. The pleasure Djuna took in her capitulations to love, to desire. Lillian breathed out through Djuna. What took place in Djuna's being which Lillian could not reach, she at least reached by way of Djuna.

"The first time a boy hurt me," said Lillian to Djuna, "it was in school. I don't remember what he did. But I wept. And he laughed at me. Do you know what I did? I went home and dressed in my brother's suit. I tried to feel as the boy felt. Naturally as I put on the suit I felt I was putting on a costume of strength. It made me feel sure, as the boy was, confident, impudent. The mere fact of putting my hands in the pockets made me feel arrogant. I thought then that to be a boy meant one did not suffer. That it was being a girl that was responsible for the suffering. Later I felt the same way. I thought man had found a way out of suffering by objectivity. What the man called being reasonable. When my husband said: Lillian, let's be reasonable, it meant he had none of the feeling I had, that he could be objective. What a power! Then there was another thing. When I felt his great choking anguish I discovered one relief, and that was action. I felt like the women who had to sit and wait at home while there was a war going on. I felt if only I could join the war, participate, I wouldn't feel the anguish and the fear. All through the last war as a child I felt: if only they would let me be Joan of Arc. Joan of Arc wore a suit of armor, she sat on a horse, she fought side by side with the men. She must have gained their strength. Then it was the same way about men. At a dance, as a girl, the moment of waiting before they asked me seemed intolerable, the suspense, and the insecurity; perhaps they were not going to ask me! So I rushed forward, to cut the suspense. I rushed. All my nature became rushed, propelled by the anxiety, merely to cut through all the moment of anxious uncertainty."

Djuna looked tenderly at her, not the strong Lillian, the overwhelming Lillian, the aggressive Lillian, but the hidden, secret, frightened Lillian who had created such a hard armor and disguise around her weakness.

Djuna saw the Lillian hidden in her coat of armor, and all of Lillian's armor lay broken around her, like cruel pieces of mail which had wounded her more than they had protected her from the enemy. The mail had melted, and revealed the bruised feminine flesh. At the first knowledge of the weakness Lillian had picked up the mail, wrapped herself in it and had taken up a lance. The lance! The man's lance. Uncertainty resolved, relieved by the activity of attack!

The body of Lillian changed as she talked, the fast coming words accelerating the dismantling. She was taking off the shell, the covering, the defenses, the coat of mail, the activity.

Suddenly Lillian laughed. In the middle of tears, she laughed: "I'm remembering a very comical incident. I was about sixteen. There was a boy in love with me. Shyly, quietly in love. We were in the same school but he lived quite far away. We all used bicycles. One day we were going to be separated for a week by the holidays. He suggested we both bicycle together towards a meeting place between the two towns. The week of separation seemed too unbearable. So it

38

was agreed: at a certain hour we would leave the house together and meet half way."

Lillian started off. At first at a normal pace. She knew the rhythm of the boy. A rather easy, relaxed rhythm. Never rushed. Never precipitate. She at first adopted his rhythm. Dreaming of him, of his slow smile, of his shy worship, of his expression of this worship, which consisted mainly in waiting for her here, there. Waiting. Not advancing, inviting, but waiting. Watching her pass by.

She pedaled slowly, dreamily. Then slowly her pleasure and tranquillity turned to anguish: suppose he did not come? Suppose she arrived before him? Could she bear the sight of the desolate place of their meeting, the failed meeting? The exaltation that had been increasing in her, like some powerful motor, what could she do with this exaltation if she arrived alone, and the meeting failed? The fear affected her in two directions. She could stop right there, and turn back, and not face the possibility of disappointment, or she could rush forward and accelerate the moment of painful suspense, and she chose the second. Her lack of confidence in life, in realization, in the fulfillment of her desires, in the outcome of a dream, in the possibility of reality corresponding to her fantasy, speeded her bicycle with the incredible speed of anxiety, a speed beyond the human body, beyond human endurance.

She arrived before him. Her fear was justified! She could not measure what the anxiety had done to her speed, the acceleration which had broken the equality of rhythm. She arrived as she had feared, at a desolate spot on the road, and the boy had become this invisible image which taunts the dreamer, a mirage that could not be made real. It had become reality eluding the dreamer, the wish unfulfilled.

The boy may have arrived later. He may have fallen asleep and not come at all. He may have had a tire puncture. Nothing mattered. Nothing could prevent her from feeling that she was not Juliet waiting on the balcony, but Romeo who had to leap across space to join her. She had leaped, she had acted Romeo, and when woman leaped she leaped into a void.

Later it was not the drama of two bicycles, of a road, of two separated towns; later it was a darkened room, and a man and woman pursuing pleasure and fusion.

At first she lay passive dreaming of the pleasure that would come out of the darkness, to dissolve and invade her. But it was not pleasure which came out of the darkness to clasp her. It was anxiety. Anxiety made confused gestures in the dark, crosscurrents of forces, short circuits, and no pleasure. A depression, a broken rhythm, a feeling such as men must have after they have taken a whore.

Out of the prone figure of the woman, apparently passive, apparently receptive, there rose a taut and anxious shadow, the shadow of the woman bicycling too fast; who, to relieve her insecurity, plunges forward as the desperado does and is defeated because this aggressiveness cannot meet its mate and unite with it. A part of the woman has not participated in this marriage, has not been taken. But was it a part of the woman, or the shadow of anxiety, which dressed itself in man's clothes and assumed man's active role to quiet its anguish? Wasn't it the woman who dressed as a man and pedalled too fast?

Jay. The table at which he sat was stained with wine. His blue eyes were inscrutable like those of a Chinese sage. He ended all his phrases in a kind of hum, as if he put his foot on the pedal of his voice and created an echo. In this way none of his phrases ended abruptly.

Sitting at the bar he immediately created a climate, a tropical day. In spite of the tension in her, Lillian felt it. Sitting at a bar with his voice rolling over, he dissolved and liquefied the hard click of silver on plates, the icy dissonances of glasses, the brittle sound of money thrown on the counter.

He was tall but he carried his tallness slackly and easily, as easily as his coat and hat, as if all of it could be discarded and sloughed off at any moment when he needed lightness or nimbleness. His body large, shaggy, as if never definitely chiselled, never quite ultimately finished, was as casually his as his passing moods and varying fancies and fortunes.

He opened his soft animal mouth a little, as if in expectancy of a drink. But instead, he said (as if he had absorbed Lillian's face and voice in place of the drink), "I'm happy. I'm too happy." Then he began to laugh, to laugh, to laugh, with his head shaking like a bear, shaking from right to left as if it were too heavy a head. "I can't help it. I can't help laughing. I'm too happy. Last night I spent the night here. It was Christmas and I didn't have the money for a hotel room. And the night before I slept at a movie house. They overlooked me, didn't sweep where I lay. In the morning I played the movie piano. In walked the furious manager, then he listened, then he gave me a contract starting this evening. Christ, Lillian, I never thought Christmas would bring me anything, yet it brought you."

How gently he had walked into her life, how quietly he seemed to be living, while all the time he was drawing bitter caricatures on the bar table, on the backs of envelopes. Drawing bums, drunks, derelicts.

"So you're a pianist . . . that's what I should have been. I'm not bad, but I would never work hard enough. I wanted also to be a painter. I might have been a writer too, if I had worked enough. I did a bit of acting too, at one time. As it is, I guess I'm the last man on earth. Why did you single me out?"

This man who would not be distinguished in a crowd, who could pass through it like an ordinary man, so quiet, so absorbed, with his hat on one side, his steps dragging a little, like a lazy devil enjoying everything, why did she see him hungry, thirsty, abandoned?

Behind this Jay, with his southern roguishness, perpetually calling for drinks, why did she see a lost man?

He sat like a workman before his drinks, he talked like a cart driver to the whores at the bar; they were all at ease with him. His presence took all the straining and willing out of Lillian. He was like the south wind: blowing when he came, melting and softening, bearing joy and abundance.

When they met, and she saw him walking towards her, she felt he would never stop walking towards her and into her very being: he would walk right into her being with his soft lazy walk and purring voice and his mouth slightly open.

She could not hear his voice. His voice rumbled over the surface of her skin, like another caress. She had no power against his voice. It came straight from him into her. She could stuff her ears and still it would find its way into her blood and make it rise.

All things were born anew when her dress fell on the floor of his room.

He said: "I feel humble, Lillian, but it is all so good, so good." He gave to the word good a mellowness which made the whole room glow, which gave a warmer color to the bare window, to the woolen shirt hung on a peg, to the single glass out of which they drank together.

Behind the yellow curtain the sun seeped in: everything was the color of a tropical afternoon.

The small room was like a deep-set alcove. Warm mist and warm blood; the high drunkenness which made Jay flushed and heavy blooded. His sensual features expanded.

"As soon as you come, I'm jubilant." And he did somersaults on the bed, two or three of them.

"This is fine wine, Lillian. Let's drink to my failure. There's no doubt about it, no doubt whatever that I'm a failure."

"I won't let you be a failure," said Lillian.

"You say: I want, as if that made things happen."

"It does."

"I don't know what I expect of you. I expect miracles." He looked up at her slyly, then mockingly, then gravely again. "I have no illusions," he said.

42

Then he sat down with his heavy shoulders bowed, and his head bowed, but Lillian caught that swift, passing flash, a moment's hope, the lightning passage of a spark of faith left in his indifference to his fate. She clung to this.

Jay—gnome and sprite and faun, and playboy of the mother-bound world. Brightly gifted, he painted while he enjoyed the painting; the accidental marvels of colors, the pleasant shock of apparitions made in a game with paint. He stopped painting where the effort began, the need for discipline or travail. He danced while he was allowed to improvise, to surprise himself and others, to stretch, laugh, and court and be courted; but stopped if there were studying, developing or disciplining or effort or repetition involved. He acted, he acted loosely, flowingly, emotionally, while nothing more difficult was demanded of him, but he evaded rehearsals, fatigue, strain, effort. He pur ued no friend, he took what came.

He gave himself to the present moment. To be with the friend, to drink with the friend, to talk with the friend, he forgot what was due the next day, and if it were something which demanded time, or energy, he could not meet it. He had not provided for it. He was asleep when he should have been awake, and tired when his energy was required, and absent when his presence was summoned. The merest expectation from a friend, the most trivial obligation, sent him running in the opposite direction. He came to the friend while there was pleasure to be had. He left as soon as the pleasure vanished and reality began. An accident, an illness, poverty, a quarrel—he was never there for them.

It was as if he smelled the climate: was it good? Was there the odor of pleasure, the colors of pleasure? Expansion, forgetfulness, abandon, enjoyment? Then he stayed. Difficulties? Then he vanished.

Lillian and Jay.

It was a merciless winter day. The wind persecuted them around the corners of the street. The snow slid into their collars. They could not talk to each other. They took a taxi.

The windows of the taxi had frosted, so they seemed completely shut off from the rest of the world. It was small and dark and warm. Jay buried his face in her fur. He made himself small. He had a way of becoming so passive and soft that he seemed to lose his height and weight. He did this now, his face in her fur, and she felt as if she were the darkness, the smallness of the taxi, and were hiding him, protecting him from the elements. Here the cold could not reach him, the snow, the wind, the daylight. He sheltered himself, she carried his head on her breast, she carried his body become limp, his hands nestling in her pocket. She was the fur, the pocket, the warmth that sheltered him. She felt immense, and strong, and illimitable, the boundless mother opening her arms and her wings, flying to carry him somewhere; she his shelter and refuge, his secret hiding place, his tent, his sky, his blanket.

The soundproof mother, the shockproof mother of man!

This passion warmer, stronger than the other passion, annihilating desire and becoming the desire, a boundless passion to surround, envelop, sustain, strengthen, uphold, to answer all needs. He closed his eyes. He almost slept in her warmth and furriness. He caressed the fur, he feared no claws, he abandoned himself, and the waves of passion inspired by his abandon intoxicated her.

44

He usually wore colored shirts to suit his fancy. Once he wore a white one, because it had been given to him. It did not suit him. Whiteness and blackness did not suit him. Only the intermediate colors.

Lillian was standing near him and they had just been discussing their life together. Jay had admitted that he would not work. He could not bear repetition, he could not bear a "boss," he could not bear regular hours. He could not bear the seriousness.

"Then you will have to be a hobo."

"I'll be a hobo, then."

"A hobo has no wife," said Lillian.

"No," he said. And added nothing. If she became part of the effort, he would not cling to her either.

"I will have to work, then," she said. "One of us has to work."

He said nothing.

Lillian was doubly disturbed by the unfamiliarity of the scene, the portentousness of it, and by the familiarity of the white shirt. The white shirt disturbed her more than his words. And then she knew. The white shirt reminded her of her husband. Just before he put on his coat she had always seen him and obscurely felt: how straight and rigid he stands in his white shirt. Black and white. Definite and starched, and always the same. But there it was. She was not sure she had liked the white shirt. From it came authority, a firm guidance, a firm construction. And now she was again facing a white shirt but with a strange feeling that there was nothing in it: no rigidity, no straight shoulders, no man. If she approached she would feel something fragile, soft and wavering: the shirt was not upheld by the body of the man. If she broke suddenly at the idea of assuming the responsibility, if she broke against this shirt it would collapse, turn to sand, trickle sand and soft laughter and elusive flickering love.

Against this white shirt of the husband she had lain her head once and heard a strong heart beat evenly, and now it was as if it were empty, and she were in a dream of falling down soft sand dunes to softer and more sliding shifty sand dunes. . . . Her head turned.

She kept herself on this new equilibrium by a great effort, fearing to touch the white shirt of weakness and to feel the yielding, the softness and the sand.

When she sewed on buttons for him she was sewing not only buttons but also sewing together the sparse, disconnected fragments of his ideas, of his inventions, of his unfinished dreams. She was weaving and sewing and mending because he carried in himself no thread of connection, no knowledge of mending, no thread of continuity or repair. If he allowed a word to pass that was poisoned like a primitive arrow, he never sought the counter-poison, he never measured its fatal consequences. She was sewing on a button and the broken pieces of his waywardness; sewing a button and his words too loosely strung; sewing their days together to make a tapestry; their words together, their moods together, which he dispersed and tore. As he tore his clothes with his precipitations towards his wishes, his wanderings, his rambles, his peripheral journeys: She was sewing together the little proofs of his devotion out of which to make a garment for her tattered love and faith. He cut into the faith with negligent scissors, and she mended and sewed and rewove and patched. He wasted, and threw away, and could not evaluate or preserve, or contain, or keep his treasures. Like his ever torn pockets, everything slipped through and was lost, as he lost gifts, mementos—all the objects from the past. She sewed his pockets that he might keep some of their days together, hold together the key to the house, to their room, to their bed. She sewed the sleeve so he could reach out his arm and hold her, when loneliness dissolved her. She sewed the lining so

46

that the warmth would not seep out of their days together, the soft inner skin of their relationship.

He always admitted and conceded to his own wishes first, before she admitted hers. Because he was sleepy, she had to become the panoply on which he rested. Her love must fan him if he were warm and be the fire if he were cold. In illness he required day and night nursing, one for the illness, the other for the pleasure he took in her attentiveness.

His helplessness made him the *"homme fatal"* for such a woman. He reached without sureness or nimbleness for the cup, for the food, Her hand flew to finish off the uncertain gesture, to supply the missing object. His hunger for anything metamorphosed her into an Aladdin's lamp: even his dreams must be fulfilled.

Towards the greater obstacles he assumed a definitely non-combatant attitude. Rather than claim his due, or face an angry landlord, or obtain a rightful privilege, his first impulse was to surrender. Move out of the house that could not be repaired, move out of the country if his papers were not in order, move out of a woman's way if another man stalked too near. Retreat, surrender.

At times Lillian remembered her husband, and now that he was no longer the husband she could see that he had been, as much as the other men she liked; handsome and desirable, and she could not understand why he had never been able to enter her being and her feelings as a lover. She had truly liked every aspect of him except the aspect of lover. When she saw him, with the clarity of distance and separation, she saw him quite outside of herself. He stood erect, and self-sufficient, and manly. He always retained his normal male largeness and upstanding protectiveness.

But Jay . . . came towards her almost as a man who limps and whom one instinctively wishes to sustain. He came as the man who did not see very well, slightly awkward, slightly stumbling. In this helplessness, in spite of his actual stature (he was the same height as her husband) he gave the air of being smaller, more fragile, more vulnerable. It was this fear in the man, who seemed inadequate in regard to life, trapped in it, the victim of it, which somehow affected her. In a smaller, weaker dimension he seemed to reach the right proportion for his being to enter into hers. He entered by the route of her compassion. She opened as the refuge opens; not conscious that it was a man who entered (man of whom she had a certain suspicion) but a child in need. Because he knocked as a beggar begging for a retreat, as a victim seeking solace, as a weakling seeking sustenance, she opened the door without suspicion.

It was in her frenzy to shelter, cover, defend him that she laid her strength over his head like an enormous starry roof, and the stretching immensity of the boundless mother was substituted for the normal image of the man covering the woman.

Jay came and he had a cold. And though he at first pretended it was of no importance, he slowly melted entirely into her, became soft and tender, waiting to be pampered, exaggerating his cough. And they wandered through the city like two lazy southerners, he said, like two convalescents. And she pampered him laughingly, ignoring time, eating when they were hungry, and seeing a radium sunlight lighting up the rain, seeing only the shimmer of the wet streets and not the greyness. He confessed that he craved a phonograph, and they shopped together and brought it back in a taxi. They slept soundly inside the warmth of this closeness, in the luxury of their contentment. It was Jay who touched everything with the magic of his contentment. It was Jay who said: isn't this ham good, isn't this salad good, isn't this wine good. Everything was good and savory, palatable and expansive.

He gave her the savor of the present, and let her care for the morrow.

This moment of utter and absolute tasting of food, of color, this moment of human breathing. No fragment detached, errant, disconnected or lost. Because as Jay gathered the food on the table, the phonograph to his room, he gathered her into the present moment.

His taking her was not to take her or master her. He was the lover inside of the woman, as the child is inside of the woman. His caresses were as if he yearned and craved to be taken in not only as a lover; not merely to satisfy his desire but to remain within her. And her yearning answered this, by her desire to be filled. She never felt him outside of herself. Her husband had stood outside of her, and had come to visit her as a man, sensually. But he had not lodged himself as Jay had done, by reposing in her, by losing himself in her, by melting within her, with such feeling of physical intermingling as she had had with her child. Her husband had come to be renewed, to emerge again, to leave her and go to his male activities, to his struggles with the world.

The maternal and the feminine cravings were all confused in her, and all she felt was that it was through this softening and through this maternal yieldingness that Jay had penetrated where she had not allowed her husband's manliness to enter, only to visit her.

He liked prostitutes. "Because one does not have to make love to them, one does not have to write them beautiful letters." He liked them, and he liked to tell Lillian how much he liked them. He had to share all this with Lillian. He could not conceal any part of it from her, even if it hurt her. He could retain and hold nothing back from her. She was his confessor and his companion, his collaborator and his guardian angel. He

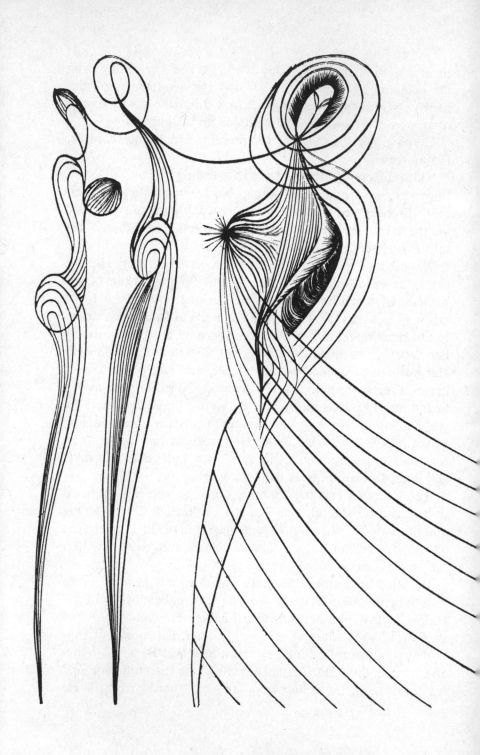

did not see her weep when he launched into descriptions. At this moment he treated her as if she were a man (or the mother). As if the spectacle of his life could amuse her. "I even think if you had seen me that time, you could have enjoyed it."

He liked her to assume the burden of their life together, its material basis. Yet when she came to him, she must be all ready to discard this mantle of responsibilities, and become a child with him. His sense of humor took wayward forms.

His favorite prank: something that could be thrown away, which others valued; something that could be broken which others preserved. Traditions, habits, possessions. His greatest enjoyment was in demolition.

One of his most joyous experiences had been when a neighbor pianist who lived on the same quiet little street with him many years ago had been obliged to visit his mother at the hospital on the same day as the piano house had promised him an exchange of pianos. The man had been looking forward to this for many months. He begged Jay to attend to this. It was a complicated affair, getting the old piano out and the new one in. It was to be done by two different houses. One, a moving man, was to take the old piano out, then the piano house was to deliver the new. Jay had laughed it all off, and walked out unconcernedly, never remembering the promise he made. When he came home he found the two pianos in the street, before the entrance of the house, and the rain pouring down on them. The sight of the two pianos in the rain sent him into an absolute state of gaiety. "It was the most surrealistic sight I have ever seen." His laughter was so contagious that Lillian laughed with him, at the same time as she felt, somehow, a kind of pain at the image of pianos drenched in rain, and a pain even for the unknown pianist's feeling on his return home.

He seized only upon the comedy of the events.

At times Lillian asked herself: what will he make of me some day, when will he hurt me? And what if he does: I will

51

try to love him gaily, more easily and loosely. To endure space
and distance and betrayals. My courage is born today. Here
lies Jay, breathing into my hair, over my neck. No hurt will
come from me. No judgment. No woman ever judged the life
stirring within her womb. I am too close to you. I will laugh
with you even if it is against me.

Against me. Now the pain about the pianos left out in the
rain suddenly touched her personally, and she understood why
she had not been able to laugh freely. Those pianos were not
only those of Jay's friend in the past, but her own too, since
she had given up playing in order to work for Jay's support.
She had surrendered any hope of becoming a concert pianist
to attend better to their immediate needs. Jay's mockery
wounded her, for it exposed his insensitiveness to anyone's
loss, and to her loss too, his incapacity to feel for others, to
understand that with the loss of her pianist self she had lost
a very large part of herself, annihilated an entire portion of
her personality, sacrificed it to him.

It was her piano Jay had left out in the rain, to be ruined. . . .

He was wearing bedroom slippers and he was painting, with
a bottle of red wine beside him. Circles of red wine on the floor.
Stains. The edge of the table was burnt by cigarette stubs.

He didn't care. He said that what he had painted today was
not as good as yesterday, but he didn't care. He was enjoying
it just the same. He wasn't worrying about art. Everything was
good, hang perfection, and he was out of cigarettes and if she
would give him one he might finish that watercolor. She had
come to interrupt him, that was good too, that was life; life
was more important than any painting, let the interruptions
come, specially in the form of a woman; let people walk in,
it was good, to paint was good, not to paint was just as good,

and eating and love making were even better, and now he was finished and he was hungry, and he wished they might go to the movies, good or bad. . . .

The room was black. Jay was asleep in her arms, now, heavily asleep. She heard the organ grinder grinding his music. It was Saturday night. Always a holiday with him, always Saturday night with the crowds laughing and shouting and the organ grinder playing.

"According to the Chinese," said Jay, awakening, "there was a realm between heaven and earth . . . this must be it."

Tornadoes of desire and exquisite calms. She felt heavy and burnt.

"I want to keep you under lock and key, Lillian."

Suddenly he leaped up with a whiplike alacrity and exuberance and began to talk about his childhood, about his life in the streets, about the women he had loved and ditched, and the women who had ditched and bitched him, as he put it. He seemed to remember everything at once, as though it was a ball inside of him which unravelled of itself, and as it unravelled made new balls which he would unravel again another day. Had he actually done all these things he was relating to Lillian with such kaleidoscopic fury and passion? Had he really killed a boy in school with a snow ball? Had he really struck his first wife down when she was with child? Had he really butted his head against a wall in sudden anger because the woman he loved had rejected him? Had he really taken abortions and thrown them off the ferry boat in order to pick up a little extra change? Had he really stolen silver from a blind news vendor?

All the layers of his past he unravelled and laid before her, his masks, his buffooneries, and she saw him pretending, driven by obscure revenges, by fears, by weaknesses.

She saw him in the past and in the world, another man from the one she knew. And like all women in love she discarded this man of the past, holding others responsible for his behavior; and thinking· before me he sheds all his poses and defenses. The legend of hardness and callousness she did not believe. She saw him innocent, as we always see the loved one, innocent and even a victim.

She felt that she knew which was the rind and which the core of the man. "You always know," he said, "what is to be laughed away."

Then he rolled over and fell asleep. No noise, no care, no work undone, no imperfection unmastered, no love scene un-resumed, no problem unsolved, ever kept him awake. He could roll over and forget. He could roll over with such grand indifference and let everything wait. When he rolled over the day ended. Nothing could be carried over into the next day. The next day would be absolutely new and clean. He just rolled over and extinguished everything. Just rolling over.

Djuna and Jay. For Djuna Jay does not look nonchalant but rather intent and listening, as if in quest of some revelation, as if he were questioning for the first time.

"I've lived so blindly. . . . No time to think much. Tons and tons of experience. Lillian always creating trouble, misery, changes, flights, dramas. No time to digest anything. And then she says I die when she leaves, that pain and war are good for me."

Djuna notices that although he is only forty years old, his hair is greying at the temple.

"Your eyes are full of wonder," he said, "as if you expected a miracle every day. I can't let you go now. I want to go places with you, obscure little places, just to be able to say: here I came with Djuna. I'm insatiable, you know. I'll ask you for the impossible. What it is, I don't know. You'll tell me, probably. You're quicker than I am. And you're the first woman with whom I feel I can be absolutely sincere. You make me happy because I can talk with you. I feel at ease with you. This is a little drunken, but you know what I mean. You always seem to know what I mean."

"You change from a wise old man to a savage. You're both timid and cruel too, aren't you?"

"There is something here it is impossible for Lillian to understand, or to break either. I feel we are friends. Don't you see? Friends. Christ, have a man and woman ever been friends, beyond love and beyond desire, and beyond everything, friends? Well, this is what I feel with you."

She hated the gaiety with which she received these words, for that condemnation of her body to be the pale watcher, the understanding one upon whom others laid their burdens, laying their heads on her lap to sleep, to be lulled from others' wounds. And even as she hated her own goodness, she heard herself say quietly, out of the very core of this sense of justice: "The destroyers do not always destroy, Jay."

"You see more, you just see more, and what you see is there all right. You get at the core of everything."

And now she was caught between them, to be the witch of words, a silent swift shadow darkened by uncanny knowledge, forgetting herself, her human needs, in the unfolding of this choking blind relationship: Lillian and Jay lacerating each other because of their different needs.

Pale beauty of the watcher shining in the dark.

Both of them now, Jay and Lillian, entered Djuna's life by gusts, and left by gusts, as they lived.

She sat for hours afterwards sailing her lingering mind like a slow river boat down the feelings they had dispersed with prodigality.

"In my case," said Jay, alone with her, "what's difficult is to keep any image of myself clear. I have never thought about myself much. The first time I saw myself full length, as it were, was in you. I have grown used to considering your image of me as the correct one. Probably because it makes me feel good. I was like a wheel without a hub."

55

"And I'm the hub, now," said Djuna, laughing.

Jay was lying on the couch in the parlor, and she had left him to dress for an evening party. When she was dressed she opened the door and then stood before her long mirror perfuming herself.

The window was open on the garden and he said: "This is like a setting for Pelleas and Melisande. It is all a dream."

The perfume made a silky sound as she squirted it with the atomizer, touching her ear lobes, her neck. "Your dress is green like a princess," he said, "I could swear it is a green I have never seen before and will never see again. I could swear the garden is made of cardboard, that the trembling of the light behind you comes from the footlights, that the sounds are music. You are almost transparent there, like the mist of perfume you are throwing on yourself. Throw more perfume on yourself, like a fixative on a water color. Let me have the atomizer. Let me put perfume all over you so that you won't disappear and fade like a water color."

She moved towards him and sat on the edge of the couch: "You don't quite believe in me as a woman," she said, with an immense distress quite out of proportion to his fancy.

"This is a setting for Pelleas and Melisande," he said, "and I know that when you leave me for that dinner I will never see you again. Those incidents last at the most three hours, and the echoes of the music maybe a day. No more."

The color of the day, the color of Byzantine paintings, that gold which did not have the firm surface of lacquer, that gold made of a fine powder easily decomposed by time, a soft powdery gold which seemed on the verge of decomposing, as if each grain of dust, held together only by atoms, was ever ready to fall apart like a mist of perfume; that gold so thin in substance that it allowed one to divine the canvas behind it, the space in the painting, the presence of reality behind its thinness, the fibrous space lying behind the illusion, the absence of color and depth, the condition of emptiness and blackness underneath the gold powder. This gold powder which had

56

fallen now on the garden, on each leaf of the trees, which was flowering inside the room, on her black hair, on the skin of his wrists, on his frayed suit sleeve, on the green carpet, on her green dress, on the bottle of perfume, on his voice, on her anxiety—the very breath of living, the very breath he and she took in to live and breathed out to live—that very breath could mow and blow it all down.

The essence, the human essence always evaporating where the dream installs itself.

The air of that summer day, when the wind itself had suspended its breathing, hung between the window and garden; the air itself could displace a leaf, could displace a word, and a displaced leaf or word might change the whole aspect of the day.

The essence, the human essence always evaporating where the dream installed itself and presided.

Every time he said he had been out the night before with friends and that he had met a woman, there was a suspense in Lillian's being, a moment of fear that he might add: I met the woman who will replace you. This moment was repeated for many years with the same suspense, the same sense of the fragility of love, without bringing any change in his love. A kind of superstition haunted her, running crosscurrent to the strength of the ties binding them, a sense of menace. At first because the love was all expansion and did not show its roots; and later, when the roots were apparent, because she expected a natural fading and death.

This fear appeared at the peak of their deepest moments, a precipice all around their ascensions. This fear appeared through the days of their tranquillity, as a sign of death rather than a sign of natural repose. It marked every moment of silence with the seal of a fatal secret. The greater the circle spanned by the attachment, the larger she saw the fissure through which human beings fall again into solitude.

The woman who personified this danger never appeared. His description gave no clues. Jay made swift portraits which he seemed to forget the next day. He was a man of many friends. His very ebullience created a warm passage but an onward flowing one, forming no grooves, fixing no image permanently. His enthusiasms were quickly burned out, sometimes in one evening. She never sought out these passing images.

Now and then he said with great simplicity: "You are the only one. You are the only one."

And then one day he said: "The other day I met a woman you would like. I was sorry you were not there. She is coming with friends this evening. Do you want to stay? You will see. She has the most extraordinary eyes."

"She has extraordinary eyes? I'll stay. I want to know her." (Perhaps if I run fast enough ahead of the present I will outdistance the shock. What is the difference between fear and intuition? How clearly I have seen what I imagine, as clearly as a vision. What is it I feel now, fear or premonition?)

Helen's knock on the door was vigorous, like an attack. She was very big and wore a severely tailored suit. She looked like a statue, but a statue with haunted eyes, inhuman eyes not made for weeping, full of animal glow. And the rest of her body a statue pinned down to its base, immobilized by a fear. She had the immobility of a Medusa waiting to transfix others into stone: hypnotic and cold, attracting others to her mineral glow.

She had two voices, one which fell deep like the voice of a man, and another light and innocent. Two women disputing inside of her.

She aroused a feeling in Lillian which was not human. She felt she was looking at a painting in which there was an infinity of violent blue. A white statue with lascivious Medusa hair. Not a woman but a legend with enormous space around her.

Her eyes were begging for an answer to an enigma. The pupils seemed to want to separate from the whites of the eyes.

Lillian felt no longer any jealousy, but a curiosity as in a dream. She did not feel any danger or fear in the meeting, only

58

an enormous blue space in which a woman stood waiting. This space and grandeur around Helen drew Lillian to her.

Helen was describing a dream she often had of being carried away by a Centaur, and Lillian could see the Centaur holding Helen's head, the head of a woman in a myth. People in myths were larger than human beings.

Helen's dreams took place in an enormous desert where she was lost among the prisons. She was tearing her hands to get free. The columns of these prisons were human beings all bound in bandages. Her own draperies were of sackcloth, the woolen robes of punishment.

And then came her questions to Lillian: "Why am I not free? I ran away from my husband and my two little girls many years ago. I did not know it then, but I didn't want to be a mother, the mother of children. I wanted to be the mother of creations and dreams, the mother of artists, the muse and the mistress. In my marriage I was buried alive. My husband was a man without courage for life. We lived as if he were a cripple, and I a nurse. His presence killed the life in me so completely that I could hardly feel the birth of my children. I became afraid of nature, of being swallowed by the mountains, stifled by the forest, absorbed by the sea. I rebelled so violently against my married life that in one day I destroyed everything and ran away, abandoning my children, my home and my native country. But I never attained the life I had struggled to reach. My escape brought me no liberation. Every night I dream the same dream of prisons and struggles to escape. It is as if only my body escaped, and not my feelings. My feelings were left over there like roots dangling when you tear a plant too violently. Violence means nothing. And it does not free one. Part of my being remained with my children, imprisoned in the past. Now I have to liberate myself wholly, body and soul, and I don't know how. The violent gestures I make only tighten the knot of resistance around me. How can one liquidate the past? Guilt and regrets can't be shed like an old coat."

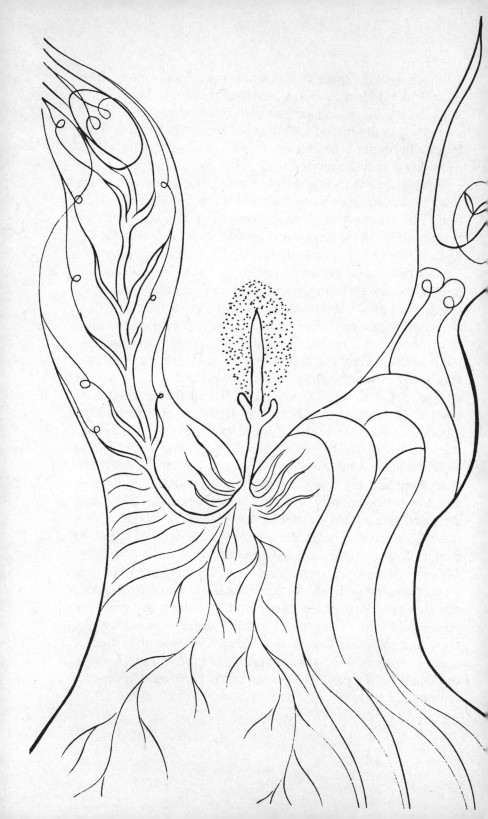

Then she saw that Lillian was affected by her story and she added: "I am grateful to Jay for having met you."

Only then Lillian remembered her painful secret. For a moment she wanted to lay her head on Helen's shoulder and confess to her: "I only came because I was afraid of you. I came because I thought you were going to take Jay away from me." But now that Helen had revealed her innermost dreams and pains, Lillian felt: perhaps she needs me more than she needs Jay. For he cannot console. He can only make her laugh.

At the same time she thought that this was equally effective. And she remembered how much Jay liked audacity in women, how some feminine part of him liked to yield, liked to be chosen, courted. Deep down he was timid, and he liked audacity in women. Helen could be given the key to his being, if Lillian told her this. If Lillian advised her to take the first step, because he was a being perpetually waiting to be ignited, never set off by himself, always seeking in women the explosion which swept him along.

All around her there were signs, signs of danger and loss.

Without knowing consciously what she was doing, Lillian began to assume the role she feared Jay might assume. She became like a lover. She was full of attentiveness and thoughtfulness. She divined Helen's needs uncannily. She telephoned her at the moment Helen felt the deepest loneliness. She said the gallant words Helen wanted to hear. She gave Helen such faith as lovers give. She gave to the friendship an atmosphere of courtship which accomplished the same miracles as love. Helen began to feel enthusiasm and hunger again. She forgot her illness to take up painting, her singing, and writing. She recreated, redecorated the place she was living in. She displayed art in her dressing, care and fantasy. She ceased to feel alone.

On a magnificent day of sun and warmth Lillian said to her: "If I were a man, I would make love to you."

Whether she said this to help Helen bloom like a flower in warmth and fervor, or to take the place of Jay and enact the courtship she had imagined, which she felt she had perhaps deprived Helen of, she did not know.

But Helen felt as rich as a woman with a new love.

At times when Lillian rang Helen's bell, she imagined Jay ringing it. And she tried to divine what Jay might feel at the sight of Helen's face. Every time she fully conceded that Helen was beautiful. She asked herself whether she was enhancing Helen's beauty with her own capacity for admiration. But then Jay too had this capacity for exalting all that he admired.

Lillian imagined him coming and looking at the paintings. He would like the blue walls. It was true he would not like her obsessions with disease, her fear of cancer. But then he would laugh at them, and his laughter might dispel her fears.

In Helen's bathroom, where she went to powder and comb her hair, she felt a greater anguish, because there she was nearer to the intimacy of Helen's life. Lillian looked at her kimono, her bedroom slippers, her creams and medicines as if trying to divine with what feelings Jay might look at them. She remembered how much he liked to go behind the scenes of people's lives. He liked to rummage among intimate belongings and dispel illusions. It was his passion. He would come out triumphantly with a jar: and this, what is this for? as if women were always seeking to delude him. He doubted the most simple things. He had often pulled at her eyelashes to make certain they were not artificial.

What would he feel in Helen's bathroom? Would he feel tenderness for her bedroom slippers? Why were there objects which inspired tenderness and others none? Helen's slippers did not inspire tenderness. Nothing about her inspired tenderness. But it might inspire desire, passion, anything else—even if she remained outside of one, like a sculpture, a painting, a form, not something which penetrated and enveloped one. But inhuman figures could inspire passion. Even if she were the statue in a Chirico painting, unable to mingle with human beings, even if she could not be impregnated by others or live inside of another all tangled in threads of blood and emotion.

62

When they went out together Lillian always expected the coincidence which would bring the three of them together to the same concert, the same exhibit, the same play. But if it never happened. They always missed each other. All winter long the coincidences of city life did not bring the three of them together. Lillian began to think that this meeting was not destined, that it was not she who was keeping them apart.

Helen's eyes grew greener and sank more and more into the myth. She could not feel. And Lillian felt as if she were keeping from her the man who might bring her back to life. Felt almost as if she were burying her alive by not giving her Jay.

Perhaps Lillian was imagining too much.

Meanwhile Helen's need of Lillian grew immense. She was not contented with Lillian's occasional visits. She wanted to fill the entire void of her life with Lillian. She wanted Lillian to stay over night when she was lonely. The burden grew heavier and heavier.

Lillian became frightened. In wanting to amuse and draw Helen away from her first interest in Jay, she had surpassed herself and become this interest.

Helen dramatized the smallest incident, suffered from insomnia, said her bedroom was haunted at night, sent for Lillian on every possible occasion.

Lillian was punished for playing the lover. Now she must be the husband, too. Helen had forgotten Jay but the exchange had left Lillian as a hostage.

Not knowing how to lighten the burden she said one day: "You ought to travel again. This city cannot be good for you. A place where you have been lonely and unhappy for so long must be the wrong place."

That very night there was a fire in Helen's house, in the apartment next to hers. She interpreted this as a sign that Lillian's intuitions for her were wise. She decided to travel again.

They parted at the corner of a street, gaily, as if for a short separation. Gaily, with green eyes flashing at one another.

They lost each other's address. It all dissolved very quickly, like a dream.

And then Lillian felt free again. Once again she had worn the warrior armor to protect a core of love. Once again she had worn the man's costume.

Jay had not made her woman, but the husband and mother of his weakness.

Lillian confessed to Jay that she was pregnant. He said: "We must find the money for an abortion." He looked irritated. She waited. She thought he might slowly evince interest in the possibility of a child. He revealed only an increased irritation. It disturbed his plans, his enjoyment. The mere idea of a child was an intrusion. He let her go alone to the doctor. He expressed resentment. And then she understood.

She sat alone one day in their darkened room.

She talked to the child inside of her.

"My little one not born yet, I feel your small feet kicking against my womb. My little one not born yet, it is very dark in the room you and I are sitting in, just as dark as it must be for you inside of me, but it must be sweeter for you to be lying in the warmth than it is for me to be seeking in this dark room the joy of not knowing, not feeling, not seeing; the joy of lying still in utter warmth and this darkness. All of us forever seeking this warmth and this darkness, this being alive without pain, this being alive without anxiety, fear or loneliness. You are impatient to live, you kick with your small feet, but you ought to die. You ought to die in warmth and darkness because you are a child without a father. You will not find on earth this father as large as the sky, big enough to hold your whole being and your fears, larger than house or church. You will not find a father who will lull you and cover you with his greatness and his warmth. It would be better if you died inside of me, quietly, in the warmth and in the darkness."

Did the child hear her? At six months she had a miscarriage and lost it.

Lillian was giving a concert in a private home which was like a temple of treasures. Paintings and people had been collected with expert and exquisite taste. There was a concentration of beautiful women so that one was reminded of a hothouse exhibit.

The floor was so highly polished there were two Lillians, two white pianos, two audiences.

The piano under her strong hands became small like a child's piano. She overwhelmed it, she tormented it, crushed it. She played with all her intensity, as if the piano must be possessed or possess her.

The women in the audience shivered before this *corps à corps.*

Lillian was pushing her vigor into the piano. Her face was full of vehemence and possessiveness. She turned her face upwards as if to direct the music upwards, but the music would not rise, volatilize itself. It was too heavily charged with passion.

She was not playing to throw music into the blue space, but to reach some climax, some impossible union with the piano, to reach that which men and women could reach together. A moment of pleasure, a moment of fusion. The passion and the blood in her rushed against the ivory notes and overloaded them. She pounded the coffer of the piano as she wanted her own body pounded and shattered. And the pain on her face was that of one who reached neither sainthood nor pleasure. No music rose and passed out of the window, but a sensual

65

cry, heavy with unspent forces. . . .

Lillian storming against her piano, using the music to tell all how she wanted to be stormed with equal strength and fervor.

This tidal power was still in her when the women moved towards her to tell her it was wonderful. She rose from the piano as if she would engulf them, the smaller women; she embraced them with all the fervor of unspent intensity that had not reached a climax—which the music, like too delicate a vessel, the piano with too delicate a frame, had not been able to contain.

It was while Lillian was struggling to tear from the piano what the piano could not possibly give her that Djuna's attention was wafted towards the window.

In the golden salon, with the crystal lamps, the tapestries and the paintings there were immense bay windows, and Djuna's chair had been placed in one of the recesses, so that she sat on the borderline between the perfumed crowd and the silent, static garden.

It was late in the afternoon, the music had fallen back upon the people like a heavy storm cloud which could not be dispersed to lighten and lift them, the air was growing heavy, when her eyes caught the garden as if in a secret exposure. As everyone was looking at Lillian, Djuna's sudden glance seemed to have caught the garden unaware, in a dissolution of peace and greens. A light rain had washed the faces of the leaves, the knots in the tree trunks stared with aged eyes, the grass was drinking, there was a sensual humidity as if leaves, trees, grass and wind were all in a state of caress.

The garden had an air of nudity.

Djuna let her eyes melt into the garden. The garden had an air of nudity, of efflorescence, of abundance, of plenitude.

The salon was gilded, the people were costumed for false roles, the lights and the faces were attenuated, the gestures were starched—all but Lillian whose nature had not been stylized, compressed or gilded, and whose nature was warring with a piano.

Music did not open doors.

Nature flowered, caressed, spilled, relaxed, slept.

In the gilded frames, the ancestors were mummified forever, and descendants took the same poses. The women were candied in perfume, conserved in cosmetics, the men preserved in their elegance. All the violence of naked truths had evaporated, volatilized within gold frames.

And then, as Djuna's eyes followed the path carpeted with detached leaves, her eyes encountered for the first time three full-length mirrors placed among the bushes and flowers as casually as in a boudoir. Three mirrors.

The eyes of the people inside could not bear the nudity of the garden, its exposure. The eyes of the people had needed the mirrors, delighted in the fragility of reflections. All the truth of the garden, the moisture, and the worms, the insects and the roots, the running sap and the rotting bark, had all to be reflected in the mirrors.

Lillian was playing among vast mirrors. Lillian's violence was attenuated by her reflection in the mirrors.

The garden in the mirror was polished with the mist of perfection. Art and artifice had breathed upon the garden and the garden had breathed upon the mirror, and all the danger of truth and revelation had been exorcised.

Under the house and under the garden there were subterranean passages and if no one heard the premonitory rumblings before the explosion, it would all erupt in the form of war and revolution.

The humiliated, the defeated, the oppressed, the enslaved. Woman's misused and twisted strength. . . .

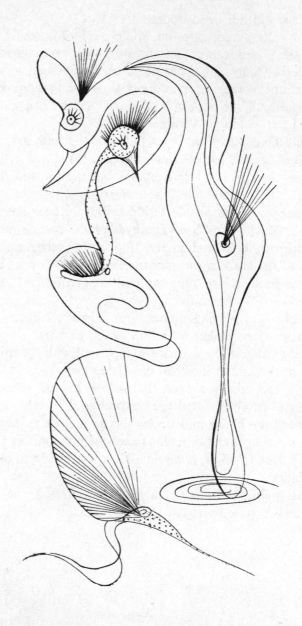

Bread and the Wafer

WHEN JAY WAS NOT TALKING or painting he sang. He sang under his breath or loudly according to his occupation. He dressed and ate to a rhythm, as if he were executing a primitive ritual with his big body that had not been quite chiselled off with the finish of a classical sculptor but whose outline had remained rugged as if it were not yet entirely separated from the wood or stone out of which it had been carved. One expected to feel the roughness of it as when one touched a clay figure before it had been thrust into the potter's oven.

He had retained so much of the animal, a graceful awkward-

69

ness in his walk, strong rhythmic gestures in full accord with the pull of the muscles, an animal love of stretching, yawning, relaxing, of sleeping anywhere, of obeying every impulse of his body. A body without nerves or tensions.

When he stood upon his well-planted, well-separated feet it was as if like a tree he would immediately take root there. As he had taken roots lustily in Paris now, in the café, in his studio, in his life with Lillian.

Wherever he found himself he was well, as if the living roots of his body could sprout in any ground, at any time, under any sky. His preference went, however, to artificial lights, crowds, and he grew, talked, and laughed best in the center of a stream of people.

If he were waiting he would fill the waiting with explosions of song, or fall into enthusiastic observations. The spectacle of the street was enough for him; whatever was there was enough for him, for his boundless satisfaction.

Placed before a simple meal he would begin his prestidigitations: this steak is wonderful . . . how *good* it is. How awfully good! And the onions. . . . He made sounds of delight. He poured his enthusiasm over the meal like a new condiment. The steak began to glow, to expand, to multiply under the warmth of his fervor. Every dish was wrapped in amorous appreciation, as if it had been brought to the table with a fire burning under it and was flaming in rum like a Christmas pudding.

"Good, good, good," said his palate, said his roseate cheeks, said his bowed assenting head, said his voice, all expanding in prodigious additions, as if he were pushing multiple buttons of delight, and colors burst from the vegetables, meat, salad, cheese and wine. Even the parsley assumed a festive air like a birthday candle on a cake. "Ah, ah, ah, the salad!" he said, pouring over it a voice like an unguent along with the olive oil.

His pleasure donned the white cap of the proud chef playing gay scales of flavors, festooning the bread and wine with the high taste of banquets.

70

The talk, too, burst its boundaries. He started a discussion, let it take fire and spread, but the moment it took too rigid a form he began to laugh, spraying it, liquefying it in a current of gaiety.

To laugh. To laugh. "I'm not laughing at you. I'm not laughing at anyone, at anybody. I just can't help myself. I don't care a bit, not a bit, who's right."

"But you must care," said Faustin, speaking through a rigid mask of sadness which made his face completely static, and one was surprised that the words could come through the closed mouth. "You must care, you must hold on to something."

"I never hold on," said Jay. "Why hold on? Whatever you hold on to dies. There comes Colette. Sit here, Colette. How was the trade today? Colette, these people are talking about holding on. You must hold on, you must care, they say. Do you hold on, Colette? They pass like a stream, don't they, and you'd be surprised if the same ones bobbed up continuously, surprised and maybe bored. It's a good stream, isn't it, just a stream that does not nestle into you to become an ulcer, a good washing stream that cleanses as it flows, and flows clean through."

With this he drank fully from his Pernod, drank indeed as if the stream of absinthe, of ideas, feelings, talk, should pass and change every day guided only by thirst.

"You're drunk," said Colette. "You don't make sense."

"Only the drunks and the insane make sense, Colette, that's where you're wrong. Only the drunks and the insane have discarded the unessential for chaos, and only in chaos there is richness."

"If you go on this way," said Faustin, his finger pointing upward like a teacher of Sanskrit, "someone will have to take care of you while you spill in all directions recklessly. You'll need taking care of, for yours is no real freedom but an illusion of freedom, or perhaps just rebellion. Chaos always turns out to be the greatest trap of all in which you'll find yourself more

71

securely imprisoned than anyone."

At the words "taking care" Jay had turned automatically towards Lillian and read in her eyes that fixed, immutable love which was his compass.

When Faustin was there at the café conversation would always start at the top of a pyramid without any gradual ascension. It would start with the problems of form, being and becoming, physiognomics, destiny versus incident, the coming of the fungoid era, the middle brain and the tertiary moon!

Faustin talked to build. He insisted that each talk should be a complete brick to add to a careful construction. He always started to draw on the marble-top table or on the tablecloth: this is our first premise, this is our second premise, and now we will reach the third. No sooner had he made on the table the semblance of a construction than there would come into Jay's eyes an absinthe glint which was not really the drink but some layer of his being which the drink had peeled away, which was hard, cruel, mischievous. His phrases would begin to break and scatter, to run wild like a machine without springs, gushing forth from the contradictory core of him which refused all crystallizations.

It happened every time the talk approached a definite conclusion, every time some meaning was about to be extracted from confusion. It was as if he felt that any attempt at understanding were a threat to the flow of life, to his enjoyment. As if understanding would threaten the tumultuous current or arrest it.

They were eating in a small café opposite the Gare St. Lazare, a restaurant wide open on the street. They were eating on the street and it was as if the street were full of people who were eating and drinking with them.

With each mouthful Lillian swallowed, she devoured the noises of the street, the voices and the echoes they dropped, the swift glances which fell on her like pieces of lighted wick from guttering candles. She was only the finger of a whole bigger body, a body hungry, thirsty, avid.

72

The wine running down her throat was passing through the throat of the world. The warmth of the day was like a man's hand on her breast, the smell of the street like a man's breath on her neck. Wide open to the street like a field washed by a river.

Shouts and laughter exploded near them from the art students on their way to the *Quatz' Arts* Ball. Egyptians and Africans in feather and jewelry, with the sweat shining on their brown painted bodies. They ran to catch the bus and it was like a heaving sea of glistening flesh shining between colored feathers and barbaric jewelry, with the muscles swelling when they laughed.

A few of them entered the restaurant, shouting and laughing. They circled around their table, like savages dancing around a stake.

The street organ was unwinding *Carmen* from its roll of tinfoil voices.

The same restaurant, another summer evening; but Jay is not there. The wine has ceased passing down Lillian's throat. It has no taste. The food does not seem rich. The street is separated from the restaurant by little green bushes she had not noticed before; the noises seem far from her, and the faces remote. Everything now happens outside, and not within her own body. Everything is distant and separated. It does not flow inside of her and carry her away.

Because Jay is not there? Does it mean it was not she who had drunk the wine, eaten the food, but that she had eaten and drunk through the pores of his pleasure and his appetite? Did she receive her pleasure, her appetite, through his gusto, his lust, his throat?

That night she had a dream: Jay had become her iron lung.

She was lying inside of him and breathing through him. She felt a great anxiety, and thought: if he leaves me then I will die. When Jay laughed she laughed; when he enjoyed she enjoyed. But all the time there was this fear that if he left her she would no longer eat, laugh or breathe.

When he welcomed friends, was at ease in groups, accepted and included all of life, she experienced this openness, this total absence of retraction through him. When alone, she still carried some constriction which interfered with deep intakes of life and people. She had thought that by yielding to him they would be removed.

She felt at times that she had fallen in love with Jay's freedom, that she had dreamed he would set her free, but that somehow or other he had been unable to accomplish this.

At night she had the feeling that she was being possessed by a cannibal.

His appetite. The gifts she made him of her feelings. How he devoured the response of her flesh, her thoughts about him, her awareness of him. As he devoured new places, new people, new impressions. His gigantic devouring spirit in quest of substance.

Her fullness constantly absorbed by him, all the changes in her, her dissolutions and rebirths, all this could be thrown into the current of his life, his work, and be absorbed like twigs by a river.

He had the appetite of the age of giants.

He could read the fattest books, tackle the most immense paintings, cover the vastest territories in his wanderings, attack the most solemn system of ideas, produce the greatest quantity of work. He excluded nothing: everything was food. He could eat the trivial and the puerile, the ephemeral and the gross, the scratchings on a wall, the phrase of a passerby, the defect on a face, the pale sonata streaming from a window, the snoring of a beggar on a bench, flowers on the wallpaper of a hotel room, the odor of cabbage on a stairway, the haunches of a bareback rider in the circus. His eyes devoured details, his

74

hands leaped to grasp.

His whole body was like a sensitive sponge, drinking, eating, absorbing with a million cells of curiosity.

She felt caught in the immense jaws of his desire, felt herself dissolving, ripping open to his descent. She felt herself yielding up to his dark hunger, her feelings smouldering, rising from her like smoke from a black mass.

Take me, take me, take my gifts and my moods and my body and my cries and my joys and my submissions and my yielding and my terror and my abandon, take all you want.

He ate her as if she were something he wanted to possess inside of his body like a fuel. He ate her as if she were a food he needed for daily sustenance.

She threw everything into the jaws of his desire and hunger. Threw all she had known, experienced and given before. She gathered all to feed his ravenousness; she went into the past and brought back her past selves, she took the present self and the future self and threw them into the jaws of his curiosity, flung them before the greed of his questions.

The red lights from a hotel sign shone into the studio. A red well. A charging, a hoofing, a clanging, a rushing through the body. Thumping. The torrent pressure of a machine, panting, sliding back and forth, back and forth.

Swing. Swing. The bed-like stillness and downiness of summer foliage. Roll. Roll. Clutch and fold. Steam. Steam. The machine on giant oiled gongs yielding honey, rivers of honey on a bed of summer foliage. The boat slicing open the lake waters, ripples extending to the tips of the hair and the roots of the toes.

No stronger sea than this sea of feelings she swam into with him, was rolled by, no waves like the waves of desire, no foam like the foam of pleasure. No sand warmer than skin, the sand and quicksands of caresses. No sun more powerful than the sun of desire, no snow like the snow of her resistance melting in blue joys, no earth anywhere as rich as flesh.

She slept, she fell into trances, she was lost, she was renewed, she was blessed, pierced by joy, lulled, burned, consumed, purified, born and reborn within the whale belly of the night.

At the beginning of their life together he had constantly reverted to his childhood as if to deposit in her hands all the mementoes of his early voyages.

In all love's beginnings this journey backwards takes place: the desire of every lover to give his loved one all of his different selves, from the beginning.

What was most vivid in Jay's memory was the treachery of his parents.

"I was about six years old when a brand-new battleship docked at the Brooklyn Navy yard. All the boys in the neighborhood had been taken to see it but me. They kept describing it in every detail until I could dream of it as if I had seen it myself. I wanted desperately for my father to take me to it. He kept postponing the visit. Then one day he told me to wash my hands and ears carefully, to put on my best suit and said he was taking me to see the battleship. I washed myself as never before. I walked beside my father neat, and proud and drunk with gaiety. I kept telling him the number of guns we would see, the number of portholes. My father listened with apparent interest. He walked me into a doctor's office instead, where I had my tonsils taken out. The pain was a million times multiplied by the shock of disillusion, of betrayal, by the violent contrast between my dream, my expectations, and the brutal reality of the operation."

As he told this story it was clear to Lillian that he still felt the shock of the deception and had never forgiven his father. The intensity of the wish had been made even greater by the poverty of his childhood which made the visit to the battleship a unique pleasure discussed by his playmates for a whole year and not easily forgotten.

"One very cold, snowy night my mother and I were walking towards the river. I was very small, five years old maybe. My mother was walking too fast for me, and I felt terribly cold, especially my hands. My mother carried a muff. Every now and then she took her right hand out of the muff to grab mine when we crossed the streets. The warmth of her hand warmed me all through. Then she would drop my hand again and nestle hers back in her muff. I began to weep: I wanted to put my hand inside of her muff but she wouldn't let me. I wept and raged as if it were a matter of life and death—probably was, for me. I wanted the warmth and her naked hands. The more I wept and pulled at the muff the harsher my mother got. Finally she slapped my hand so I would let the muff go."

As he told this his blue eyes became the eyes of an irrevocably angry child. Lillian could see clear through his open eyes as through the wrong end of a telescope, a diminutive Jay raging, cold and thwarted, with his blue frozen hands reaching for his mother's muff.

This image was not being transmitted to Lillian the woman, but to the responsive child in herself understanding and sharing his anger and disillusion. It was the child in herself who received it as it sank through and beyond the outer layer of the woman who sat there listening with a woman's full body, a woman's face. But of this response there was no outer sign showing for Jay to see: the child in her lay so deeply locked within her, so deeply buried, that no sign of its existence or of its response was apparent. It did not beckon through her eyes which showed only a woman's compassion, nor alter her gestures nor the pose of her body which was the pose of a woman listening to a child and looking at his smallness without herself changing stature. At this moment, like Jay, she could have slipped out of her maturity, of her woman's body, and exposed her child's face, eyes, movements, and then Jay would have seen it, known that he had communicated with it, touched it by way of his own childhood, and the child might have met the child and become aware of its similar needs.

By her attitude she did not become one with him in this return to his past self. What she overtly extended to him was one who seemed done with her child self and who would replace the harsh mother, extend the muff and the warm naked hands.

She became, at that instant, indelibly fixed in his eyes not as another child with possibly equal needs, but as the stronger one in possession of the power to dispense to all *his* needs.

From now on was established an inequality in power: he was the cold and hungry one, she the muff and the warm naked hands.

From now on her needs, concealed and buried as mere interferences with the accomplishment of this role, were condemned to permanent muteness. Strong direction was given to her activity as the muff, as the provider of innumerable battleships in compensation for the one he had been cheated of. Giving to him on all levels, from book to blanket to phonograph to fountain pen to food, was always and forever the battleship he had dreamed and not seen. It was the paying off of a debt to the cheated child.

Lillian did not know then that the one who believes he can pay this early debt meets a bottomless well. Because the first denial has set off a fatality of revenge which no amount of giving can placate. Present in every child and criminal is this conviction that no retribution will repair the injury done. The man who was once starved may revenge himself upon the world not by stealing just once, or by stealing only what he needs, but by taking from the world an endless toll in payment of something irreplaceable, which is the lost faith.

This diminutive Jay who appeared in the darkness when he evoked his childhood was also a personage who could come nearer to her own frightened self without hurting her than the assertive, rather ruthless Jay who appeared in the daytime when he resumed his man's life. When he described his smallness

78

and how he could enter saloons to call for his father without having to swing the doors open, it seemed to Lillian that she could encompass this small figure better in the range of her vision than the reckless, amorphous, protean Jay whose personality flowed into so many channels like swift mercury.

When Jay described the vehemence, the wildness, the hunger with which he went out into the streets to play, it seemed to her that he was simultaneously describing and explaining the vehemence, the hunger, the wildness with which he went out at night now and left her alone, so that the present became strangely innocent in her mind.

When he talked about his impulses towards other women he took on the expression not of a man who had enjoyed another woman sensually, but of a gay, irrepressible child whose acts were absolutely uncontrollable; it became no longer infidelity but a childish, desperate eagerness to "go to the street and play."

She saw him in the present as the same child needing to boast of his conquests out of a feeling of helplessness, needing to be admired, to win many friends, and thus she attenuated in herself the anxiety she experienced at his many far-flung departures from her.

When she rebelled at times he looked completely baffled by her rebellions, as if there were nothing in his acts which could harm her. She always ended by feeling guilty: he had given her his entire self to love, including the child, and now, out of noblesse oblige, she could not possibly act . . . like his harsh mother!

He looked at the sulphur-colored Pernod and drank it.

He was in the mood to paint his self-portrait for anyone who wanted to listen: this always happened after someone had attacked his painting, or claimed some overdue debt.

So Jay drank Pernod and explained: "I'm like Buddha who chose to live in poverty. I abandoned my first wife and child for a religious life. I now depend on the bowl of rice given to me by my followers."

"What do you teach?" asked a young man who was not susceptible to the contagion of Jay's gaiety.

"A life from which all suffering is absent."

But to the onlooker who saw them together, Lillian, ever alert to deflect the blows which might strike at him, it seemed much more as if Jay had merely unburdened all sadnesses upon her rather than as if he had found a secret for eliminating them altogether. His disciples inevitably discovered they, too, must find themselves a Lillian to achieve his way of life.

"I'm no teacher," said Jay. "I'm just a happy man. I can't explain how I arrived at such a state." He pounded his chest with delight. "Give me a bowl of rice and I will make you as joyous as I am."

This always brought an invitation to dinner.

"Nothing to worry about," he always said to Lillian. "Someone will always invite me to dinner."

In return for the dinner Jay took them on a guided tour of his way of life. Whoever did not catch his mood could go overboard. He was no initiator. Let others learn by osmosis!

But this was only one of his self-portraits. There were other days when he did not like to present himself as a laughing man who communicated irresponsibility and guiltlessness, but as the great barbarian. In this mood he exulted the warrior, the invaders, the pillagers, the rapers. He believed in violence. He saw himself as Attila avenging the impurities of the world by bloodshed. He saw his paintings then as a kind of bomb.

As he talked he became irritated with the young man who had asked him what he taught, for Jay noticed that he walked back and forth constantly but not the whole length of the studio. He would take five long steps, stop mechanically, and turn back like an automaton. The nervous compulsion disturbed Jay and he stopped him: "I wish you'd sit down."

"Excuse me, I'm really sorry," he said, stopping dead. A look of anxiety came to his face. "You see, I've just come out of jail. In jail I could only walk five steps, no more. Now when I'm in a large room, it disturbs me. I want to explore it,

80

familiarize myself with it, at the same time I feel compelled to walk no further."

"You make me think of a friend I had," said Jay, "who was very poor and a damned good painter and of the way he escaped from his narrow life. He was living at the Impasse Rouet, and as you know probably, that's the last step before you land at the Hospital, the Insane Asylum or the Cemetery. He lived in one of those houses set far back into a courtyard, full of studios as bare as cells. There was no heat in the house and most of the windows were cracked and let the wind blow through. Those who owned stoves, for the most part, didn't own any coal. Peter's studio had an additional anomaly: it had no windows, only a transom. The door opened directly on the courtyard. He had no stove, a cot whose springs showed through the gored mattress. No sheets, and only one old blanket. No doorbell, of course. No electricity, as he couldn't pay the bill. He used candles, and when he had no money for candles he got fat from the butcher and burnt it. The concierge was like an old octopus, reaching everywhere at once with her man's voice and inquisitive whiskers. Peter was threatened with eviction when he hit upon an idea. Every year, as you know, foreign governments issued prizes for the best painting, the best sculpture. Peter got one of the descriptive pamphlets from the Dutch embassy where he had a friend. He brought it to the concierge and read it to her, then explained: Fact one: he was the only Dutch painter in Paris. Fact two: a prize would be given to the best painting produced by a Dutchman, amounting to half a million francs. The concierge was smart enough to see the point. She agreed to let the rent slide for a month, to lend him money for paints and a little extra change for cigarettes while he painted something as big as the wall of his cell. In return, with the prize money, he promised to buy her a little house in the country for her old age—with garden. Now he could paint all day. It was spring; he left his door open and the concierge settled in the courtyard with her heavy red hands at rest on her lap and thought that each brush stroke added to her house and garden. After two months she got impatient. He was still painting, but he was also eating, smoking cigarettes, drinking aperitifs and even sleeping at times more than eight hours. Peter rushed to the embassy and asked his friend to pay him an official call. The friend managed to borrow the official car with the Dutch coat of arms and paid the painter a respectful visit. This reassured her for another month. Every evening they read the booklet together: "the prize will be handed over in cash one week after the jury decides upon its value. . . ." The concierge's beatitude was contagious. The entire house benefited from her mellowness. Until one morning when the newspapers published the name and photograph of the genuine Dutch painter who had actually won the prize and then without warning she turned into a cyclone. Peter's door was locked. She climbed on a chair to look through the transom to make sure he was not asleep or drunk. To her great horror she saw a body hanging from the ceiling. He had hanged himself! She called for help. The police forced the door open. What they cut down was a mannequin of wax and old rags, carefully painted by Peter.

"The funny thing," added Jay after a pause, "is that after this his luck turned. When he hanged his effigy he seemed to have killed the self who had been a failure."

The visitors left.

Then all the laughter in him subsided into a pool of serenity. His voice became soft. Just as he loved the falsities of his roles, he loved also to rest from these pranks and attitudes and crystallize in the white heat of Lillian's faith.

And when all the gestures and talk seemed lulled, suddenly he sprang up again with a new mood, a fanatic philosopher who walked up and down the studio punctuating the torrent of his ideas with fist blows on the tables. A nervous lithe walk, while he churned ideas like leaves on a pyre which never turned to ash.

Then all the words, the ideas, the memories, were drawn together like the cords of a hundred kites and he said:

82

"I'd like to work now."

Lillian watched the transformation in him. She watched the half open mouth close musingly, the scattered talk crystallizing. This man so easily swayed, caught, moved, now collecting his strength again. At that moment she saw the big man in him, the man who appeared to be merely enjoying recklessly, idling, roaming, but deep down set upon a terribly earnest goal: to hand back to life all the wealth of material he had collected, intent on making restitution to the world for what he had absorbed with his enormous creator's appetite.

There remained in the air only the echoes of his resonant voice, the hot breath of his words, the vibration of his pounding gestures.

She rose to lock the door of the studio upon the world. She drew in long invisible bolts. She pulled in rustless shutters. Silence. She imprisoned within herself that mood and texture of Jay which would never go into his work, or be given or exposed to the world, that which she alone could see and know.

While Lillian slept Jay reassembled his dispersed selves.

At this moment the flow in him became purposeful.

In his very manner of pressing the paint tube there was intensity; often it spurted like a geyser, was wasted, stained his clothes and the floor. The paint, having appeared in a minor explosion, proceeded to cause a major one on the canvas.

The explosion caused not a whole world to appear, but a shattered world of fragments. Bodies, objects, cities, trees, animals were all splintered, pierced, impaled.

It was actually a spectacle of carnage.

The bodies were dismembered and every part of them misplaced. In the vast dislocation eyes were placed where they had never visited a body, the hands and feet were substituted

83

for the face, the faces bore four simultaneous facets with one empty void between. Gravity was lost, all relation between the figures were like those of acrobats. Flesh became rubber, trees flesh, bones became plumage, and all the life of the interior, cells, nerves, sinew lay exposed as by a merely curious surgeon not concerned with closing the incisions. All his painter's thrusts opening, exposing, dismembering in the violent colors of reality.

The vitality with which he exploded, painted dissolution and disintegration, with which his energy broke familiar objects into unfamiliar components, was such that people who walked into a room full of his painting were struck only with the power and force of these brilliant fragments as by an act of birth. That they were struck only by broken pieces of an exploded world, they did not see. The force of the explosion, the weight, density and brilliance was compelling.

To each lost, straying piece of body or animal was often added the growth and excrescences of illness, choking moss on southern trees, cocoons of the unborn, barnacles and parasites.

It was Jay's own particular jungle in which the blind warfare of insects and animals was carried on by human beings. The violence of the conflicts distorted the human body. Fear became muscular twistings like the tangled roots of trees, dualities sundered them in two separate pieces seeking separate lives. The entire drama took place at times in stagnant marshes, in petrified forests where every human being was a threat to the other.

The substance that could weld them together again was absent. Through the bodies irretrievable holes had been drilled and in place of a heart there was a rubber pump or a watch.

The mild, smiling Jay who stepped out of these infernos always experienced a slight tremor of uneasiness when he passed from the world of his painting to Lillian's room. If she was awake she would want to see what he had been doing. And she was always inevitably shocked. To see the image of her

84

inner nightmares exposed affected her as the sight of a mirror affects a cat or a child. There was always a moment of strained silence.

This underground of hostility she carried in her being, of which her body felt only the blind impacts, the shocks, was now clearly projected.

Jay was always surprised at her recoil, for he could see how Lillian was a prolongation of this warfare on canvas, how at the point where he left violence and became a simple, anonymous, mild-mannered man, it was she who took up the thread and enacted the violence directly upon people.

But Lillian had never seen herself doing it.

Jay would say: "I wish you wouldn't quarrel with everyone, Lillian."

"I wish you wouldn't paint such horrors. Why did you paint Faustin without a head? That's what he's proudest of—his head."

"Because that's what he should lose, to come alive. You hate him too. Why did you hand him his coat the other night in such a way that he was forced to leave?"

In the daylight they repudiated each other. At night their bodies recognized a familiar substance: gunpowder, and they made their peace together.

In the morning it was he who went out for bread, butter and milk for breakfast, while she made the coffee.

When she locked the studio for the night, she locked out anxiety. But when Jay got into his slack morning working clothes and stepped out jauntily, whistling, he had a habit of locking the door again—and in between, anxiety slipped in again.

He locks the door, he has forgotten that I am here.

Thus she interpreted it, because of her feeling that once he had taken her, he deserted her each time anew. No contact was ever continuous with him. So he locked the door, forgot she was there, deserted her.

When she confessed this to Djuna, Djuna who had continued to write for Lillian the Chinese dictionary of counter-interpretations, she laughed: "Lillian, have you ever thought that he might be locking you in to keep you for himself?"

Lillian was accurate in her feeling that when Jay left the studio he was disassociated from her, and not from her alone, but from himself.

He walked out in the street and became one with the street. His mood became the mood of the street. He dissolved and became eye, ear, smile.

There are days when the city exposes only its cripples, days when the bus must stop close to the curb to permit a one-legged man to board it, days when a man without legs rests his torso on a rolling stand and propels himself with his hands, days when a head is held up by a pink metal truss, days when blind men ask to be guided, and Jay knew as he looked, absorbing every detail, that he would paint them, even though had he been consulted all the cripples of the world would be destroyed excepting the smiling old men who sat on benches beatifically drunk, because they were his father. He had so many fathers, for he was one to see the many. *I believe we have a hundred fathers and mothers and lovers all interchangeable, and that's the flaw in Lillian, for her there is only one mother, one father, one husband, one lover, one son, one daughter, irreplaceable, unique—her world is too small. The young girl who just passed me with lightning in her eyes is my daughter. I could take her home as my daughter in place of the one I lost. The world is full of fathers, whenever I need one I only need to stop and talk to one ... this one sitting there with a white beard and a captain's cap ...*

"Do you want a cigarette, Captain?"

"I'm no captain, Monsieur, I was a Legionnaire, as you can

see by my beard. Are you sure you haven't a butt or two? I'd rather have a butt. I like my independence, you know, I collect butts. A cigarette is charity. I'm a hobo, you know, not a beggar."

His legs were wrapped in newspapers. "Because of the varicose veins. They sort of bother me in the winter. I could stay with the nuns, they would take care of me. But imagine having to get up every morning at six at the sound of a bell, of having to eat exactly at noon, and then at seven and having to sleep at nine. I'm better here. I like my independence." He was filling his pipe with butts.

Jay sat beside him.

"The nuns are not bad to me. I collect crusts of old bread from the garbage cans and I sell them to the hospital for the soup they serve to pregnant women."

"Why did you leave the Legion?"

"During my campaigns I received letters from an unknown godmother. You can't imagine what those letters were, Monsieur, I haven't got them because I wore them out reading them there, in the deserts. They were so warm I could have heated my hands over them if I had been fighting in a cold country. Those letters made me so happy that on my first furlough I looked her up. That was quite a task, believe me, she had no address! She sold bananas from a little cart, and she slept under the bridges. I spent my furlough sitting with her like this with a bottle of red wine. It was a good life; I deserted the Legion."

He again refused a cigarette and Jay walked on.

The name of a street upon an iron plate, Rue Dolent, Rue Dolent decomposed for him into dolorous, doliente, douleur. The plate is nailed to the prison wall, the wall of China, of our chaos and our mysteries, the wall of Jericho, of our religions and our guilts, the wall of lamentation, the wall of the prison of Paris. Wall of soot, encrusted dust. No prison breaker ever crumbled this wall, the darkest and longest of all leaning heavily upon the little Rue Dolent Doliente Douleur which,

although on the free side of the wall, is the saddest street of
all Paris. On one side are men whose crimes were accomplished
in a moment of rage, rebellion, violence. On the other, grey
figures too afraid to hate, to rebel, to kill openly. On the free
side of the wall they walk with iron bars in their hearts and
stones on their feet carrying the balls and chains of their ob-
sessions. Prisoners of their weakness, of their self-inflicted ill-
nesses and slaveries. No need of guards and keys! They will
never escape from themselves, and they only kill others with
the invisible death rays of their impotence.

He did not know any longer where he was walking. The
personages of the street and the personages of his paintings
extended into each other, issued from one to fall into the other,
fell into the work, or out of it, stood now with, now without,
frames. The man on the sliding board, had he not seen him
before in Coney Island when he was a very young man and
walking with a woman he loved? This half-man had followed
them persistently along the boardwalk, on a summer night made
for caresses, until the woman had recoiled from his pursuit
and left both the half-man and Jay. Again the man on wheels
had appeared in his dream, but this time it was his mother in
a black dress with black jet beads on it as he had seen her
once about to attend a funeral. Why he should deprive his
mother of the lower half of her body, he didn't know. No fear
of incest had ever barred his way to women, and he had always
been able to want them all, and the more they looked like his
mother the better.

He saw the seven hard benches of the pawnshop where he
had spent so many hours of his life in Paris waiting to borrow
a little cash on his paintings, and felt the bitterness he had
tasted when they underestimated his work! The man behind
the counter had eyes dilated from appraising objects. Jay
laughed out loud at the memory of the man who had pawned
his books and continued to read them avidly until the last
minute like one condemned to future starvation. He had
painted them all pawning their arms and legs, after seeing

them pawn the stove that would keep them warm, the coat that would save them from pneumonia, the dress that would attract customers. A grotesque world, hissed the Dean of Critics. A distorted world. *Well and good. Let them sit for three hours on one of the seven benches of the Paris pawnshop. Let them walk through the Rue Dolent. Perhaps I should not be allowed to go free, perhaps I should be jailed with the criminals. I feel in sympathy with them. My murders are committed with paint. Every act of murder might awaken people to the state of things that produced it, but soon they fall asleep again, and when the artist awakens them they are quick to take revenge. Very good that they refuse me money and honors, for thus they keep me in these streets and exposing what they do not wish me to expose. My jungle is not the innocent one of Rousseau. In my jungle everyone meets his enemy. In the underworld of nature debts must be paid in the same specie: no false money accepted. Hunger with hunger, pain with pain, destruction with destruction.*

The artist is there to keep accounts.

From his explorations of the Dome, the Select, the Rotonde, Jay once brought back Sabina, though with these two people it would be difficult to say which one guided the other home or along the street, since both of them had this aspect of overflowing rivers rushing headlong to cover the city, making houses, cafés, streets and people seem small and fragile, easily swept along. The uprooting power of Jay's impulses added to Sabina's mobility reversed the whole order of the city.

Sabina brought in her wake the sound and imagery of fire engines as they tore through the streets of New York alarming the heart with the violent gong of catastrophe.

All dressed in red and silver, the tearing red and silver siren cutting a pathway through the flesh. The first time one looked at Sabina one felt: everything will burn!

Out of the red and silver and the long cry of alarm, to the poet who survives in a human being as the child survives in him, to this poet Sabina threw an unexpected ladder in the middle of the city and ordained: climb!

As she appeared, the orderly alignment of the city gave way before this ladder one was invited to climb, standing straight in space like the ladder of Baron Münchhausen which led to the sky.

Only Sabina's ladder led to fire.

As she walked heavily towards Lillian from the darkness of the hallway into the light of the door Lillian saw for the first time the woman she had always wanted to know. She saw Sabina's eyes burning, heard her voice so rusty and immediately felt drowned in her beauty. She wanted to say: I recognize you. I have often imagined a woman like you.

Sabina could not sit still. She talked profusely and continuously with feverish breathlessness, like one in fear of silence. She sat as if she could not bear to sit for long, and when she walked she was eager to sit down again. Impatient, alert, watchful, as if in dread of being attacked; restless and keen, making jerking gestures with her hands, drinking hurriedly, speaking rapidly, smiling swiftly and listening to only half of what was said to her.

Exactly as in a fever dream, there was in her no premeditation, no continuity, no connection. It was all chaos—her erratic gestures, her unfinished sentences, her sulky silences, her sudden walks through the room, her apologizing for futile reasons (I'm sorry, I lost my gloves), her apparent desire to be elsewhere.

She carried herself like one totally unfettered who was rushing and plunging on some fiery course. She could not stop to reflect.

She unrolled the film of her life stories swiftly, like the accelerated scenes of a broken machine, her adventures, her

90

escapes from drug addicts, her encounters with the police, parties at which indistinct incidents took place, hazy scenes of flagellations in which no one could tell whether she had been the flagellator or the victim, or whether or not it had happened at all.

A broken dream, with spaces, reversals, contradictions, galloping fantasies and sudden retractions. She would say: "he lifted my skirt," or "we had to take care of the wounds," or "the policeman was waiting for me and I had to swallow the drug to save my friends," and then as if she had written this on a blackboard she took a huge sponge and effaced it all by a phrase which was meant to convey that perhaps this story had happened to someone else, or she may have read it, or heard it at a bar, and as soon as this was erased she began another story of a beautiful girl who was employed in a night club and whom Sabina had insulted, but if Jay asked why she shifted the scene, she at once effaced it, cancelled it, to tell about something else she had heard and not seen at the night club at which she worked.

The faces and the figures of her personages appeared only half drawn, and when one just began to perceive them another face and figure were interposed, as in a dream, and when one thought one was looking at a woman it was a man, an old man, and when one approached the old man who used to take care of her, it turned out to be the girl she lived with who looked like a younger man she had first loved and this one was meta-morphosed into a whole group of people who had cruelly humiliated her one evening. Somewhere in the middle of the scene Sabina appeared as the woman with gold hair, and then later as a woman with black hair, and it was equally impossible to keep a consistent image of whom she had loved, betrayed, escaped from, lived with, married, lied to, forgotten, deserted.

She was impelled by a great confessional fever which forced her to lift a corner of the veil, but became frightened if anyone listened or peered at the exposed scene, and then she took a giant sponge and rubbed it all out, to begin somewhere else, thinking that in confusion there was protection. So Sabina beckoned and lured one into her world, and then blurred the passageways, confused the images and ran away in fear of detection.

From the very first Jay hated her, hated her as Don Juan hates Doña Juana, as the free man hates the free woman, as man hates in woman this freedom in passion which he grants solely to himself. Hated her because he knew instinctively that she regarded him as he regarded woman: as a possible or impossible lover.

He was not for her a man endowed with particular gifts, standing apart from other men, irreplaceable as Lillian saw him, unique as his friends saw him. Sabina's glance measured him as he measured women: endowed or not endowed as lovers.

She knew as he did, that none of the decorations or dignities conferred upon a man or woman could alter the basic talent or lack of talent as a lover. No title of architect emeritus will confer upon them the magic knowledge of the body's structure. No prestidigitation with words will replace the knowledge of the secret places of responsiveness. No medals for courage will confer the graceful audacities, the conquering abductions, the exact knowledge of the battle of love, when the moment for seduction, when for consolidation, when for capitulation.

The trade, art and craft that cannot be learned, which requires a divination of the fingertips, the accurate reading of signals from the fluttering of an eyelid, an eye like a microscope to catch the approval of an eyelash, a seismograph to catch the vibrations of the little blue nerves under the skin, the capacity to prognosticate from the direction of the down as from the inclination of the leaves some can predict rain, tell where storms are brooding, where floods are threatening, tell which regions to leave alone, which to invade, which to lull and which to take by force.

No decorations, no diplomas for the lover, no school and no traveller's experience will help a man who does not hear the beat, tempo and rhythms of the body, catch the ballet leaps of desire at their highest peak, perform the acrobatics of tenderness and lust, and know all the endless virtuosities of silence.

Sabina was studying his potentialities with such insolence, weighing the accuracy of his glance. For there is a black lover's glance well known to women versed in this lore, which can strike at the very center of woman's body, which plants its claim as in a perfect target.

Jay saw in her immediately the woman without fidelity, capable of all desecrations. That a woman should do this, wear no wedding ring, love according to her caprice and not be in bondage to the one. (A week before he was angry with Lillian for considering him as the unique and irreplaceable one, because it conferred on him a responsibility he did not wish to assume, and he was wishing she might consider an understudy who would occasionally relieve him of his duties!)

For one sparkling moment Jay and Sabina faced each other in the center of the studio, noting each other's defiance, absorbing this great mistrustfulness which instantly assails the man and women who recognize in each other the law-breaking lovers; erecting on this basic mutual mistrust the future violent attempts to establish certitude.

Sabina's dress at first like fire now appeared, in the more tangible light of Lillian's presence, as made of black satin, the texture most similar to skin. Then Lillian noticed a hole in Sabina's sleeve, and suddenly she felt ashamed not to have a hole in her sleeve too, for somehow, Sabina's poverty, Sabina's worn sandals, seemed like the most courageous defiance of all, the choice of a being who had no need of flawless sleeves or new sandals to feel complete.

Lillian's glance which usually remained fixed upon Jay, grazing lightly over others, for the first time absorbed another human being as intently.

Jay looked uneasily at them. This fixed attention of Lillian revolving around him had demanded of him, the mutable one, something he could not return, thus making him feel like a man accumulating a vast debt in terms he could never meet.

In Sabina's fluctuating fervors he met a challenge: she gave him a feeling of equality. She was well able to take care of herself and to answer treachery with treachery.

Lillian waited at the corner of the Rue Auber. She would see Sabina in full daylight advancing out of a crowd. She would make certain that such an image could materialize, that Sabina was not a mirage which would melt in the daylight.

She was secretly afraid that she might stand there at the corner of the Rue Auber exactly as she had stood in other places watching the crowd, knowing no figure would come out of it which would resemble the figures in her dreams. Waiting for Sabina she experienced the most painful expectancy: she could not believe Sabina would arrive by these streets, cross such a boulevard, emerge from a mass of faceless people. What a profound joy to see her striding forward, wearing her shabby sandals and her shabby black dress with royal indifference.

"I hate daylight," said Sabina, and her eyes darkened with anger. The dark blue rings under her eyes were so deep they marked her flesh. It was as if the flesh around her eyes had been burned away by the white heat and fever of her glance.

They found the place she wanted, a place below the level of the street.

Her talk like a turbulent river, like a broken necklace spilled around Lillian.

"It's a good thing I'm going away. You would soon unmask me."

At this Lillian looked at Sabina and her eyes said so clearly: "I want to become blind with you," that Sabina was moved and turned her face away, ashamed of her doubts.

"There are so many things I would love to do with you, Lillian. With you I would take drugs. I would not be afraid."

"You afraid?" said Lillian, incredulously. But one word rose persistently to the surface of her being, one word which was like a rhythm more than a word, which beat its tempo as soon as Sabina appeared. Each step she took with Sabina was marked as by a drum beat with the word: danger danger danger danger.

"I have a feeling that I want to be you, Sabina. I never wanted to be anyone but myself before."

"How can you live with Jay, Lillian? I hate Jay. I feel he is like a spy. He enters your life only to turn around afterwards and caricature. He exposes only the ugly."

"Only when something hurts him. It's when he gets hurt that he destroys. Has he caricatured you?"

"He painted me as a whore. And you know that isn't me. He has such an interest in evil that I told him stories. . . . I hate him."

"I thought you loved him," said Lillian simply.

All Sabina's being sought to escape Lillian's directness in a panic. Behind the mask a thousand smiles appeared, behind the eyelids ageless deceptions.

This was the moment. If only Sabina could bring herself to say what she felt: Lillian, do not trust me. I want Jay. Do not love me, Lillian, for I am like him. I take what I want no matter who is hurt.

"You want to unmask me, Lillian."

"If I were to unmask you, Sabina, I would only be revealing myself: you act as I would act if I had the courage. I see you exactly as you are, and I love you. You should not fear exposure, not from me."

This was the moment to turn away from Jay who was bringing her not love, but another false role of play, to turn towards Lillian with the truth, that a real love might take place.

Sabina's face appeared to Lillian as that of a child drowning behind a window. She saw Sabina as a child struggling with her terror of the truth, considering before answering what might come closest to the best image of herself she might give Lillian. Sabina would not say the truth but whatever conformed to what she imagined Lillian expected of her, which was in reality not at all what Lillian wanted of her, but what she, Sabina, thought necessary to her idealized image of herself. What Sabina was feverishly creating always was the reverse of what she acted out: a woman of loyalty and faithfulness. To maintain this image at all costs she ceased responding to Lillian's soft appeal to the child in need of a rest from pretenses.

"I don't deny Jay is a caricaturist, but only out of revengefulness. What have you done to deserve his revenge?"

Again Sabina turned her face away.

"I know you're not a *femme fatale,* Sabina. But didn't you want him to think you were?"

With this peculiar flair she had for listening to the buried child in human beings, Lillian could hear the child within Sabina whining, tired of its inventions grown too cumbersome, weary of its adornments, of its disguises. Too many costumes, valances, gold, brocade, veils, to cover Sabina's direct thrusts towards what she wanted, and meanwhile it was this audacity, this directness, this unfaltering knowledge of her wants which Lillian loved in her, wanted to learn from her.

But a smile of immeasurable distress appeared in Sabina, and then was instantly effaced by another smile: the smile of seduction. When Lillian was about to seize upon the distress, to enter the tender, vulnerable regions of her being, then Sabina concealed herself again behind the smile of a woman of seduction.

Pity, protection, solace, they all fell away from Lillian like gifts of trivial import, because with the smile of seduction Sabina assumed simultaneously the smile of an all-powerful enchantress.

Lillian forgot the face of the child in distress, hungrily demanding a truthful love, and yet, in terror that this very truth might destroy the love. The child face faded before this potent

96

smile to which Lillian succumbed.

She no longer sought the meaning of Sabina's words. She looked at Sabina's blonde hair tumbling down, at her eyebrows peaked upward, at her smile slanting perfidiously, a gem-like smile which made a whirlpool of her feelings.

A man passed by and laughed at their absorption.

"Don't mind, don't mind," said Sabina, as if she were familiar with this situation. "I won't do you any harm."

"You can't do me any harm."

Sabina smiled. "I destroy people without meaning to. Everywhere I go things become confused and terrifying. For you I would like to begin all over again, to go to New York and become a great actress, to become beautiful again. I won't appear any more with clothes that are held together with safety pins! I've been living stupidly, blindly, doing nothing but drinking, smoking, talking. I'm afraid of disillusioning you, Lillian."

They walked down the streets aimlessly, unconscious of their surroundings, arm in arm with a joy that was rising every moment, and with every word they uttered. A swelling joy that mounted with each step they took together and with the occasional brushing of their hips as they walked.

The traffic eddied around them but everything else, houses and trees were lost in a fog. Only their voices distinct, carrying such phrases as they could utter out of their female labyrinth of oblique perceptions.

Sabina said: "I wanted to telephone you last night. I wanted to tell you how sorry I was to have talked so much. I knew all the time I couldn't say what I wanted to say."

"You too have fears, although you seem so strong," said Lillian.

"I do everything wrong. It's good that you don't ever ask questions about facts. Facts don't matter. It's the essence that matters. You never ask the kind of question I hate: what city? what man? what year? what time? Facts. I despise them."

Bodies close, arm in arm, hands locked together over her

breast. She had taken Lillian's hand and held it over her breast as if to warm it.

The city had fallen away. They were walking into a world of their own for which neither could find a name.

They entered a softly lighted place, mauve and diffuse, which enveloped them in velvet closeness.

Sabina took off her silver bracelet and put it around Lillian's wrist.

"It's like having your warm hand around my wrist. It's still warm, like your own hand. I'm your prisoner, Sabina."

Lillian looked at Sabina's face, the fevered profile taut, so taut that she shivered a little, knowing that when Sabina's face turned towards her she could no longer see the details of it for its blazing quality. Sabina's mouth always a little open, pouring forth that eddying voice which gave one vertigo.

Lillian caught an expression on her face of such knowingness that she was startled. Sabina's whole body seemed suddenly charged with experience, as if discolored from it, filled with violet shadows, bowed down by weary eyelids. In one instant she looked marked by long fevers, by an unconquerable fatigue. Lillian could see all the charred traces of the fires she had traversed. She expected her eyes and hair to turn ashen.

But the next moment her eyes and hair gleamed more brilliantly than ever, her face became uncannily clear, completely innocent, an innocence which radiated like a.gem. She could shed her whole life in one moment of forgetfulness, stand absolutely washed of it, as if she were standing at the very beginning of it.

So many questions rushed to Lillian's mind, but now she knew Sabina hated questions. Sabina's essence slipped out between the facts. So Lillian smiled and was silent, listening merely to Sabina's voice, the way its hoarseness changed from rustiness to a whisper, a faint gasp, so that the hotness of her breath touched her face.

She watched her smoke hungrily, as if smoking, talking and moving were all desperately necessary to her, like breathing, and she did them all with such reckless intensity.

When Lillian and Sabina met one night under the red light of the café they recognized in each other similar moods: they would laugh at him, the man.

"He's working so hard, so hard he's in a daze," said Lillian. "He talks about nothing but painting."

She was lonely, deep down, to think that Jay had been at his work for two weeks without noticing either of them. And her loneliness drew her close to Sabina.

"He was glad we were going out together, he said it would give him a chance to work. He hasn't any idea of time—he doesn't even know what day of the week it is. He doesn't give a damn about anybody or anything."

A feeling of immense loneliness invaded them both.

They walked as if they wanted to walk away from their mood, as if they wanted to walk into another world. They walked up the hill of Montmartre with little houses lying on the hillside like heather. They heard music, music so off tune that they did not recognize it as music they heard every day. They slid into a shaft of light from where this music came—into a room which seemed built of granified smoke and crystallized human breath. A room with a painted star on the ceiling, and a wooden, pock-marked Christ nailed to the wall. Gusts of weary, petrified songs, so dusty with use. Faces like empty glasses. The musicians made of rubber like the elastic rubber-soled night.

We hate Jay tonight. We hate man.

The craving for caresses. Wanting and fighting the want. Both frightened by the vagueness of their desire, the indefiniteness of their craving.

A rosary of question marks in their eyes.

Sabina whispered: "Let's take drugs tonight."

She pressed her strong knee against Lillian, she inundated her with the brilliance of her eyes, the paleness of her face.

Lillian shook her head, but she drank, she drank. No drink equal to the state of war and hatred. No drink like bitterness.

Lillian looked at Sabina's fortuneteller's eyes, and at the taut profile.

"It takes all the pain away; it wipes out reality."

She leaned over the table until their breaths mingled.

"You don't know what a relief it is. The smoke of opium like fog. It brings marvelous dreams and gaiety. Such gaiety, Lillian. And you feel so powerful, so powerful and content. You don't feel any more frustration, you feel that you are lording it over the whole world with marvelous strength. No one can hurt you then, humiliate you, confuse you. You feel you're soaring over the world. Everything becomes soft, large, easy. Such joys, Lillian, as you have never imagined. The touch of a hand is enough . . . the touch of a hand is like going the whole way. . . . And time . . . how time flies. The days pass like an hour. No more straining, just dreaming and floating. Take drugs with me, Lillian."

Lillian consented with her eyes. Then she saw that Sabina was looking at the Arab merchant who stood by the door with his red Fez, his kimono, his slippers, his arms loaded with Arabian rugs and pearl necklaces. Under the rugs protruded a wooden leg with which he was beating time to the jazz.

Sabina laughed, shaking her whole body with drunken laughter. "You don't know, Lillian . . . this man . . . with his wooden leg . . . you never can tell . . . he may have some. There was a man once, with a wooden leg like that. He was arrested and they found that his wooden leg was packed with snow. I'll go and ask him."

And she got up with her heavy, animal walk, and talked to the rug merchant, looking up at him alluringly, begging, smiling up at him in the same secret way she had of smiling at Lillian. A burning pain invaded Lillian to see Sabina begging. But the merchant shook his head, smiled innocently, shook his head firmly, smiled again, offered his rugs and the necklaces.

When she saw Sabina returning empty handed, Lillian drank again, and it was like drinking fog, long draughts of fog.

They danced together, the floor turning under them like a

phonograph record. Sabina dark and potent, leading Lillian.

A gust of jeers seemed to blow through the place. A gust of jeers. But they danced, cheeks touching, their cheeks chalice white. They danced and the jeers cut into the haze of their dizziness like a whip. The eyes of the men were insulting them. The eyes of men called them by the name the world had for them. Eyes. Green, jealous. Eyes of the world. Eyes sick with hatred and contempt. Caressing eyes, participating. Eyes ransacking their conscience. Stricken yellow eyes of envy caught in the flare of a match. Heavy torpid eyes without courage, without dreams. Mockery, frozen mockery from the frozen glass eyes of the loveless.

Lillian and Sabina wanted to strike those eyes, break them, break the bars of green wounded eyes, condemning them. They wanted to break the walls confining them, suffocating them. They wanted to break out from the prison of their own fears, break every obstacle. But all they found to break were glasses. They took their glasses and broke them over their shoulders and made no wish, but looked at the fragments of the glasses on the floor wonderingly as if their mood of rebellion might be lying there also, in broken pieces.

Now they danced mockingly, defiantly, as if they were sliding beyond the reach of man's hands, running like sand between their insults. They scoffed at those eyes which brimmed with knowledge for they knew the ecstasy of mystery and fog, fire and orange fumes of a world they had seen through a slit in the dream. Spinning and reeling and falling, spinning and turning and rolling down the brume and smoke of a world seen through a slit in the dream.

The waiter put his ham-colored hand on Sabina's bare arm: "You've got to get out of here, you two!"

They were alone.

They were alone without daylight, without past, without any thought of the resemblance between their togetherness and the union of other women. The whole world was being pushed to one side by their faith in their own uniqueness. All comparisons proudly discarded.

Sabina and Lillian alone, innocent of knowledge, and innocent of other experiences. They remembered nothing before this hour: they were innocent of associations. They forgot what they had read in books, what they had seen in cafés, the laughter of men and the mocking participation of other women. Their individuality washed down and effaced the world: they stood at the beginning of everything, naked and innocent of the past.

They stood before the night which belonged to them as two women emerging out of sleep. They stood on the first steps of their timidity, of their faith, before the long night which belonged to them. Blameless of original sin, of literary sins, of the sin of premeditation.

Two women. Strangeness. All the webs of ideas blown away. New bodies, new souls, new minds, new words. They would create it all out of themselves, fashion their own reality. Innocence. No roots dangling into other days, other nights, other men or women. The potency of a new stare into the face of their desire and their fears.

Sabina's sudden timidity and Lillian's sudden awkwardness. Their fears. A great terror slashing through the room, cutting icily through them like a fallen sword. A new voice. Sabina's breathless and seeking to be lighter so as to touch the lightness of Lillian's voice like a breath now, an exhalation, almost a voicelessness because they were so frightened.

Sabina sat heavily on the edge of the bed, her earthly weight like roots sinking into the earth. Under the weight of her stare Lillian trembled.

Their bracelets tinkled.

The bracelets had given the signal. A signal like the first

tinkle of beads on a savage neck when they enter a dance. They took their bracelets off and put them on the table, side by side.

The light. Why was the light so still, like the suspense of their blood? Still with fear. Like their eyes. Shadeless eyes that dared neither open, nor close, nor melt.

The dresses. Sabina's dress rolled around her like long sea weed. She wanted to turn and drop it on the floor but her hands lifted it like a Bayadere lifting her skirt to dance and she lifted it over her head.

Sabina's eyes were like a forest; the darkness of a forest, a watchfulness behind ambushes. Fear. Lillian journeyed into the darkness of them, carrying her blue eyes into the red-brown ones. She walked from the place where her dress had fallen holding her breasts as if she expected to be mortally thrust.

Sabina loosened her hair and said: "You're so extraordinarily white." With a strange sadness, like a weight, she spoke, as if it were not the white substance of Lillian but the whiteness of her newness to life which Sabina seemed to sigh for. "You're so white, so white and smooth." And there were deep shadows in her eyes, shadows of one old with living: shadows in the neck, in her arms, on her knees, violet shadows.

Lillian wanted to reach out to her, into these violet shadows. She saw that Sabina wanted to be she as much as she wanted to be Sabina. They both wanted to exchange bodies, exchange faces. There was in both of them the dark strain of wanting to become the other, to deny what they were, to transcend their actual selves. Sabina desiring Lillian's newness, and Lillian desiring Sabina's deeply marked body.

Lillian drank the violet shadows, drank the imprint of others, the accumulation of other hours, other rooms, other odors, other caresses. How all the other loves clung to Sabina's body, even though her face denied this and her eyes repeated: I have forgotten all. How they made her heavy with the loss of herself, lost in the maze of her gifts. How the lies, the loves, the dreams, the obscenities, the fevers weighed down her body, and how Lillian wanted to become leadened with her, poisoned with her.

Sabina looked at the whiteness of Lillian's body as into a mirror and saw herself as a girl, standing at the beginning of her life unblurred, unmarked. She wanted to return to this early self. And Lillian wanted to enter the labyrinth of knowledge, to the very bottom of the violet wells.

Through the acrid forest of her being there was a vulnerable opening. Lillian trod into it lightly. Caresses of down, moth invasions, myrrh between the breasts, incense in their mouths. Tendrils of hair raising their heads to the wind in the finger tips, kisses curling within the conch-shell necks. Tendrils of hair bristling and between their closed lips a sigh.

"How soft you are, how soft you are," said Sabina.

They separated and saw it was not this they wanted, sought, dreamed. Not this the possession they imagined. No bodies touching would answer this mysterious craving in them to become each other. Not to possess each other but to become each other. Not to take, but to imbibe, absorb, change themselves. Sabina carried a part of Lillian's being, Lillian a part of Sabina, but they could not be exchanged through an embrace. It was not that.

Their bodies touched and then fell away, as if both of them had touched a mirror, their own image upon a mirror. They had felt the cold wall, they had felt the mirror that never appeared when they were taken by man. Sabina had merely touched her own youth, and Lillian her free passions.

As they lay there the dawn entered the room, a grey dawn which showed the dirt on the window panes, the crack in the table, the stains on the walls. Lillian and Sabina sat up as if the dawn had opened their eyes. Slowly they descended from dangerous heights, with the appearance of daylight and the weight of their fatigue.

With the dawn it was as if Jay had entered the room and were now lying between them. Every cell of their dream seemed to burst at once, with the doubt which had entered Lillian's mind.

104

If she had wanted so much to be Sabina so that Jay might love in her what he admired in Sabina, could it be that Sabina wanted of Lillian this that made Jay love her?

"I feel Jay in you," she said.

The taste of sacrilege came to both their mouths. The mouths he kissed. The women whose flavor he knew. The one man within two women. Jealousy, dormant all night; now lying at their side, between their caresses, slipping in between them like an enemy.

(Lillian, Lillian, if you arouse hatred between us, you break a magic alliance! He is not as aware of us as we are of each other. We have loved in each other all he has failed to love and see. Must we awake to the great destructiveness of rivalry, of war, when this night contained all that slipped between his fingers!)

But jealousy had stirred in Lillian's flesh. Doubt was hardening and crystallizing in Lillian, crystallizing her features, her eyes, tightening her mouth, stiffening her body. She shivered with cold, with the icy incision of this new day which was laying everything bare.

Bare eyes looking at each other with naked, knife-pointed questions.

To stare at each other they had to disentangle their hair, Sabina's long hair having curled around Lillian's neck.

Lillian left the bed. She took the bracelets and flung them out of the window.

"I know, I know," she said violently, "you wanted to blind me. If you won't confess, he will. It's Jay you love, not me. Get up. I don't want him to find us here together. And he thought we loved each other!"

"I do love you, Lillian."

"Don't you dare say it," shouted Lillian violently, all her being now craving wildly for complete devastation.

They both began to tremble.

Lillian was like a foaming sea, churning up wreckage, the debris of all her doubts and fears.

Their room was in darkness. Then came Jay's laughter, creamy and mould-breaking. In spite of the darkness Lillian could feel all the cells of his body alive in the night, vibrating with abundance. Every cell with a million eyes seeing in the dark.

"A fine dark night in which an artist might well be born," he said. "He must be born at night, you know, so that no one will notice that his parents gave him only seven months of human substance. No artist has the patience to remain nine months in the womb. He must run away from home. He is born with a mania to complete himself, to create himself. He is so multiple and amorphous that his central self is constantly falling apart and is only recomposed by his work. With his imagination he can flow into all the moulds, multiply and divide himself, and yet whatever he does, he will always be two."

"And require two wives?" asked Lillian.

"I need you terribly," he said.

Would the body of Sabina triumph over her greater love?

"There are many Sabinas in the world, but only one like you," said Jay.

How could he lie so close and know only what she chose to tell him, knowing nothing of her, of her secret terrors and fear of loss.

He was only for the joyous days, the days of courage, when she could share with him all the good things he brought with his passion for novelty and change.

But he knew nothing of her; he was no companion to her sadness. He could never imagine anyone else's mood, only his own. His own were so immense and loud, they filled his world and deafened him to all others. He was not concerned to know whether she could live or breathe within the dark caverns of his whale-like being, within the whale belly of his ego.

Somehow he had convinced her that this expansiveness was a sign of bigness. A big man could not belong to one person. He had merely overflowed into Sabina, out of over-richness.

106

And they would quarrel some day. Already he was saying: "I suspect that when Sabina gives one so many lies it is because she has nothing else to give but mystery, but fiction. Perhaps behind her mysteries there is nothing."

But how blinded he was by false mysteries! Because Sabina made such complicated tangles of everything—mixing personalities, identities, missing engagements, being always elsewhere than where she was expected to be, chaotic in her hours, elusive about her occupations, implying mystery and suspense even when she said goodbye . . . calling at dawn when everyone was asleep, and asleep when everyone else was awake. Jay with his indefatigable curiosity was easily engaged in unravelling the tangle, as if every tangle had a meaning, a mystery.

But Lillian knew, too, how quickly he could turn about and ridicule if he were cheated, as he often was, by his blind enthusiasms. How revengeful he became when the mysteries were false.

"If only Sabina would die," thought Lillian, "if she would only die. She does not love him as I do."

Anxiety oppressed her. Would he push everything into movement again, disperse her anxieties with his gaiety, carry her along in his reckless course?

Lillian's secret he did not detect: that of her fear. Once her secret had almost pierced through, once when Jay had stayed out all night. From her room she could see the large lights of the Boulevard Montparnasse blinking maliciously, Montparnasse which he loved and those lights, and the places where he so easily abandoned himself as he gave himself to everything that glittered,—rococo women, spluttering men in bars, anyone who smiled, beckoned, had a story to tell.

She had waited with the feeling that where her heart had been there was now a large hole; no heart or blood beating anymore but a drafty hole made by a precise and rather large bullet.

Merely because Jay was walking up and down Montparnasse

107

in one of his high drunken moods which had nothing to do with drink but with his insatiable thirst for new people, new smiles, new words, new stories.

Each time the white lights blinked she saw his merry smile in his full mouth, each time the red lights blinked she saw his cold blue eyes detached and mocking, annihilating the mouth in a daze of blue, iced gaiety. The eyes always cold, the mouth warm, the eyes mocking and the mouth always repairing the damage done. His eyes that would never turn inward and look into the regions of deep events, the regions of personal explorations: his eyes intent on not seeing discords or dissolutions, not seeing the missing words, the lost treasures, the wasted hours, the shreds of the dispersed self, the blind mobilities.

Not to see the dark night of the self his eyes rose frenziedly to the surface seeking in fast-moving panoramas merely the semblance of riches. . . .

"Instead of love there is appetite," thought Lillian. "He does not say: 'I love you,' but 'I need you.' Our life is crowded like a railroad station, like a circus. He does not feel things where I feel them: the heart is definitely absent. That's why mine is dying, it has ceased to pound tonight, it is being slowly killed by his hardness."

Away from him she could always say: he does not feel. But as soon as he appeared she was baffled. His presence carried such a physical glow that it passed for warmth. His voice was warm like the voice of feeling. His gestures were warm, his hands liked touch. He laid his hands often on human beings, and one might think it was love. But it was just a physical warmth, like the summer. It gave off heat like a chemical, but no more.

"He will die of hardness, and I from feeling too much. Even when people knock on the door I have a feeling they are not knocking on wood but on my heart. All the blows fall directly on my heart."

Even pleasure had its little stabs upon the heart. The perpetual heart-murmur of the sensibilities.

"I wish I could learn his secret. I would love to be able to go out for a whole night without feeling all the threads that bind me to him, feeling my love for him all around me like a chastity belt."

And now he was lying still on the breast of her immutable love and she had no immutable love upon which to lay her head, no one to return to at dawn.

He sat up lightly saying: "Oh, Sabina has no roots!"

"And I'm strangling in my roots," thought Lillian.

He had turned on the light to read now, and she saw his coat hugging the back of the chair, revealing in the shape of its shoulders the roguish spirit that had played in it. If she could only take the joys he gave her, his soft swagger, the rough touch of his coat, the effervescence of his voice when he said: that's good. Even his coat seemed to be stirring with his easy flowing life, even to his clothes he gave the imprint of his liveliness.

To stem his outflowing would be like stemming a river of life. She would not be the one to do it. When a man had decided within himself to live out every whim, every fancy, every impulse, it was a flood for which no Noah's Ark had ever been provided.

Lillian and Djuna were walking together over dead autumn leaves that crackled like paper. Lillian was weeping and Djuna was weeping with her and for her.

They were walking through the city as it sank into twilight and it was as if they were both going blind together with the bitterness of their tears. Through this blurred city they walked hazily and half lost, the light of a street lamp striking them now and then like a spotlight throwing into relief Lillian's distorted mouth and the broken line of her neck where her head fell forward heavily.

The buses came upon them out of the dark, violently, with a deafening clatter, and they had to leap out of their way, only to continue stumbling through dark streets, crossing bridges, passing under heavy arcades, their feet unsteady on the uneven cobblestones as if they had both lost their sense of gravity.

Lillian's voice was plaintive and monotonous, like a lamentation. Her blue eyes wavered but always fixed on the ground as if the whole structure of her life lay there and she were watching its consummation.

Djuna was looking straight before her, through and beyond the dark, the lights, the traffic, beyond all the buildings. Eyes fixed, immobile like glass eyes, as if the curtain of tears had opened a new realm.

Lillian's phrases surged and heaved like a turgid sea. Unformed, unfinished, dense, heavy with repetitions, with recapitulations, with a baffled, confused bitterness and anger.

Djuna found nothing to answer, because Lillian was talking about God, the God she had sought in Jay.

"Because he had the genius," she said, "I wanted to serve him, I wanted to make him great. But he is treacherous, Djuna. I am more confused and lost now than before I knew him. It isn't only his betrayals with women, Djuna, it's that he sees no one as they are. He only adds to everyone's confusions. I put myself wholly in his hands. I wanted to serve someone who would create something wonderful, and I also thought he would help me to create myself. But he is destructive, and he is destroying me."

This seeking of man the guide in a dark city, this aimless wandering through the streets touching men and seeking the guide—this was a fear all women had known . . . seeking the guide in men, not in the past, or in mythology, but a guide with a living breath who might create one, help one to be born as a woman, a guide they wished to possess for themselves alone, in their own isolated woman's soul. The guide for woman was still inextricably woven with man and with man's creation.

Lillian had thought that Jay would create her because he was the artist, that he would be able to see her as clearly as she had seen in him the great painter, but Jay's inconsistencies bewildered her. She had placed her own image in his hands for him to fashion: make of me a big woman, someone of value.

His own chaos had made this impossible.

"Lillian, no one should be entrusted with one's image to fashion, with one's self-creation. Women are moving from one circle to another, rising towards independence and self-creation. What you're really suffering from is from the pain of parting with your faith, with your old love when you wish to renew this faith and preserve the passion. You're being thrust out of one circle into another and it is this which causes you so much fear. You know you cannot lean on Jay, but you don't know what awaits you, and you don't trust your own awareness."

Lillian thought that she was weeping because Jay had said: Leave me alone, or let me work, or let me sleep.

"Oh, Lillian, it's such a struggle to emerge from the past clean of regrets and memories and of the desire to regress. No one can accept failure."

She wanted to take Lillian's hand and make her raise her head and lead her into a new circle, raise her above the pain and confusion, above the darkness of the present.

These sudden shafts of light upon them could not illumine where the circle of pain closed and ended and woman was raised into another circle. She could not help Lillian emerge out of the immediacy of her pain, leap beyond the stranglehold of the present.

And so they continued to walk unsteadily over what Lillian saw merely as the dead leaves of his indifference.

Jay and Lillian lived in the top floor studio of a house on the Rue Montsouris, on the edge of Montparnasse—a small street without issue lined with white cubistic villas.

When they gave a party the entire house opened its doors from the ground floor to the roof, since all the artists knew each other. The party would branch off into all the little street with its quiet gardens watched by flowered balconies.

The guests could also walk down the street to the Park Montsouris lake, climb on a boat and fancy themselves attending a Venetian feast.

First came the Chess Player, as lean, brown, polished, and wooden in his gestures as a chess piece; his features sharply carved and his mind set upon a perpetual game.

For him the floors of the rooms were large squares in which the problem was to move the people about by the right word. To control the temptation to point such a person to another he kept his hands in his pockets and used merely his eyes. If he were talking to someone his eyes would design a path in the air which his listener could not help but follow. His glance having caught the person he had selected made the invisible alliance in space and soon the three would find themselves on the one square until he chose to move away and leave them together.

What his game was no one knew, for he was content with the displacements and did not share in the developments. He would then stand in the corner of the room again and survey the movements with a semitone smile.

No one ever thought of displacing him, of introducing him to strangers.

But he thought it imperative to bring about an encounter between the bearded Irish architect and Djuna, because he had conceived a house for many moods, a house whose sliding panels made it one day very large for grandiose states of being, one day very small for intimate relationships. He had topped it with a removable ceiling which allowed the sky to play roof, and designed both a small spiral staircase for secret escapades

112

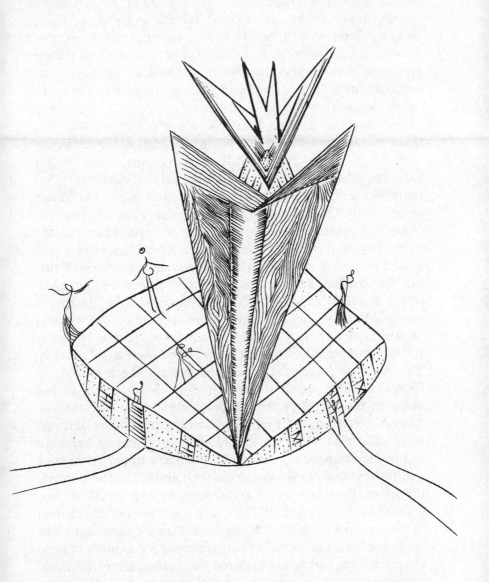

and a vast one for exhibitionism. Besides, it turned on a pivot to follow the changing whims of the sun, and who but Djuna should know this house which corresponded to her many moods, to her smiling masks and refusal to show her night face, her shadows and her darkness, she who turned on artificial pivots always towards the light, who was adept at sliding panels to make womb enclosures suitable to intimate confessions, and equally capable of opening them all at once to admit the entire world.

Djuna smiled at the Chess Player's accuracy, and he left them standing on the square while the Irish architect began with silken mouthfuls of words to design this house around Djuna as if he were spewing a cocoon and she would leave the party like a snail with a house built around her to the image of her needs. On her black dress he was drawing a blue print.

On this square something was being constructed and so the Chess Player moved on, his eyes made of the glass one could look through without being seen and now he seized upon Faustin, the Zombie, the one who had died under the first blow struck at him by experience. Most of those who die like this in the middle of their life await a resuscitation, but Faustin awaited nothing: every line of his body sagged with acceptance, the growing weight of his flesh cushioned inertia, submission. The blood no longer circulated and one could see the crystal formations of fear and stagnation as in those species of fish living in the deepest waters without eyes, ears, fins, motion, shaped like loaves of bread, nourishing themselves through static cells of the skin. His one obsession was not to free himself of his death but to stand like a black sentinel at the gate and prevent others escaping from their traps. He lived among the artists, the rebels, never acquiescing in their rebellions, but waiting for the moment of Jay's fullest sunburst of enthusiasm to puncture it with irony, waiting for Lillian's wildest explosions to shame her as an exhibitionist, watching for Djuna's blurred absences from reality to point out her delinquencies from the present. His very expression set the stage for the murder; he

114

had a way of bearing himself which was like the summation of all the prohibitions: do not trespass, do not smoke, do not spit, do not lean out of the window, no thoroughfare, do not speed.

With his black eyes and pale face set for homicide he waited in a corner. Wherever he was, a black moth would enter the room and begin its flights of mourning, black-gloved, black-creped, black-soled, inseminating the white walls with future sadnesses. The silence which followed his words clearly marked the withering effect of them and the time it took for the soil to bloom again. Always at midnight he left, following a rigid compulsion, and the Chess Player knew he must act hastily if he were going to exploit the Zombie's death rays and test their effect upon the living.

He walked the Zombie towards the fullest bloom of all, towards the camellia face of Sabina which opened at a party like the crowned prize-winner of the flower shows and gave every man the sensation he held the tip of a breast in his teeth. Would Sabina's face close when the shadow of Faustin fell across it, when the black moth words and the monotonous voice fell upon her ears curtained intricately by her anarchic hair?

She merely turned her face away: she was too richly nourished with pollen, seeds and sap to wither before any man, even a dead one. Too much love and desire had flown through the curves of her body, too many sighs, whispers, lay folded in the cells of her skin. Through the many rivers of her veins too much pleasure had coursed; she was immune.

Faustin the Zombie felt bitterly defeated, for he loved to walk in the traces of Jay's large patterns and collect his discarded mistresses. He loved to live Jay's discarded lives, like a man accepting a second-hand coat. There was always a little warmth left in them.

From the moment of his defeat, he ceased to attend the Party, even in his role of zombie, and the Chess Player whose role it was to see that the Party was attended at all cost, even at the cost of pretending, was disturbed to see this shadowy figure walking now always between the squares, carefully setting his foot on that rim of Saturn, the rim of nowhere which surrounds all definite places. One fallen piece.

The Chess Player's eyes fell on Djuna but she had escaped all seizure by dissolving into the music. This was a game he could not play: giving yourself. Djuna gave herself in the most unexpected ways. She lived in the cities of the interior, she had no permanent abode. She was always arriving and leaving undetected, as through a series of trap doors. The life she led there no one knew anything about. It never reached the ears of reporters. The statisticians of facts could never interview her. Then unexpectedly, in a public place, in a concert hall, a dance hall, at a lecture, at a party, she gave the immodest spectacle of her abandon to Stravinsky, her body's tense identification with the dancer, or revealed a passionate interest in the study of phosphenes.

And now she sat very neatly shaped in the very outline of the guitar played by Rango, her body tuned by the keys of her fingers as if Rango were playing on the strands of her hair, of her nerves, and the black notes were issuing from the black pupils of her eyes.

At least she could be considered as attending the party: her eyes were not closed, as they had been a half hour earlier when she was telling the Chess Player about phosphenes: phosphenes are the luminous impressions and circles seen with the eyelids closed, after the sudden compression of the eyeball. "Try it!"

The guitar distilled its music. Rango played it with the warm sienna color of his skin, with the charcoal pupil of his eyes, with the underbrush thickness of his black eyebrows, pouring into the honey-colored box the flavors of the open road on which he lived his gypsy life: thyme, rosemary, oregano, marjoram and sage. Pouring into the resonant sound-box the sensual swing of his hammock hung across the gypsy-cart and the dreams born on his mattress of black horsehair.

Idol of the night clubs, where men and women barred the doors and windows, lit candles, drank alcohol, and drank from his voice and his guitar the potions and herbs of the open road,

116

the charivaris of freedom, the drugs of leisure and laziness, the maypole dance of the fireflies, the horse's neighing fanfaronade, the fandangoes and ridottos of sudden lusts.

Shrunken breasts, vacillating eyes, hibernating virilities, all drank out of Rango's guitar and sienna voice. At dawn, not content with the life transfusion through cat guts, filled with the sap of his voice which had passed into their veins, at dawn the women laid hands upon his body like a tree. But at dawn Rango swung his guitar over his shoulder and walked away.

Will you be here tomorrow, Rango?

Tomorrow he might be playing and singing to his black horse's philosophically swaying tail on the road to the south of France.

Now arrived a very drunken Jay with his shoal of friends: five pairs of eyes wide open and vacant, five men wagging their heads with felicity because they are five. One a Chinese poet, tributary of Lao Tze; one Viennese poet, echo of Rilke; Hans the painter derived from Paul Klee; an Irish writer feebly stemming from Joyce. What they will become in the future does not concern them: at the present moment they are five praising each other and they feel strong and they are tottering with felicity.

They had had dinner at the Chinese restaurant, a rice without salt and meat with tough veins, but because of the shoal beatitude Jay proclaimed he had never eaten such rice, and five minutes later forgetting himself he said: "Rice is for the dogs!" The Chinese poet was hurt, his eyelids dropped humbly.

Now as they walked up the stairs he explained in neat phrases the faithfulness of the Chinese wife and Jay foamed with amazement: oh, such beautiful faithfulness!—he would marry a Chinese woman. Then the Chinese poet added: In China all tables are square. Jay almost wept with delight at this, it was the sign of a great civilization. He leaned over perilously and said with intimate secretiveness: In New Jersey when I was a boy tables were always round; I always hated round tables.

Their feet were not constructed for ascensions at the present moment; they might as well remain midway and call at Soutine's studio.

On the round stairway they collided with Stella susurrating in a tafetta skirt and eating fried potatoes out of a paper bag. Her long hair swayed as if she sat on a child's swing.

Her engaging gestures had lassoed an artist known for his compulsion to exhibit himself unreservedly, but he was not yet drunk enough and was for the moment content with strumming on his belt. Stella, not knowing what spectacle was reserved for her in his imagination, took the offering pose of women in Florentine paintings, extending the right hip like a holy water stand, both hands open as if inviting pigeons to eat from her palms, stylized, liturgical, arousing in Manuel the same impulse which had once made him set fire to a ballet skirt with a cigarette.

But Manuel was displaced by a figure who moved with stately politeness, his long hair patined with brilliantine, his face set in large and noble features by the men who carved the marble faces in the hall of fame.

He bowed graciously over women's hands with the ritualistic deliberateness of a Pope. His decrees, issued with handkissing, with soothing opening and closing of doors, extending of chairs, were nevertheless fatal: he held full power of decision over the delicate verdict: is it tomorrow's art?

No one could advance without his visa. He gave the passports to the future. Advance . . . or else: My dear man, you are a mere echo of the past.

Stella felt his handkissing charged with irony, felt herself installed in a museum *not* of modern art—blushed. To look at her in this ironic manner while scrupulously adhering to medieval salutations this man must know that she was one to keep faded flowers.

For he passed on with royal detachment and gazed seriously for relief at the steel and wood mobiles turning gently in the breeze of the future, like small structures of nerves vibrating in the air without their covering of flesh, the new cages of our future sorrows, so abstract they could not even contain a sob.

Jay was swimming against the compact stream of visitors looking for re-enforcement to pull out the Chinese poet who had stumbled into a very large garbage can in the front yard, and who was neatly folded in two, severely injured in his dignity. But he was arrested on his errand by the sight of Sabina and he thought why are there women in whom the sediment of experience settles and creates such a high flavor that when he had taken her he had also possessed all the unexplored regions of the world he had wanted to know, the men and women he would never have dared to encounter. Women whose bodies were a labyrinth so that when he was lying beside her he had felt he was taking a journey through the ancient gorge where Paracelsus dipped his sick people in fishing nets into lukewarm water, like a journey back into the womb, and he had seen several hundred feet above his head the little opening in the cathedral archway of the rocks through which the sun gleamed like a knife of gold.

But too late now to dwell on the panoramic, great voyage flavors of Sabina's body: the Chinese poet must be saved.

At this moment Sabina intercepted a look of tenderness between Jay and Lillian, a tenderness he had never shown her. The glance with which Lillian answered him was thrown around him very much like a safety net for a trapezist, and Sabina saw how Jay, in his wildest leaps, never leaped out of range of the net of protectiveness extended by Lillian.

The Chess Player noted with a frown that Sabina picked up her cape and made her way to the imitation Italian balcony. She was making a gradual escape; from the balcony to balcony, she would break the friendly efforts made to detain her, and reach the exit. He could not allow this to go on, at a Party everyone should pursue nothing but his individual drama. Because Lillian and Jay had stood for a moment on the same square and Sabina had caught Jay leaping spuriously into the safety net of Lillian's protectiveness, now Sabina acted like one

119

pierced by a knife and left the game for a balcony.

Where she stood now the noises of the Party could not reach her. She heard the wind and rain rushing through the trees like the lamentation of reeds in shallow tropical waters.

Sabina was lost.

The broken compass which inhabited her and whose wild fluctuations she had always obeyed, making for tumult and motion in place of direction, was suddenly fractured so that she no longer knew the relief of tides, ebbs and flows and dispersions.

She felt lost.

The dispersion had become too vast, too extended. For the first time a shaft of pain appeared cutting through the nebulous pattern. Pain lies only in reflection, in awareness. Sabina had moved so fast that all pain had passed swiftly as through a sieve, leaving a sorrow like children's sorrows, soon forgotten, soon replaced by a new interest. She had never known a pause.

And suddenly in this balcony, she felt alone.

Her cape, which was more than a cape, which was a sail, which was the feelings she threw to the four winds to be swelled and swept by the wind in motion, lay becalmed.

Her dress was becalmed.

It was as if now she wore nothing that the wind could catch, swell and propel.

For Sabina, to be becalmed meant to die.

Jealousy had entered her body and refused to run through it like sand through an hourglass. The silvery holes of her sieve against sorrow granted her at birth through which everything passed through and out painlessly, had clogged. Now the pain had lodged itself inside of her.

She had lost herself somewhere along the frontier between her inventions, her stories, her fantasies, and her true self. The boundaries had become effaced, the tracks lost, she had walked into pure chaos, and not a chaos which carried her like the wild gallopings of romantic riders in operas and legends, but a cavalcade which suddenly revealed the stage prop: a papier-mâché horse.

120

She had lost her boat, her sails, her cape, her horse, her seven-league boots, and all of them at once, leaving her stranded on a balcony, among dwarfed trees, diminished clouds, a miserly rainfall.

In the semi-darkness of that winter evening, her eyes were blurred. And then as if all the energy and warmth had been drawn inward for the first time, killing the senses, the ears, the touch, the palate, all movements of the body, all its external ways of communicating with the exterior, she suddenly felt a little deaf, a little blind, a little paralyzed; as if life, in coiling upon itself into a smaller, slower inward rhythm, were thinning her blood.

She shivered, with the same tremor as the leaves, feeling for the first time some small withered leaves of her being detaching themselves.

The Chess Player placed two people on a square.

As they danced a magnet pulled her hair and his together, and when they pulled their heads away, the magnet pulled their mouths together and when they separated the mouths, the magnet clasped their hands together and when they unclasped the hands their hips were soldered. There was no escape. When they stood completely apart then her voice spiralled around his, and his eyes were caught in the net grillage which barred her breasts.

They danced off the square and walked into a balcony.

Mouth meeting mouth, and pleasure striking like a gong, once, twice, thrice, like the beating wings of large birds. The bodies traversed by a rainbow of pleasure.

By the mouth they flowed into each other, and the little grey street ceased to be an impasse in Montparnasse. The balcony was now suspended over the Mediterranean, the Aegean sea, the Italian lakes, and through the mouth they flowed and coursed through the world.

While on the wall of the studio there continued to hang a large painting of a desert in smoke colors, a desert which parched the throat. Imbedded in the sand many little bleached

121

bones of lovelessness.

"The encounter of two is pure, in two there is some hope of truth," said the Chess Player catching the long floating hair of Stella as she passed and confronting her with a potential lover.

Behind Stella hangs a painting of a woman with a white halo around her head. Anxiety had carved diamond holes through her body and her airiness came from this punctured faith through which serenity had flown out.

What Stella gave now was only little pieces of herself, pieces carefully painted in the form of black circles of wit, squares of yellow politeness, triangles of blue friendliness, or the mock orange of love: desire. Only little pieces from her external armor. What she gave now was a self which a man could only carry across the threshold of an abstract house with only one window on the street and this street a desert with little white bones bleaching in the sun.

Deserts of mistrust.

The houses are no longer hearths, they hang like mobiles turning to the changing breeze while they love each other like ice skaters on the top layers of their invented selves, blinded with the dust of attic memories, within the windowless houses of their fears.

The guests hang their coats upon a fragile structure like the bar upon which ballet dancers test their limb's wit.

The Party spreads like an uneasy octopus that can no longer draw in his tentacles to seize and strangle the core of its destructiveness.

In each studio there is a human being dressed in the full regalia of his myth fearing to expose a vulnerable opening, spreading not his charms but his defences, plotting to disrobe, somewhere along the night—his body without the aperture of the heart or his heart with a door closed to his body. Thus keeping one compartment for refuge, one uninvaded cell.

And if you feel a little compressed, a little cramped in your daily world, you can take a walk through a Chirico painting. The houses have only facades, so escape is assured; the colonnades, the volutes, valances extend into the future and you can walk into space.

The painters peopled the world with a new variety of fruit and tree to surprise you with the bitterness of what was known for its sweetness and the sweetness of what was known for its bitterness, for they all deny the world as it is and take you back to the settings and scenes of your dreams. You slip out of a Party into the past or the future.

This meandering led the Chess Player to stray from his geometrical duties, and he was not able to prevent a suicide. It was Lillian who stood alone on a square; Lillian who had begun the evening like an African dancer donning not only all of her Mexican silver jewelry but a dress of emerald green of a starched material which had a bristling quality like her mood.

She had moved from one to another with gestures of her hands inciting others to foam, to dance. She teased them out of their nonchalance or detachment. People would awaken from their lethargies as in a thunderstorm; stand, move, ignite, catching her motions, her hands beating a meringue of voices, a soufflé of excitement. When they were ready to follow her into some kind of tribal dance, she left them, to fall again into limpness or to walk behind her enslaved, seeking another electrical charge.

She could not even wait for the end of the Party to commit her daily act of destruction. So she stood alone in her square defended by her own bristles and began: "No one is paying any attention to me. I should not have worn this green dress: it's too loud. I've just said the wrong thing to Brancusi. All these people have accomplished something and I have not. They put me in a panic. They are all so strong and so sure of themselves. I feel exactly as I did in my dream last night: I had been asked to play at a concert. There were so many people. When I went to play, the piano had no notes, it was a lake, and I tried to play on the water and no sound came. I felt defeated and humiliated. I hate the way my hair gets wild. Look at Stella's hair so smooth and clinging to her face. Why did I tease her? She looked so tremulous, so frightened, as if pleading not to be hurt. Why do I rush and speak before thinking? My dress is too short."

In this invisible hara-kiri she tore off her dress, her jewels, tore off every word she had uttered, every smile, every act of the evening. She was ashamed of her talk, of her silences, of what she had given, and of what she had not given, to have confided and not to have confided.

And now it was done. A complete house-wrecking service. Every word, smile, act, silver jewel, lying on the floor, with the emerald green dress, and even Djuna's image of Lillian to which she had often turned for comfort, that too lay shattered on the ground. Nothing to salvage. A mere pile of flaws. A little pile of ashes from a bonfire of self-criticism.

The Chess Player saw a woman crumpling down on a couch as if her inner frame had collapsed, smiled at her drunkenness and took no note of the internal suicide.

Came the grey-haired man who makes bottles, Lawrence Vail, saying: "I still occasionally and quite frequently and very perpetually empty a bottle. This is apt to give one a guilty feeling. Is it not possible I moaned and mooned that I have neglected the exterior (of the bottle) for the interior (of the bottle)? Why cast away empty bottles? The spirits in the bottle are not necessarily the spirit of the bottle. The spirit of the spirits of the bottle are potent, potential substances that should not be discarded, eliminated in spleen, plumbing and hangover. Why not exteriorize these spirits on the body of the bottle. . . ."

The Chess Player saw it was going to happen.

He saw Djuna slipping off one of the squares and said: "Come here! Hold hands with Jay's warm winey white-trash friends. It is too early in the evening for you to be slipping off."

Djuna gave him a glance of despair, as one does before falling.

She knew it was now going to happen.

This dreaded mood which came, warning her by dimming the lights, muffling the sounds, effacing the faces as in great snowstorms.

She would be inside of the Party as inside a colored ball, being swung by red ribbons, swayed by indigo music. All the objects of the Fair around her—the red wheels, the swift chariots, the dancing animals, the puppet shows, the swinging trapezes, words and faces swinging, red suns bursting, birds singing, ribbons of laughter floating and catching her, teasing hands rustling in her hair, the movements of the dance like all the motions of love: taking, bending, yielding, welding and unwelding, all the pleasures of collisions, every human being opening the cells of his gaiety.

And then wires would be cut, lights grow dim, sounds muffled, colors paled.

At this moment, like the last message received through her inner wireless from the earth, she always remembered this scene: she was sixteen years old. She stood in a dark room brushing her hair. It was a summer night. She was wearing her nightgown. She leaned out of the window to watch a party taking place across the way.

The men and women were dressed in rutilant festive colors she had never seen before, or was she dressing them with the intense light of her own dreaming, for she saw their gaiety, their relation to each other as something unparalleled in splendor. That night she yearned so deeply for this unattainable party, fearing she would never attend it, or else that if she did she would not be dressed in those heightened colors, she would not be so shining, so free. She saw herself attending but invisible, made invisible by timidity.

Now when she had reached this Party, where she had been visible and desired, a new danger threatened her: a mood which came and carried her off like an abductor, back into darkness.

This mood was always provoked by a phrase out of a dream: "This is not the place."

(What place? Was it the first party she wanted and none other, the one painted out of the darkness of her solitude?)

The second phrase would follow: "He is not the one."

Fatal phrase, like a black magic potion which annihilated the present. Instantly she was outside, locked out, thrust out by no one but herself, by a mood which cut her off from fraternity.

Merely by wishing to be elsewhere, where it might be more marvelous, made the near, the palpable seem then like an obstruction, a delay to the more marvelous place awaiting her, the more wonderful personage kept waiting. The present was murdered by this insistent, whispering, interfering dream, this invisible map constantly pointing to unexplored countries, a compass pointing to mirage.

But as quickly as she was deprived of ears, eyes, touch and placed adrift in space, as quickly as warm contact broke, she was granted another kind of ear, eye, touch, and contact.

She no longer saw the Chess Player as made of wood directed by a delicate geometric inner apparatus, as everyone saw him. She saw him before his crystallization, saw the incident which alchemized him into wood, into a chess player of geometric patterns. There, where a blighted love had made its first incision and the blood had turned to tree sap to become wood and move with geometric carefulness, there she placed her words calling to his warmth before it had congealed.

But the Chess Player was irritated. He addressed a man he did not recognize.

From the glass bastions of her city of the interior she could see all the excrescences, deformities, disguises, but as she moved among their hidden selves she incurred great angers.

"You demand we shed our greatest protections!"

"I demand nothing. I wanted to attend a Party. But the Party had dissolved in this strange acid of awareness which only dissolves the callouses, and I see the beginning."

"Stand on your square," said the Chess Player. "I shall bring you someone who will make you dance."

"Bring me one who will rescue me! Am I dreaming or dying? Bring me one who knows that between the dream and death there is only one frail step, one who senses that between this murder of the present by a dream, and death, there is only one shallow breath. Bring me one who knows that the dream without exit, without explosion, without awakening, is the passageway to the world of the dead! I want my dress torn and stained!"

A drunken man came up to her with a chair. Of all the chairs in the entire house he had selected a gold one with a red brocade top.

Why couldn't he bring me an ordinary chair?

To single her out for this hierarchic offering was to condemn her.

Now it was going to happen, inevitably.

The night and the Party had barely begun and she was being whisked away on a gold chair with a red brocade top by an abductor who would carry her back to the dark room of her adolescence, to the long white nightgown and hair brush, and to dream of a Party that she could never attend.

Children
of the Albatross

The Sealed Room

STEPPING OFF THE BUS at Montmartre Djuna arrived in the center of the ambulant Fair and precisely at the moment when she set her right foot down on the cobblestones the music of the merry-go-round was unleashed from its mechanical box and she felt the whole scene, her mood, her body, transformed by its gaiety exactly as in her childhood her life in the orphan asylum had been suddenly transformed from a heavy nightmare to freedom by her winning of a dance scholarship.

As if, because of so many obstacles her childhood and adolescence had been painful, heavy walking on crutches and

130

had suddenly changed overnight into a dance in which she discovered the air, space and the lightness of her own nature.

Her life was thus divided into two parts: the bare, the pedestrian one of her childhood, with poverty weighing her feet, and then the day when her interior monologue set to music led her feet into the dance.

Pointing her toe towards the floor she would always think: I danced my way out of the asylum, out of poverty, out of my past.

She remembered her feet on the bare floor of their first apartment. She remembered her feet on the linoleum of the orphan asylum. She remembered her feet going up and down the stairs of the home where she had been "adopted" and had suffered her jealousy of the affection bestowed on the legitimate children. She remembered her feet running away from that house.

She remembered her square-toed lusterless shoes, her mended stockings, and her hunger for new and shining shoes in shop windows.

She remembered the calluses on her feet from house work, from posing for painters, from working as a mannequin, from cold, from clumsy mendings and from ill-fitting shoes.

She remembered the day that her dreaming broke into singing, and became a monologue set to music, the day when the dreams became a miniature opera shutting out the harsh or dissonant sounds of the world.

She remembered the day when her feet became restless in their prison of lusterless leather and they began to vibrate in obedience to inner harmonizations, when she kicked off her shoes and as she moved her worn dress cracked under her arms and her skirt slit at the knees.

The flow of images set to music had descended from her head to her feet and she ceased to feel as one who had been split into two pieces by some great invisible saber cut.

In the external world she was the woman who had submitted to mysterious outer fatalities beyond her power to alter, and in her interior world she was a woman who had built many tunnels deeper down where no one could reach her, in which she deposited her treasures safe from destruction and in which she built a world exactly the opposite of the one she knew.

But at the moment of dancing a fusion took place, a welding, a wholeness. The cut in the middle of her body healed, and she was all one woman moving.

Lifted and impelled by an inner rhythm, with a music box playing inside her head, her foot lifted from drabness and immobility, from the swamps and miasmas of poverty, carried her across continents and oceans, depositing her on the cobblestones of a Paris square on the day of the Fair, among shimmering colored tents, the flags of pleasure at full mast, the merry-go-rounds turning like dervish dancers.

She walked to a side street, knocked on a dark doorway opened by a disheveled concierge and ran down the stairway to a vast underground room.

As she came down the stairway she could already hear the piano, feet stamping, and the ballet master's voice. When the piano stopped there was always his voice scolding, and the whispering of smaller voices.

Sometimes as she entered the class was dissolving, and a flurry of little girls brushed by her in their moth ballet costumes, the little girls from the Opera, laughing and whispering, fluttering like moths on their dusty ballet slippers, flurries of snow in the darkness of the vast room, with drops of dew from exertion.

Djuna went down with them along the corridors to the dressing rooms which at first looked like a garden, with the puffed white giant daisies of ballet skirts, the nasturtiums and poppies of Spanish skirts, the roses of cotton, the sunflowers, the spider webs of hair nets.

The small dressing room overflowed with the smell of cold cream, face powder, and cheap cologne, with the wild confusion of laughter, confessions from the girls, with old dancing slippers, faded flowers and withering tulle.

132

As soon as Djuna cast off her city clothes it was the trepidating moment of metamorphosis.

The piano slightly out of tune, the floor's vibrations, the odor of perspiration swelled the mood of excitement born in this garden of costumes to the accompaniment of whisperings and laughter.

When she extended her leg at the bar, the ballet master placed his hand on it as if to guide the accuracy of her pointed toe.

He was a slender, erect, stylized man of forty, not handsome in face; only in attitudes and gestures. His face was undefined, his features blurred. It was as if the dance were a sculptor who had taken hold of him and had carved style, form, elegance out of all his movements, but left the face unimportant.

She always felt his hand exceptionally warm whenever he placed it on her to guide, to correct, improve or change a gesture.

When he placed his hand on her ankle she became intensely aware of her ankle, as if he were the magician who caused the blood to flow through it; when he placed his hand on her waist she became intensely aware of her waist as if he were the sculptor who indented it.

When his hand gave the signal to dance then it was not only as if he had carved the form of her body and released the course of her blood but as if his hand had made the co-ordination between blood and gestures and form, and the *leçon de danse* became a lesson in living.

So she obeyed, she danced, she was flexible and yielding in his hands, plying her body, disciplining it, awakening it.

It became gradually apparent that she was the favorite. She was the only one at whom he did not shout while she was dressing. He was more elated at her progress, and less harsh about her faults.

She obeyed his hands, but he found it more imperative than with other pupils to guide her by touch or by tender inflections of his voice.

133

He gave of his own movements as if he knew her movements would be better if he made them with her.

The dance gained in perfection, a perfection born of an accord between their gestures; born of her submission and his domination.

When he was tired she danced less well. When his attention was fixed on her she danced magnificently.

The little girls of the ballet troupe, mature in this experience, whispered and giggled: you are the favorite!

Yet not for a moment did he become for her a man. He was the ballet master. If he ruled her body with this magnetic rulership, a physical prestige, it was as a master of her dancing for the purpose of the dance.

But one day after the lessons, when the little girls from the Opera had left and there still hung in the air only an echo of the silk, flurry, snow and patter of activities, he followed her into the dressing room.

She had not yet taken off the voluminous skirt of the dance, the full-blown petticoat, the tight-fitting panties, so that when he entered the dressing room it seemed like a continuation of the dance. A continuation of the dance when he approached her and bent one knee in gallant salutation, and put his arms around her skirt that swelled like a huge flower. She laid her hand on his head like a queen acknowledging his worship. He remained on one knee while the skirt like a full-blown flower opened to allow a kiss to be placed at the core.

A kiss enclosed in the corolla of the skirt and hidden away, then he returned to the studio to speak with the pianist, to tell her at what time to come the next day, and to pay her, while Djuna dressed, covering warmth, covering her tremor, covering her fears.

He was waiting for her at the door, neat and trim.

He said: "Why don't you come and sit at the café with me?"

She followed him. Not far from there was the Place Clichy, always animated but more so now as the site of the Fair.

The merry-go-rounds were turning swiftly. The gypsies were

reading fortunes in little booths hung with Arabian rugs.

Workmen were shooting clay pigeons and winning cut-glass dishes for their wives.

The prostitutes were enjoying their watchful promenades, and the men their loitering.

The ballet master was talking to her: "Djuna (and suddenly as he said her name, she felt again where he had deposited his tribute), I am a simple man. My parents were shoemakers in a little village down south. I was put to work as a boy in an iron factory where I handled heavy things and was on the way to becoming deformed by big muscles. But during my lunch hour I danced. I wanted to be a ballet dancer, and I practiced at one of the iron bars in front of a big furnace. And today— look!" He handed her a cigarette case all engraved with names of famous ballet dancers. "Today," he said proudly, "I have been the partner of all these women. If you would come with me, we could be happy. I am a simple man, but we could dance in all the cities of Europe. I am no longer young but I have a lot of dancing in me still. We could be happy. . . ."

The merry-go-round turned and her feelings with it, riding again the wooden horses of her childhood in the park, which was so much like flying, riding around from city to city reaching eagerly for the prizes, for bouquets, for clippings, for fame, flinging all of one's secret desires for pleasure on the outside like a red shawl, with this joyous music at the center always, the body recovered, the body dancing. (Hadn't she been the woman in quest of her body once lost by a shattering blow— submerged, and now floating again on the surface where uncrippled human beings lived in a world of pleasure like the Fair?)

How to explain to this simple man, how to explain? *There is something broken inside of me.* I cannot dance, live, love as easily as others. Surely enough, if we traveled around the world, I would break my leg somewhere. Because this inner break is invisible and unconvincing to others, I would not rest until I had broken something for everyone to see, to under-

135

stand. How to explain to this simple man, I could dance continuously with success, without breaking. *I am the dancer who falls,* always, into traps of depression, breaking my heart and my body almost at every turn, losing my tempo and my lightness, falling out of groups, out of grace, out of perfection. There is too often something wrong. Something you cannot help me with. . . . Supposing we found ourselves in a strange country, in a strange hotel. You are alone in a hotel room. Well, what of that? You can talk to the bar man, or you can sit before your glass of beer and read the papers. Everything is simple. But when I am alone in a hotel room something happens to me at times which must be what happens to children when the lights are turned out. Animals and children. But the animals howl their solitude, and children can call for their parents and for lights. But I. . . .

"What a long time it takes you to answer me," said the ballet master.

"I'm not strong enough," said Djuna.

"That's what I thought when I first saw you. I thought you couldn't take the discipline of a dancer's life. But it isn't so. You look fragile and all that, but you're healthy. I can tell healthy women by their skin. Yours is shining and clear. No, I don't think you have the strength of a horse, you're what we call *'une petite nature.'* But you have energy and guts. And we'll take it easy on the road."

In the middle of a piece of music the merry-go-round suddenly stopped. Something had gone wrong with the motor! The horses slowed down their pace. The children lost their hilarity. The boss looked troubled, and the mechanic was called and like a doctor came with his bag.

The Fair lost its spinning frenzy.

When the music stopped, one could hear the dry shots of the amateur hunters and the clay pigeons falling behind the cardboard walls.

136

The dreams which Djuna had started to weave in the asylum as if they were the one net in which she could exist, leaping thus always out of reach of unbearable happenings and creating her own events parallel to the ones her feelings could not accept, the dreams which gave birth to worlds within worlds, which, begun at night when she was asleep, continued during the day as an accompaniment to acts which she now discovered were rendered ineffectual by this defensive activity, with time became more and more violent.

For at first the personages of the dream, the cities which sprang up, were distinct and bore no resemblance to reality. They were images which filled her head with the vapors of fever, a drug-like panorama of incidents which rendered her insensible to cold, hunger and fatigue.

The day her mother was taken to the hospital to die, the day her brother was injured while playing in the street and developed a gentle insanity, the day at the asylum when she fell under the tyranny of the only man in the place, were days when she noted an intensification of her other world.

She could still weep at these happenings, but as people might lament just before they go under an anesthetic. "It still hurts," says the voice as the anesthetic begins to take effect and the pain growing duller, the body complaining more out of a mere remembrance of pain, automatically, just before sinking into a void.

She even found a way to master her weeping.

No mirrors were allowed in the orphan asylum, but girls had made one by placing black paper behind one of the small windows. Once a week they set it up and took turns looking at their faces.

Djuna's first glimpse of her adolescent face was in this black mirror, where the clear coloring of her skin was as if touched with mourning, as if reflected at the bottom of a well.

Even long afterwards it was difficult for her to overcome this first impression of her face painted upon black still waters.

But she discovered that if she was weeping, and she looked

137

at the weeping in a mirror, the weeping stopped. It ceased to be her own. It belonged to another.

Henceforth she possessed this power: whatever emotion would ravish or torment her, she could bring it before a mirror, look at it, and separate herself from it. And she thought she had found a way to master sorrow.

There was a boy of her age who passed under her window and who had the power to move her. He had a lean, eager face, eyes which seemed liquid with tenderness, and his gestures were full of gentleness.

His passage had the power to make her happy or unhappy, warm or cold, rich or poor. Whether he walked abstractedly on the other side of the street or on her side, whether he looked up at her window or forgot to look up, determined the mood of her day.

Because of his manner, she felt she trusted him entirely, that if he should come to the door and ask her to follow him she would do so without hesitation.

In her dreams at night she dissolved in his presence, lost herself in him. Her feelings for him were the opposite of an almost continuous and painful tension whose origin she did not know.

In contrast to this total submission to the unknown boy's gentleness, her first encounter with man was marked with defiance, fear, hostility.

The man, called the Watchman by the girls, was about forty years old when Djuna was sixteen. He was possessed of unlimited power because he was the lover of the Directress. His main attribute was power. He was the only man in the asylum, and he could deal privileges, gifts, and give permissions to go out at night.

This unique role gave him a high prestige. He was polite, carried himself with confidence, and was handsome in a neutral way which adapted him easily to any kind of image the orphans wished to fashion of him.

He could pass for the tall man, the brown-haired man, the

138

blond man; given a little leeway, he answered all the descriptions of gypsy card readers.

An added piquancy was attained by the common knowledge that he was the favorite of the Directress, who was very much hated. In winning his favor, one struck indirect blows at her authority, and achieved a subtle revenge for her severity.

The girls thought of him as possessing an even greater power than hers, for she who submitted to no one, had often been seen bowing her head before his reproaches.

The one he chose felt endowed immediately with greater beauty, greater charm and power than the other girls. He was appointed the arbiter, the connoisseur, the bestower of decorations.

To be chosen by the Watchman was to enter the realm of protection. No girl could resist this.

Djuna could distinguish his steps at a great distance. It seemed to her that he walked more evenly than anyone she knew, evenly and without stops or change of rhythm. He advanced through the hallways inexorably. Other people could be stopped, or eluded. But his steps were those of absolute authority.

He knew at what time Djuna would be passing through this particular hallway alone. He always came up to her, not a yard away, but exactly beside her.

His glance was always leveled at her breasts, and two things would happen simultaneously: he would offer her a present without looking at her face, as if he were offering it to her breasts, and then he would whisper: "Tonight I will let you out if you are good to me."

And Djuna would think of the boy who passed by under her window, and feel a wild beating of her heart at the possibility of meeting him outside, of talking to him, and her longing for the boy, for the warm liquid tenderness of his eyes was so violent that no sacrifice seemed too great—her longing and her feeling that if he knew of this scene, he would rescue her, but that there was no other way to reach him, no other way to defeat authority to reach him than by this concession to authority.

In this barter there was no question of rebellion. The way the Watchman stood, demanded, gestured, was all part of a will she did not even question, a continuation of the will of the father. There was the man who demanded, and outside was the gentle boy who demanded nothing, and to whom she wanted to give everything, whose silence even, she trusted, whose way of walking she trusted with her entire heart, while this man she did not trust.

It was the *droit du seigneur.*

She slipped the Watchman's bracelet around the lusterless cotton of her dress, while he said: "The poorer the dress the more wonderful your skin looks, Djuna."

Years later when Djuna thought the figure of the Watchman was long since lost she would hear echoes of his heavy step and she would find herself in the same mood she had experienced so many times in his presence.

No longer a child, and yet many times she still had the feeling that she might be overpowered by a will stronger than her own, might be trapped, might be somehow unable to free herself, unable to escape the demands of man upon her.

Her first defeat at the hands of man the father had caused her such a conviction of helplessness before tyranny that although she realized that she was now in reality no longer helpless, the echo of this helplessness was so strong that she still dreaded the possessiveness and willfulness of older men. They benefited from this regression into her past, and could override her strength merely because of this conviction of unequal power.

It was as if maturity did not develop altogether and completely, but by little compartments like the airtight sections of a ship. A part of her being would mature, such as her insight, or interpretative faculties, but another could retain a childhood conviction that events, man and authority together were stronger than one's capacity for mastering them, and that

140

one was doomed to become a victim of one's pattern.

It was only much later that Djuna discovered that this belief in the great power of others became the fate itself and caused the defeats.

But for years, she felt harmed and defeated at the hands of men of power, and she expected the boy, the gentle one, the trusted one, to come and deliver her from tyranny.

Ever since the day of Lillian's concert when she had seen the garden out of the window, Djuna had wanted a garden like it.

And now she possessed a garden and a very old house on the very edge of Paris, between the city and the Park.

But it was not enough to possess it, to walk through it, sit in it. One still had to be able to live in it.

And she found she could not live in it.

The inner fever, the restlessness within her corroded her life in the garden.

When she was sitting in a long easy chair she was not at ease.

The grass seemed too much like a rug awaiting footsteps, to be trampled with hasty incidents. The rhythm of growth too slow, the falling of the leaves too tranquil.

Happiness was an absence of fever. The garden was feverless and without tension to match her tensions. She could not unite or commune with the plants, the languor, the peace. It was all contrary to her inward pulse. Not one pulsation of the garden corresponded to her inner pulsation which was more like a drum beating feverish time.

Within her the leaves did not wait for autumn, but were torn off prematurely by unexpected sorrows. Within her, leaves did not wait for spring to sprout but bloomed in sudden hothouse exaggerations. Within her there were storms contrary to the lazy moods of the garden, devastations for which nature had no equivalent.

Peace, said the garden, peace.

The day began always with the sound of gravel crushed by automobiles.

141

The shutters were pushed open by the French servant, and the day admitted.

With the first crushing of the gravel under wheels came the barking of the police dog and the carillon of the church bells.

Cars entered through an enormous green iron gate, which had to be opened ceremoniously by the servant.

Everyone else walked through the small green gate that seemed like the child of the other, half covered with ivy. The ivy did not climb over the father gate.

When Djuna looked at the large gate through her window it took on the air of a prison gate. An unjust feeling, since she knew she could leave the place whenever she wanted, and since she knew more than anyone that human beings placed upon an object, or a person this responsibility of being the obstacle, when the obstacle lay within one's self.

In spite of this knowledge, she would often stand at the window staring at the large closed iron gate as if hoping to obtain from this contemplation a reflection of her inner obstacles to a full open life.

She mocked its importance; the big gate had a presumptuous creak! Its rusty voice was full of dissonant affectations. No amount of oil could subdue its rheumatism, for it took a historical pride in its own rust: it was a hundred years old.

But the little gate, with its overhanging ivy like disordered hair over a running child's forehead, had a sleepy and sly air, an air of always being half open, never entirely locked.

Djuna had chosen the house for many reasons, because it seemed to have sprouted out of the earth like a tree, so deeply grooved it was within the old garden. It had no cellar and the rooms rested right on the ground. Below the rugs, she felt, was the earth. One could take root here, feel as one with the house and garden, take nourishment from them like the plants.

She had chosen it too because its symmetrical façade covered by a trellis overrun by ivy showed twelve window faces. But one shutter was closed and corresponded to no room. During some transformation of the house it had been walled up.

142

Djuna had taken the house because of this window which led to no room, because of this impenetrable room, thinking that someday she would discover an entrance to it.

In front of the house there was a basin which had been filled, and a well which had been sealed up. Djuna set about restoring the basin, excavated an old fountain and unsealed the well.

Then it seemed to her that the house came alive, the flow was re-established.

The fountain was gay and sprightly, the well deep.

The front half of the garden was trim and stylized like most French gardens, but the back of it some past owner had allowed to grow wild and become a miniature jungle. The stream was almost hidden by overgrown plants, and the small bridge seemed like a Japanese bridge in a glass-bowl garden.

There was a huge tree of which she did not know the name, but which she named the Ink Tree for its black and poisonous berries.

One summer night she stood in the courtyard. All the windows of the house were lighted.

Then the image of the house with all its windows lighted— all but one—she saw as the image of the self, of the being divided into many cells. Action taking place in one room, now in another, was the replica of experience taking place in one part of the being, now in another.

The room of the heart in Chinese lacquer red, the room of the mind in pale green or the brown of philosophy, the room of the body in shell rose, the attic of memory with closets full of the musk of the past.

She saw the whole house on fire in the summer night and it was like those moments of great passion and deep experience when every cell of the self lighted simultaneously, a dream of fullness, and she hungered for this that would set aflame every room of the house and of herself at once!

In herself there was one shuttered window.

She did not sleep soundly in the old and beautiful house.

She was disturbed.

143

She could hear voices in the dark, for it is true that on days of clear audibility there are voices which come from within and speak in multiple tongues contradicting each other. They speak out of the past, out of the present, the voices of awareness—in dialogues with the self which mark each step of living.

There was the voice of the child in herself, unburied, who had long ago insisted: I want only the marvelous.

There was the low-toned and simple voice of the human being Djuna saying: I want love.

There was the voice of the artist in Djuna saying: I will create the marvelous.

Why should such wishes conflict with each other, or annihilate each other?

In the morning the human being Djuna sat on the carpet before the fireplace and mended and folded her stockings into little partitioned boxes, keeping the one perfect unmended pair for a day of high living, partitioning at the same time events into little separate boxes in her head, dividing (that was one of the great secrets against shattering sorrows), allotting and rearranging under the heading of one word a constantly fluid, mobile and protean universe whose multiple aspects were like quicksands.

This exaggerated sense, for instance, of a preparation for the love to come, like the extension of canopies, the unrolling of ceremonial carpets, the belief in the state of grace, of a perfection necessary to the advent of love.

As if she must first of all create a marvelous world in which to house it, thinking it befell her adequately to receive this guest of honor.

Wasn't it too oriental, said a voice protesting with mockery —such elaborate receptions, such costuming, as if love were such an exigent guest?

She was like a perpetual bride preparing a trousseau. As other women sew and embroider, or curl their hair, she embellished her cities of the interior, painted, decorated, prepared a great *mise en scène* for a great love.

144

It was in this mood of preparation that she passed through her kingdom the house, painting here a wall through which the stains of dampness showed, hanging a lamp where it would throw Balinese theater shadows, draping a bed, placing logs in the fireplaces, wiping the dull-surfaced furniture that it might shine. Every room in a different tone like the varied pipes of an organ, to emit a wide range of moods—lacquer red for vehemence, gray for confidences, a whole house of moods with many doors, passageways, and changes of level.

She was not satisfied until it emitted a glow which was not only that of the Dutch interiors in Dutch paintings, a glow of immaculateness, but an effulgence which had caused Jay to discourse on the gold dust of Florentine paintings.

Djuna would stand very still and mute and feel: my house will speak for me. My house will tell them I am warm and rich. The house will tell them inside of me there are these rooms of flesh and Chinese lacquer, sea greens to walk through, inside of me there are lighted candles, live fires, shadows, spaces, open doors, shelters and air currents. Inside of me there is color and warmth.

The house will speak for me.

People came and submitted to her spell, but like all spells it was wonderful and remote. Not warm and near. No human being, they thought, made this house, no human being lived here. It was too fragile and too unfamiliar. There was no dust on her hands, no broken nails, no sign of wear and tear.

It was the house of the myth.

It was the ritual they sensed, tasted, smelled. Too different from the taste and smell of their own houses. It took them out of the present. They took on an air of temporary guests. No familiar landscape, no signpost to say: this is your home as well.

All of them felt they were passing, could not remain. They were tourists visiting foreign lands. It was a voyage and not a port.

Even in the bathroom there were no medicine bottles on

the shelves proclaiming: soda, castor oil, cold cream. She had transferred all of them to alchemist bottles, and the homeliest drug assumed an air of philter.

This was a dream and she was merely a guide.

None came near enough.

There were houses, dresses, which created one's isolation as surely as those tunnels created by ferrets to elude pursuit by the male.

There were rooms and costumes which appeared to be made to lure but which were actually effective means to create distance.

Djuna had not yet decided what her true wishes were, or how near she wanted them to come. She was apparently calling to them but at the same time, by a great ambivalence and fear of their coming too near, of invading her, of dominating or possessing her, she was charming them in such a manner that the human being in her, the warm and simple human being, remained secure from invasion. She constructed a subtle obstacle to invasion at the same time as she constructed an appealing scene.

None came near enough. After they left she sat alone, and deserted, as lonely as if they had not come.

She was alone as everyone is every morning after a dream.

What was this that was weeping inside of her costume and house, something smaller and simpler than the edifice of spells?

She did not know why she was left hungry.

The dream took place. Everything had contributed to its perfection, even her silence, for she would not speak when she had nothing meaningful to say (like the silence in dreams between fateful events and fateful phrases, never a trivial word spoken in dreams!).

The next day, unknowing, she began anew.

She poured medicines from ugly bottles into alchemist bottles, creating minor mysteries, minor transmutations.

Insomnia. The nights were long.

Who would come and say: that is *my* dream, and take up

146

the thread and make all the answers?

Or are all dreams made alone?

Lying in the fevered sheets of insomnia, there was a human being cheated by the dream.

Insomnia came when one must be on the watch, when one awaited an important visitor.

Everyone, Djuna felt, saw the dancer on light feet but no one seized the moment when she vacillated, fell. No one perceived or shared her difficulties, the mere technical difficulties of loving, dancing, believing.

When she fell, she fell alone, as she had in adolescence.

She remembered feeling this mood as a girl, that all her adolescence had proceeded by oscillations between weakness and strength. She remembered, too, that whenever she became entangled in too great a difficulty she had these swift regressions into her adolescent state. Almost as if in the large world of maturity, when the obstacle loomed too large, she shrank again into the body of a young girl for whom the world had first appeared as a violent and dangerous place, forcing her to retreat, and when she retreated she fell back into smallness.

She returned to the adolescent deserts of mistrust of love.

Walking through snow, carrying her muff like an obsolete wand no longer possessed of the power to create the personage she needed, she felt herself walking through a desert of snow.

Her body muffled in furs, her heart muffled like her steps, and the pain of living muffled as by the deepest rich carpets, while the thread of Ariadne which led everywhere, right and left, like scattered footsteps in the snow, tugged and pulled within her memory and she began to pull upon this thread (silk for the days of marvel and cotton for the bread of everyday living which was always a little stale) as one pulls upon a spool, and she heard the empty wooden spool knock against the floor of different houses.

Holding the silk or cotton began to cut her fingers which bled from so much unwinding, or was it that the thread of Ariadne had led into a wound?

147

The thread slipped through her fingers now, with blood on it, and the snow was no longer white.

Too much snow on the spool she was unwinding from the tightly wound memories. Unwinding snow as it lay thick and hard around the edges of her adolescence because the desire of men did not find a magical way to open her being.

The only words which opened her being were the muffled words of poets so rarely uttered by human beings. They alone penetrated her without awakening the bristling guards on watch at the gateways, costumed like silver porcupines armed with mistrust, barring the way to the secret recesses of her thoughts and feelings.

Before most people, most places, most situations, most words, Djuna's being, at sixteen, closed hermetically into muteness. The sentinels bristled: someone is approaching! And all the passages to her inner self would close.

Today as a mature woman she could see how these sentinels had not been content with defending her, but they had constructed a veritable fort under this mask of gentle shyness, forts with masked holes concealing weapons built by fear.

The snow accumulated every night all around the rim of her young body.

Blue and crackling snowbound adolescence.

The young men who sought to approach her then, drawn by her warm eyes, were startled to meet with such harsh resistance.

This was no mere flight of coquetry inviting pursuit. It was a fort of snow (for the snowbound, dream-swallower of the frozen fairs). An unmeltable fort of timidity.

Yet each time she walked, muffled, protected, she was aware of two young women walking: one intent on creating trap doors of evasion, the other wishing someone might find the entrance that she might not be so alone.

148

With Michael it was as if she had not heard him coming, so gentle were his steps, his words. Not the walk or words of the hunter, of the man of war, the determined entrance of older men, not the dominant walk of the father, the familiar walk of the brother, not like any other man she knew.

Only a year older than herself, he walked into her blue and white climate with so light a tread that the guards did not hear him!

He came into the room with a walk of vulnerability, treading softly as upon a carpet of delicacies. He would not crush the moss, no gravel would complain under his feet, no plant would bow its head or break.

It was a walk like a dance in which the gentleness of the steps carried him through air, space and silence in a sentient minuet in accord with his partner's mood, his leaf-green eyes obeying every rhythm, attentive to harmony, fearful of discord, with an excessive care for the other's intent.

The path his steps took, his velvet words, miraculously slipped between the bristles of her mistrust, and before she had been fully aware of his coming, by his softness he had entered fully into the blue and white climate.

The mists of adolescence were not torn open, not even disturbed by his entrance.

He came with poems, with worship, with flowers not ordered from the florist but picked in the forest near his school.

He came not to plunder, to possess, to overpower. With great gentleness he moved towards the hospitable regions of her being, towards the peaceful fields of her interior landscape, where white flowers placed themselves against green backgrounds as in Botticelli paintings of spring.

At his entrance her head remained slightly inclined towards the right, as it was when she was alone, slightly weighed down by pensiveness, whereas on other occasions, at the least approach of a stranger, her head would raise itself tautly in preparation for danger.

And so he entered into the flowered regions behind the forts,

149

having easily crossed all the moats of politeness.

His blond hair gave him the befitting golden tones attributed to most legendary figures.

Djuna never knew whether this light of sun he emitted came out of his own being or was thrown upon him by her dream of him, as later she had observed the withdrawal of this light from those she had ceased to love. She never knew whether two people woven together by feelings answering each other as echoes threw off a phosphorescence, the chemical sparks of marriage, or whether each one threw upon the other the spotlight of his inner dream.

Transient or everlasting, inner or outer, personal or magical, there was now this lighting falling upon both of them and they could only see each other in its spanning circle which dazzled them and separated them from the rest of the world.

Through the cocoon of her shyness her voice had been hardly audible, but he heard every shading of it, could follow its nuances even when it retreated into the furthest impasse of the ear's labyrinth.

Secretive and silent in relation to the world, she became exalted and intense once placed inside of this inner circle of light.

This light which enclosed two was familiar and natural to her.

Because of their youth, and their moving still outside of the center of their own desires blindly, what they danced together was not a dance in which either took possession of the other, but a kind of minuet, where the aim consisted in *not* appropriating, *not* grasping, *not* touching, but allowing the maximum space and distance to flow between the two figures. To move in accord without collisions, without merging. To encircle, to bow in worship, to laugh at the same absurdities, to mock their own movements, to throw upon the walls twin shadows which will never become one. To dance around this danger: the danger of becoming one! To dance keeping each to his own path. To allow parallelism, but no loss of the self into the

150

other. To play at marriage, step by step, to read the same book together, to dance a dance of elusiveness on the rim of desire, to remain within circles of heightened lighting without touching the core that would set the circle on fire.

A deft dance of unpossession.

They met once at a party, imprinted on each other forever the first physical image: she saw him tall, with an easy bearing, an easily flowing laughter. She saw all: the ivory color of the skin, the gold metal sheen of the hair, the lean body carved with meticulous economy as for racing, running, leaping; tender fingers touching objects as if all the world were fragile; tender inflections of the voice without malice or mockery; eyelashes always ready to fall over the eyes when people spoke harshly around him.

He absorbed her dark, long, swinging hair, the blue eyes never at rest, a little slanted, quick to close their curtains too, quick to laugh, but more often thirsty, absorbing like a mirror. She allowed the pupil to receive these images of others but one felt they did not vanish altogether as they would on a mirror: one felt a thirsty being absorbing reflections and drinking words and faces into herself for a deep communion with them.

She never took up the art of words, the art of talk. She remained always as Michael had first seen her: a woman who talked with her Naiad hair, her winged eyelashes, her tilted head, her fluent waist and rhetorical feet.

She never said: I have a pain. But laid her two arms over the painful area as if to quiet a rebellious child, rocking and cradling this angry nerve. She never said: I am afraid. But entered the room on tiptoes, her eyes watching for ambushes.

She was already the dancer she was to become, eloquent

151

with her body.

They met once and then Michael began to write her letters as soon as he returned to college.

In these letters he appointed her Isis and Arethusa, Iseult and the Seven Muses.

Djuna became the woman with the face of all women.

With strange omissions: he was neither Osiris nor Tristram, nor any of the mates or pursuers.

He became uneasy when she tried to clothe *him* in the costume of myth figures.

When he came to see her during vacations they never touched humanly, not even by a handclasp. It was as if they had found the most intricate way of communicating with each other by way of historical personages, literary passions, and that any direct touch even of finger tips would explode this world.

With each substitution they increased the distance between their human selves.

Djuna was not alarmed. She regarded this with feminine eyes: in creating this world Michael was merely constructing a huge, superior, magnificent nest in some mythological tree, and one day he would ask her to step into it with him, carrying her over the threshold all costumed in the trappings of his fantasy, and he would say: this is our home!

All this to Djuna was an infinitely superior way of wooing her, and she never doubted its ultimate purpose, or climax, for in this the most subtle women are basically simple and do not consider mythology or symbolism as a substitute for the climaxes of nature, merely as adornments!

The mist of adolescence, prolonging and expanding the wooing, was merely an elaboration of the courtship. His imagination continued to create endless detours as if they had to live first of all through all the loves of history and fiction before they could focus on their own.

But the peace in his moss-green eyes disturbed her, for in her eyes there now glowed a fever. Her breasts hurt her at night, as if from overfullness.

His eyes continued to focus on the most distant points of all, but hers began to focus on the near, the present. She would dwell on a detail of his face. On his ears for instance. On the movements of his lips when he talked. She failed to hear some of his words because she was following with her eyes and her feelings the contours of his lips moving as if they were moving on the surface of her skin.

She began to understand for the first time the carnation in Carmen's mouth. Carmen was eating the mock orange of love: the white blossoms which she bit were like skin. Her lips had pressed around the mock-orange petals of desire.

In Djuna all the moats were annihilated: she stood perilously near to Michael glowing with her own natural warmth. Days of clear visibility which Michael did not share. His compass still pointed to the remote, the unknown.

Djuna was a woman being dreamed.

But Djuna had ceased to dream: she had tasted the mock orange of desire.

More baffling still to Djuna grown warm and near, with her aching breasts, was that the moss-green serenity of Michael's eyes was going to dissolve into jealousy without pausing at desire.

He took her to a dance. His friends eagerly appropriated her. From across the room full of dancers, for the first time he saw not her eyes but her mouth, as vividly as she had seen him. Very clear and very near, and he felt the taste of it upon his lips.

For the first time, as she danced away from him, encircled by young men's arms, he measured the great space they had been swimming through, measured it exactly as others measure the distance between planets.

The mileage of space he had put between himself and Djuna. The lighthouse of the eyes alone could traverse such immensity!

And now, after such elaborations in space, so many figures interposed between them, the white face of Iseult, the burning

153

face of Catherine, all of which he had interpreted as mere elaborations of his enjoyment of her, now suddenly appeared not as ornaments but as obstructions to his possession of her.

She was lost to him now. She was carried away by other young men, turning with them. They had taken her waist as he never had, they bent her, plied her to the movements of the dance, and she answered and responded: they were mated by the dance.

As she passed him he called out her name severely, reproachfully, and Djuna saw the green of his eyes turned to violet with jealousy.

"Djuna! I'm taking you home."

For the first time he was willful, and she liked it.

"Djuna!" He called again, angrily, his eyes darkening with anger.

She had to stop dancing. She came gently towards him, thinking: "He wants me all to himself," and she was happy to yield to him.

He was only a little taller than she was, but he held himself very erect and commanding.

On the way home he was silent.

The design of her mouth had vanished again, his journey towards her mouth had ceased the moment it came so near in reality to his own. It was as if he dared to experience a possibility of communion only while the obstacle to it was insurmountable, but as the obstacle was removed and she walked clinging to his arm, then he could only commune with her eyes, and the distance was again reinstated.

He left her at her door without a sign of tenderness, with only the last violet shadows of jealousy lurking reproachfully in his eyes. That was all.

Djuna sobbed all night before the mystery of his jealousy, his anger, his remoteness.

She would not question him. He confided nothing. They barred all means of communication with each other. He would not tell her that at this very dance he had discovered an intermediate world from which all the figures of women were absent. A world of boys like himself in flight away from woman, mother, sister, wife or mistress.

In her ignorance and innocence then, she could not have pierced with the greatest divination where Michael, in his flight from her, gave his desire.

In their youthful blindness they wounded each other. He excused his coldness towards her: "You're too slender. I like plump women." Or again: "You're too intelligent. I feel better with stupid women." Or another time he said: "You're too impulsive, and that frightens me."

Being innocent, she readily accepted the blame.

Strange scenes took place between them. She subdued her intelligence and became passive to please him. But it was a game, and they both knew it. Her ebullience broke through all her pretenses at quietism.

She swallowed countless fattening pills, but could only gain a pound or two. When she proudly asked him to note the improvements, his eyes turned away.

One day he said: "I feel your clever head watching me, and you would look down on me if I failed."

Failed?

She could not understand.

With time, her marriage to another, her dancing which took her to many countries, the image of Michael was effaced.

But she continued to relate to other Michaels in the world. Some part of her being continued to recognize the same gentleness, the same elusiveness, the same mystery.

Michael reappeared under different bodies, guises, and each time she responded to him, discovering each time a little more until she pierced the entire mystery open.

But the same little dance took place each time, a little dance of insolence, a dance which said to the woman: "I dance alone, I will not be possessed by a woman."

The kind of dance tradition had taught woman as a ritual to provoke aggression! But this dance made by young men

155

before the women left them at a loss for it was not intended to be answered.

Years later she sat at a café table in Paris between Michael and Donald.

Why should she be sitting between Michael and Donald?

Why were not all cords cut between herself and Michael when she married and when he gave himself to a succession of Donalds?

When they met in Paris again, he had this need to invent a trinity: to establish a connecting link between Djuna and all the changing, fluctuating Donalds.

As if some element were lacking in his relation to Donald.

Donald had a slender body, like an Egyptian boy. Dark hair wild like that of a child who had been running. At moments the extreme softness of his gestures made him appear small, at others when he stood stylized and pure in line, erect, he seemed tall and firm.

His eyes were large and entranced, and he talked flowingly like a medium. His eyelids fell heavily over his eyes like a woman's, with a sweep of the eyelashes. He had a small straight nose, small ears, and strong boyish hands.

When Michael left for cigarettes they looked at each other, and immediately Donald ceased to be a woman. He straightened his body and looked at Djuna unflinchingly.

With her he asserted his strength. Was it her being a woman which challenged his strength? He was now like a grave child in the stage of becoming a man.

With the smile of a conspirator he said: "Michael treats me as if I were a woman or a child. He wants me not to work and to depend on him. He wants to go and live down south in a kind of paradise."

156

"And what do you want?"

"I am not sure I love Michael. . . ."

That was exactly what she expected to hear. Always this admission of incompleteness. Always one in flight or the three sitting together, always one complaining or one loving less than the other.

All this accompanied by the most complicated harmonization of expressions Djuna had ever seen. The eyes and mouth of Donald suggesting an excitement familiar to drug addicts, only in Donald it did not derive from any artificial drugs but from the strange flavor he extracted from difficulties, from the maze and detours and unfulfillments of his loves.

In Donald's eyes shone the fever of futile watches in the night, intrigue, pursuits of the forbidden, all the rhythms and moods unknown to ordinary living. There was a quest for the forbidden and it was this flavor he sought, as well as the strange lighting which fell on all the unknown, the unfamiliar, the tabooed, all that could remind him of those secret moments of childhood when he sought the very experiences most forbidden by the parents.

But when it came to the selection of one, to giving one's self to one, to an open simplicity and an effort at completeness, some mysterious impulse always intervened and destroyed the relationship. A hatred of permanency, of anything resembling marriage.

Donald was talking against Michael's paradise as it would destroy the bitter-sweet, intense flavor he sought.

He bent closer to Djuna, whispering now like a conspirator. It was his conspiracy against simplicity, against Michael's desire for a peaceful life together.

"If you only knew, Djuna, the first time it happened! I expected the whole world to change its face, be utterly transformed, turned upside down. I expected the room to become inclined, as after an earthquake, to find that the door no longer led to a stairway but into space, and the windows overlooked the sea. Such excitement, such anxiety, and such a fear of not achieving fulfillment. At other times I have the feeling that I am escaping a prison, I have a fear of being caught again and punished. When I signal to another like myself in a café I have the feeling that we are two prisoners who have found a laborious way to communicate by a secret code. All our messages are colored with the violent colors of danger. What I find in this devious way has a taste like no other object overtly obtained. Like the taste of those dim and secret afternoons of our childhood when we performed forbidden acts with great anxiety and terror of punishment. The exaltation of danger, I'm used to it now, the fever of remorse. This society which condemns me . . . do you know how I am revenging myself? I am seducing each one of its members slowly, one by one. . . ."

He talked softly and exultantly, choosing the silkiest words, not disguising his dream of triumphing over all those who had dared to forbid certain acts, and certain forms of love.

At the same time when he talked about Michael there came to his face the same expression women have when they have seduced a man, an expression of vain glee, a triumphant, uncontrollable celebration of her power. And so Donald was celebrating the feminine wiles and ruses and charms by which he had made Michael fall so deeply in love with him.

In his flight from woman, it seemed to Djuna, Michael had merely fled to one containing all the minor flaws of women.

Donald stopped talking and there remained in the air the feminine intonations of his voice, chanting and never falling into deeper tones.

Michael was back and sat between them offering cigarettes.

As soon as Michael returned Djuna saw Donald change, become woman again, tantalizing and provocative. She saw Donald's body dilating into feminine undulations, his face open in all nakedness. His face expressed a dissolution like that of a woman being taken. Everything revealed, glee, the malice, the vanity, the childishness. His gestures like those of a second-rate actress receiving flowers with a batting of the eyelashes, with an oblique glance like the upturned cover of

158

a bedspread, the edge of a petticoat.

He had the stage bird's turns of the head, the little dance of alertness, the petulance of the mouth pursed for small kisses that do not shatter the being, the flutter and perk of prize birds, all adornment and change, a mockery of the evanescent darts of invitation, the small gestures of alarm and promise made by minor women.

Michael said: "You two resemble each other. I am sure Donald's suits would fit you, Djuna."

"But Donald is more truthful," said Djuna, thinking how openly Donald betrayed that he did not love Michael, whereas she might have sought a hundred oblique routes to soften this truth.

"Donald is more truthful because he loves less," said Michael.

Warmth in the air. The spring foliage shivering out of pure coquetry, not out of discomfort. Love flowing now between the three, shared, transmitted, contagious, as if Michael were at last free to love Djuna in the form of a boy, through the body of Donald to reach Djuna whom he could never touch directly, and Djuna through the body of Donald reached Michael—and the missing dimension of their love accomplished in space like an algebra of imperfection, an abstract drama of incompleteness at last resolved for one moment by this trinity of woman sitting between two incomplete men.

She could look with Michael's eyes at Donald's finely designed body, the narrow waist, the square shoulders, the stylized gestures and dilated expression.

She could see that Donald did not give his true self to Michael. He acted for him a caricature of woman's minor petulances and caprices. He ordered a drink and then changed his mind, and when the drink came he did not want it at all.

Djuna thought: "He is like a woman without the womb in which such great mysteries take place. He is a travesty of a marriage that will never take place."

Donald rose, performed a little dance of salutation and

159

flight before them, eluding Michael's pleading eyes, bowed, made some whimsical gesture of apology and flight, and left them.

This little dance reminded her of Michael's farewells on her doorsteps when she was sixteen.

And suddenly she saw all their movements, hers with Michael, and Michael's with Donald, as a ballet of unreality and unpossession.

"Their greatest form of activity is flight!" she said to Michael.

To the tune of Debussy's *"Ile Joyeuse,"* they gracefully made all the steps which lead to no possession.

(When will I stop loving these airy young men who move in a realm like the realm of the birds, always a little quicker than most human beings, always a little above, or beyond humanity, always in flight, out of some great fear of human beings, always seeking the open space, wary of enclosures, anxious for their freedom, vibrating with a multitude of alarms, always sensing danger all around them. . . .)

"Birds," said a research scientist, "live their lives with an intensity as extreme as their brilliant colors and their vivid songs. Their body temperatures are regularly as high as 105 to 110 degrees, and anyone who has watched a bird at close range must have seen how its whole body vibrates with the furious pounding of its pulse. Such engines must operate at forced draft: and that is exactly what a bird does. The bird's indrawn breath not only fills its lungs, but also passes on through myriads of tiny tubules into air sacs that fill every space in the bird's body not occupied by vital organs. Furthermore the air sacs connect with many of the bird's bones, which are not filled with marrow as animals' bones are, but are hollow. These reserve air tanks provide fuel for the bird's intensive life, and at the same time add to its buoyancy in flight."

160

Paul arrived as the dawn arrives, mist-laden, uncertain of his gestures. The sun was hidden until he smiled. Then the blue of his eyes, the shadows under his eyes, the sleepy eyelids, were all illuminated by the wide, brilliant smile. Mist, dew, the uncertain hoverings of his gestures were dispelled by the full, firm mouth, the strong even teeth.

Then the smile vanished again, as quickly as it had come. When he entered her room he brought with him this climate of adolescence which is neither sun nor full moon but the intermediate regions.

Again she noticed the shadows under his eyes, which made a soft violet-tinted halo around the intense blue of the pupils.

He was mantled in shyness, and his eyelids were heavy as if from too much dreaming. His dreaming lay like the edges of a deep slumber on the rim of his eyelids. One expected them to close in a hypnosis of interior fantasy as mysterious as a drugged state.

This constant passing from cloudedness to brilliance took place within a few instants. His body would sit absolutely still, and then would suddenly leap into gaiety and lightness. Then once again his face would close hermetically.

He passed in the same quick way between phrases uttered with profound maturity to sudden innocent inaccuracies.

It was difficult to remember he was seventeen.

He seemed more preoccupied with uncertainty as to how to carry himself through this unfamiliar experience than with absorbing or enjoying it.

Uncertainty spoiled his pleasure in the present, but Djuna felt he was one to carry away his treasures into secret chambers of remembrance and there he would lay them all out like the contents of an opium pipe being prepared, these treasures no longer endangered by uneasiness in living, the treasures becoming the past, and there he would touch and caress every word, every image, and make them his own.

In solitude and remembrance his real life would begin. Everything that was happening now was merely the preparation of the opium pipe that would later send volutes into space to enchant his solitude, when he would be lying down away from danger and unfamiliarity, lying down to taste of an experience washed of the dross of anxiety.

He would lie down and nothing more would be demanded of the dreamer, no longer expected to participate, to speak, to act, to decide. He would lie down and the images would rise in chimerical visitations and from a tale more marvelous in every detail than the one taking place at this moment marred by apprehension.

Having created a dream beforehand which he sought to preserve from destruction by reality, every movement in life became more difficult for the dreamer, for Paul, his fear of errors being like the opium dreamer's fear of noise or daylight.

And not only his dream of Djuna was he seeking to preserve like some fragile essence easily dispelled but even more dangerous, his own image of what was expected of him by Djuna, what he imagined Djuna expected of him—a heavy demand upon a youthful Paul, his own ideal exigencies which he did not know to be invented by himself creating a difficulty in every act or word in which he was merely re-enacting scenes rehearsed in childhood in which the child's naturalness was always defeated by the severity of the parents giving him the perpetual feeling that no word and no act came up to this impossible standard set for him. A more terrible compression than when the Chinese bound the feet of their infants, bound them with yards of cloth to stunt the natural growth. Such tyrannical cloth worn too long, unbroken, uncut, would in the end turn one into a mummy. . . .

Djuna could see the image of the mother binding Paul in the story he told her: He had a pet guinea pig, once, which he loved. And his mother had forced him to kill it.

She could see all the bindings when he added: "I destroyed a diary I kept in school."

"Why?"

"Now that I was home for a month, my parents might have

162

read it."

Were the punishments so great that he was willing rather to annihilate living parts of himself, a loved pet, a diary reflecting his inner self?

"There are many sides of yourself you cannot show your parents."

"Yes," An expression of anxiety came to his face. The effect of their severity was apparent in the way he sat, stood— even in the tone of resignation in which he said: "I have to leave soon."

Djuna looked at him and saw him as the prisoner he was— a prisoner of school, of parents.

"But you have a whole month of freedom now."

"Yes," said Paul, but the word freedom had no echo in his being.

"What will you do with it?"

He smiled then. "I can't do much with it. My parents don't want me to visit dancers."

"Did you tell them you were coming to visit me?"

"Yes."

"Do they know you want to be a dancer yourself?"

"Oh, no." He smiled again, a distressed smile, and then his eyes lost their direct, open frankness. They wavered, as if he had suddenly lost his way.

This was his most familiar expression: a nebulous glance, sliding off people and objects.

He had the fears of a child in the external world, yet he gave at the same time the impression of living in a larger world. This boy, thought Djuna tenderly, is lost. But he is lost in a large world. His dreams are vague, infinite, formless. He loses himself in them. No one knows what he is imagining and thinking. He does not know, he cannot say, but it is not a simple world. It expands beyond his grasp, he senses more than he knows, a bigger world which frightens him. He cannot confide or give himself. He must have been too often harshly condemned.

Waves of tenderness flowed out to him from her eyes as they sat without talking. The cloud vanished from his face. It was as if he sensed what she was thinking.

Just as he was leaving Lawrence arrived breathlessly, embraced Djuna effusively, pranced into the studio and turned on the radio.

He was Paul's age, but unlike Paul he did not appear to carry a little snail house around his personality, a place into which to retreat and vanish. He came out openly, eyes aware, smiling, expectant, in readiness for anything that might happen. He moved propelled by sheer impulse, and was never still.

He was carrying a cage which he laid in the middle of the room. He lifted its covering shaped like a miniature striped awning.

Djuna knelt on the rug to examine the contents of the cage and laughed to see a blue mouse nibbling at a cracker.

"Where did you find a turquoise mouse?" asked Djuna.

"I bathed her in dye," said Lawrence. "Only she licks it all away in a few days and turns white again, so I had to bring her this time right after her bath."

The blue mouse was nibbling eagerly. The music was playing. They were sitting on the rug. The room began to glitter and sparkle.

Paul looked on with amazement.

(This pet, his eyes said, need not be killed. Nothing is forbidden here.)

Lawrence was painting the cage with phosphorescent paint so that it would shine in the dark.

"That way she won't be afraid when I leave her alone at night!"

While the paint dried Lawrence began to dance.

Djuna was laughing behind her veil of long hair.

Paul looked at them yearningly and then said in a toneless voice: "I have to leave now." And he left precipitately.

"Who is the beautiful boy?" asked Lawrence.

"The son of tyrannical parents who are very worried he

should visit a dancer."

"Will he come again?"

"He made no promise. Only if he can get away."

"We'll go and visit him."

Djuna smiled. She could imagine Lawrence arriving at Paul's formal home with a cage with a blue mouse in it and Paul's mother saying: "You get rid of that pet!"

Or Lawrence taking a ballet leap to touch the tip of a chandelier, or singing some delicate obscenity.

"C'est une jeune fille en fleur," he said now, clairvoyantly divining Djuna's fear of never escaping from the echoes and descendants of Michael.

Lawrence shrugged his shoulders. Then he looked at her with his red-gold eyes, under his red-gold hair. Whenever he looked at her it was contagious: that eager, ardent glance falling amorously on everyone and everything, dissolving the darkest moods.

No sadness could resist this frenzied carnival of affection he dispensed every day, beginning with his enthusiasm for his first cup of coffee, joy at the day's beginning, an immediate fancy for the first person he saw, a passion at the least provocation for man, woman, child or animal. A warmth even in his collisions with misfortunes, troubles and difficulties.

He received them smiling. Without money in his pocket he rushed to help. With generous excess he rushed to love, to desire, to possess, to lose, to suffer, to die the multiple little deaths everyone dies each day. He would even die and weep and suffer and lose with enthusiasm, with ardor. He was prodigal in poverty, rich and abundant in some invisible chemical equivalent to gold and sun.

Any event would send him leaping and prancing with gusto: a concert, a play, a ballet, a person. Yes, yes, yes, cried his young firm body every morning. No retractions, no hesitations, no fears, no caution, no economy. He accepted every invitation.

His joy was in movement, in assenting, in consenting, in expansion.

165

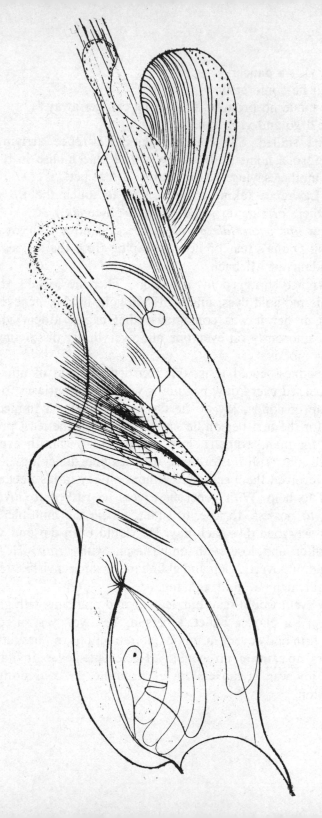

Whenever he came he lured Djuna into a swirl. Even in sadness they smiled at each other, expanding in sadness with dilated eyes and dilated hearts.

"Drop every sorrow and dance!"

Thus they healed each other by dancing, perfectly mated in enthusiasm and fire.

The waves which carried him forward never dropped him on the rocks. He would always come back smiling: "Oh, Djuna, you remember Hilda? I was so crazy about her. Do you know what she did? She tried to palm off some false money on me. Yes, with all her lovely eyes, manners, sensitiveness, she came to me and said so tenderly: let me have change for this ten-dollar bill. And it was a bad one. And then she tried to hide some drugs in my room, and to say I was the culprit. I nearly went to jail. She pawned my typewriter, my box of paints. She finally took over my room and I had to sleep for the night on a park bench."

But the next morning he was again full of faith, love, trust, impulses.

Dancing and believing.

In his presence she was again ready to believe.

To believe in Paul's eyes, the mystery and the depth in them, the sense of some vast dream lying coiled there, undeciphered.

Lawrence had finished the phosphorescent painting. He closed the curtains and the cage shone in the dark. Now he decided to paint with phosphorescence everything paintable in the room.

The next day Lawrence appeared with a large pot of paint and he was stirring it with a stick when Paul telephoned: "I can get away for a while. May I come?"

"Oh, come, come," said Djuna.

"I can't stay very late. . . ." His voice was muffled, like that of a sick person. There was a plaintiveness in it so plainly audible to Djuna's heart.

"The prisoner is allowed an hour's freedom," she said.

When Paul came Lawrence handed him a paintbrush and

in silence the two of them worked at touching up everything paintable in the room. They turned off the lights. A new room appeared.

Luminous faces appeared on the walls, new flowers, new jewels, new castles, new jungles, new animals, all in filaments of light.

Mysterious translucence like their unmeasured words, their impulsive acts, wishes, enthusiasms. Darkness was excluded from their world, the darkness of loss of faith. It was now the room with a perpetual sparkle, even in darkness.

(They are making a new world for me, felt Djuna, a world of greater lightness. It is perhaps a dream and I may not be allowed to stay. They treat me as one of their own, because I believe what they believe, I feel as they do. I hate the father, authority, men of power, men of wealth, all tyranny, all authority, all crystallizations. I feel as Lawrence and Paul: outside there lies a bigger world full of cruelties, dangers and corruptions, where one sells out one's charms, one's playfulness, and enters a rigid world of discipline, duty, contracts, accountings. A thick opaque world without phosphorescence. I want to stay in this room forever not with man the father but with man the son, carving, painting, dancing, dreaming, and always beginning, born anew every day, never aging, full of faith and impulse, turning and changing to every wind like the mobiles. I do not love those who have ceased to flow, to believe, to feel. Those who can no longer melt, exult, who cannot let themselves be cheated, laugh at loss, those who are bound and frozen.)

She laid her head on Lawrence's shoulder with a kind of gratitude.

(Nowhere else as here with Lawrence and with Paul was there such an iridescence in the air; nowhere else so far from the threat of hardening and crystallizing. Everything flowing. . . .)

Djuna was brushing her hair with her fingers, in long pensive strokes, and Lawrence was talking about the recurrent big

168

problem of a job. He had tried so many. How to work without losing one's color, one's ardor, personal possessions and freedom. He was very much like a delicate Egyptian scarab who dreaded to lose his iridescence in routine, in duty, in monotony. The job could kill one, or maim one, make one a robot, an opaque personage, a future undertaker, a man of power with gouty limbs and a hardening of the arteries of faith!

Lawrence was now working in a place which made decorations for shop windows. He liked to work at night, to go on strange expeditions in the company of mannequins, papier-mâché horses, to live on miniature stages building jungles, sea landscapes, fabulous animals. To flirt with naked mannequins whose arms came off as easily as other women's gloves, who deposited their heads on the floor and took off their wigs when they took off their hats. He became an expert at dismantling women!

Lawrence lived and breathed color and there was no danger of his dying of drabness, for even accidents took on a most vivid shade and a spilled pot of *gouache* was still a delight to the eyes.

He brought Djuna gifts of chokers, headdresses, earrings made of painted clay which crumbled quickly like the trappings for a costume play.

She had always liked objects without solidity. The solid ones bound her to permanency. She had never wanted a solid house, enduring furniture. All these were traps. Then you belonged to them forever. She preferred stage trappings which she could move into and out of easily, without regret. Soon after they fell apart and nothing was lost. The vividness alone survived.

She remembered once hearing a woman complain that armchairs no longer lasted twenty years, and Djuna answered: "But I couldn't love an armchair for twenty years!"

And so change, mutations like the rainbow, and she preferred Lawrence's gifts from which the colored powder and crystals fell like the colors on the wings of butterflies after yielding their maximum of charm.

Paul was carving a piece of copper, making such fine incisions with the scissors that the bird which finally appeared between his slender fingers bristled with filament feathers.

He stood on the table and hung it by a thread to the ceiling. The slightest breath caused it to turn slowly.

Paul had the skin of a child that had never been touched by anything of this earth: no soap, no washrag, no brush, no human kiss could have touched his skin! Never scrubbed, rubbed, scratched, or wrinkled by a pillow. The transparency of the child skin, of the adolescent later to turn opaque. What do children nourish themselves with that their skin has this transparency, and what do they eat of later which brings on opaqueness?

The mothers who kiss them are eating light.

There is a phosphorescence which comes from the magic world of childhood.

Where does this illumination go later? Is it the substance of faith which shines from their bodies like phosphorescence from the albatross, and what kills it?

Now Lawrence had discovered a coiled measuring tape of steel in Djuna's closet while delving for objects useful for charades.

When entirely pulled out of its snail covering it stretched like a long snake of steel which under certain manipulations could stand rigid like a sword or undulate like silver-tipped waves, or flash like lightning.

Lawrence and Paul stood like expert swordsmen facing each other for a duel of light and steel.

The steel band flexed, then hardened between them like a bridge, and at each forward movement by one it seemed as if the sword had pierced the body of the other.

At other moments it wilted, wavered like a frightened snake, and then it looked bedraggled and absurd and they both laughed.

But soon they learned never to let it break or waver and it became like a thunderbolt in their hands. Paul attacked with audacity and Lawrence parried with swiftness.

At midnight Paul began to look anxious. His luminosity clouded, he resumed his hesitant manner. He ceased to occupy the center of the room and moved out of the focus of light and laughter. Like a sleepwalker, he moved away from gaiety.

Djuna walked with him towards the door. They were alone and then he said: "My parents have forbidden me to come here."

"But you were happy here, weren't you?"

"Yes, I was happy."

"This is where you belong."

"Why do you think I belong here?"

"You're gifted for dancing, for painting, for writing. And this is your month of freedom."

"Yes, I know. I wish . . . I wish I were free. . . ."

"If you wish it deeply enough you will find a way."

"I would like to run away, but I have no money."

"If you run away we'll all take care of you."

"Why?"

"Because we believe in you, because you're worth helping."

"I have nowhere to go."

"We'll find you a room somewhere, and we will adopt you. And you will have your month of life."

"Of life!" he repeated with docility.

"But I don't want you to do it unless you feel ready, unless you want it so much that you're willing to sacrifice everything else. I only want you to know you can count on us, but it must be your decision, or it will not mean anything."

"Thank you." This time he did not clasp her hand, he laid his hand within hers as if nestling it there, folded, ivory smooth and gentle, at rest, in an act of trustingness.

Then before leaving the place he looked once more at the room as if to retain its enfolding warmth. At one moment he had laughed so much that he had slid from his chair. Djuna had made him laugh. At that moment many of his chains must have broken, for nothing breaks chains like laughter, and

171

Djuna could not remember in all her life a greater joy than this spectacle of Paul laughing like a released prisoner.

Two days later Paul appeared at her door with his valise.

Djuna received him gaily as if this were the beginning of a holiday, asked him to tie the velvet bows at her wrist, drove him to where Lawrence lived with his parents and where there was an extra room.

She would have liked to shelter him in her own house, but she knew his parents would come there and find him.

He wrote a letter to his parents. He reminded them that he had only a month of freedom for himself before leaving for India on the official post his father had arranged for him, that during this month he felt he had a right to be with whatever friends he felt a kinship with. He had found people with whom he had a great deal to share and since his parents had been so extreme in their demands, forbidding him to see his friends at all, he was being equally extreme in his assertion of his freedom. Not to be concerned about him, that at the end of the month he would comply with his father's plans for him.

He did not stay in his room. It had been arranged that he would have his meals at Djuna's house. An hour after he had laid down his valise in Lawrence's room he was at her house.

In his presence she did not feel herself a mature woman, but again a girl of seventeen at the beginning of her own life. As if the girl of seventeen had remained undestroyed by experience—like some deeper layer in a geological structure which had been pressed but not obliterated by the new layers.

(He seems hungry and thirsty for warmth, and yet so fearful. We are arrested by each other's elusiveness. Who will take flight first? If we move too hastily fear will spring up and separate us. I am fearful of his innocence, and he of what he

172

believes to be my knowingness. But neither one of us knows what the other wants, we are both arrested and ready to vanish, with such a fear of being hurt. His oscillations are like mine, his muteness like mine at his age, his fears like my fears.)

She felt that as she came nearer there was a vibration through his body. Through all the mists as her body approached to greet him there was an echo of her movements within him.

With his hand within hers, at rest, he said: "Everyone is doing so much for me. Do you think that when I grow up I will be able to do the same for someone else?"

"Of course you will." And because he had said so gently "when I grow up" she saw him suddenly as a boy, and her hand went out swiftly towards the strand of boyish hair which fell over his eyes and pulled it.

That she had done this with a half-frightened laugh as if she expected retaliation made him feel at ease with her.

He did retaliate by trying jiujitsu on her arm until she said: "You hurt me." Then he stopped, but the discovery that her bones were not as strong as the boys' on whom he had tested his knowledge made him feel powerful. He had more strength than he needed to handle her. He could hurt her so easily, and now he was no longer afraid when her face came near his and her eyes grew larger and more brilliant, or when she danced and her hair accidentally swung across her face like a silk whip, or when she sat like an Arab holding conversation over the telephone in answer to invitations which might deprive him of her presence. No matter who called, she always refused, and stayed at home to talk with him.

The light in the room became intensely bright and they were bathed in it, bright with the disappearance of his fear.

He felt as ease to sit and draw, to read, to paint, and to be silent. The light around them grew warm and dim and intimate.

By shedding in his presence the ten years of life which created distance between them, she felt herself re-entering a smaller house of innocence and faith, and that what she shed was merely a role: she played a role of woman, and this had been the torment, she had been pretending to be a woman, and now she knew she had not been at ease in this role, and now with Paul she felt she was being transformed into a stature and substance nearer to her true state.

With Paul she was passing from an insincere pretense at maturity into a more vulnerable world, escaping from the more difficult role of tormented woman to a smaller room of warmth.

For one moment, sitting there with Paul, listening to the Symphony in D Minor of César Franck, through his eyes she was allowed behind the mirror into a smaller silk-lined house of faith.

In art, in history, man fights his fears, he wants to live forever, he is afraid of death, he wants to work with other men, he wants to live forever. He is like a child afraid of death. The child is afraid of death, of darkness, of solitude. Such simple fears behind all the elaborate constructions. Such simple fears as hunger for light, warmth, love. Such simple fears behind the elaborate constructions of art. Examine them all gently and quietly through the eyes of a boy. There is always a human being lonely, a human being afräid, a human being lost, a human being confused. Concealing and disguising his dependence, his needs, ashamed to say: I am a simple human being in too vast and too complex a world. Because of all we have discovered about a leaf . . . it is still a leaf. Can we relate to a leaf, on a tree, in a park, a simple leaf: green, glistening, sun-bathed or wet, or turning white because the storm is coming. Like the savage, let us look at the leaf wet or shining with sun, or white with fear of the storm, or silvery in the fog, or listless in too great heat, or falling in the autumn, drying, reborn each year anew. Learn from the leaf: simplicity. In spite of all we know about the leaf: its nerve structure phyllome cellular papilla parenchyma stomata venation. Keep a human relation—leaf, man, woman, child. In tenderness. No matter how immense the world, how elaborate, how contradictory,

174

there is always man, woman, child, and the leaf. Humanity makes everything warm and simple. Humanity. Let the waters of humanity flow through the abstract city, through abstract art, weeping like rivulets, cracking rocky mountains, melting icebergs. The frozen worlds in empty cages of mobiles where hearts lie exposed like wires in an electric bulb. Let them burst at the tender touch of a leaf.

The next morning Djuna was having breakfast in bed when Lawrence appeared.

"I'm broke and I'd like to have breakfast with you."

He had begun to eat his toast when the maid came and said: "There's a gentleman at the door who won't give his name."

"Find out what he wants. I don't want to dress yet."

But the visitor had followed the servant to the door and stood now in the bedroom.

Before anyone could utter a protest he said in the most classically villainous tone: "Ha, ha, having breakfast, eh?"

"Who are you? What right have you to come in here," said Djuna.

"I have every right: I'm a detective."

"A detective!"

Lawrence's eyes began to sparkle with amusement.

The detective said to him: "And what are you doing here, young man?"

"I'm having breakfast." He said this in the most cheerful and natural manner, continuing to drink his coffee and buttering a piece of toast which he offered Djuna.

"Wonderful!" said the detective. "So I've caught you. Having breakfast, eh? While your parents are breaking their hearts over your disappearance. Having breakfast, eh? When you're not eighteen yet and they can force you to return home and never let you out again." And turning to Djuna he added: "And what may your interest in this young man be?"

Then Djuna and Lawrence broke into irrepressible laughter.

"I'm not the only one," said Lawrence.

At this the detective looked like a man who had not expected his task to be so easy, almost grateful for the collaboration.

"So you're not the only one!"

Djuna stopped laughing. "He means anyone who is broke can have breakfast here."

"Will you have a cup of coffee?" said Lawrence with an impudent smile.

"That's enough talk from you," said the detective. "You'd better come along with me, Paul."

"But I'm not Paul."

"Who are you?"

"My name is Lawrence."

"Do you know Paul—? Have you seen him recently?"

"He was here last night for a party."

"A party? And where did he go after that?"

"I don't know," said Lawrence. "I thought he was staying with his parents."

"What kind of a party was this?" asked the detective.

But now Djuna had stopped laughing and was becoming angry. "Leave this place immediately," she said.

The detective took a photograph out of his pocket, compared it with Lawrence's face, saw there was no resemblance, looked once more at Djuna's face, read the anger in it, and left.

As soon as he left her anger vanished and they laughed again. Suddenly Djuna's playfulness turned into anxiety. "But this may become serious, Lawrence. Paul won't be able to come to my house any more. And suppose it had been Paul who had come for breakfast!"

And then another aspect of the situation struck her and her face became sorrowful. "What kind of parents has Paul that they can consider using force to bring him home."

She took up the telephone and called Paul. Paul said in a shocked voice: "They can't take me home by force!"

"I don't know about the law, Paul. You'd better stay away from my house. I will meet you somewhere—say at the ballet theater—until we find out."

For a few days they met at concerts, galleries, ballets. But no one seemed to follow them.

Djuna lived in constant fear that he would be whisked away and that she might never see him again. Their meetings took on the anxiety of repeated farewells. They always looked at each other as if it were for the last time.

Through this fear of loss she took longer glances at his face, and every facet of it, every gesture, every inflection of his voice thus sank deeper into her, to be stored away against future loss—deeper and deeper it penetrated, impregnated her more as she fought against its vanishing.

She felt that she not only saw Paul vividly in the present but Paul in the future. Every expression she could read as an indication of future power, future discernment, future completion. Her vision of the future Paul illumined the present. Others could see a young man experiencing his first drunkenness, taking his first steps in the world, oscillating or contradicting himself. But she felt herself living with a Paul no one had seen yet, the man of the future, willful, and with a power in him which appeared intermittently.

When the clouds and mists of adolescence would vanish, what a complete and rich man he would become, with this mixture of sensibility and intelligence motivating his choices, discarding shallowness, never taking a step into mediocrity, with an unerring instinct for the extraordinary.

To send a detective to bring him home by force, how little his parents must know this Paul of the future, possessed of that deep-seated mine of tenderness hidden below access but visible to her.

She was living with a Paul no one knew as yet, in a secret relationship far from the reach of the subtlest detectives, beyond the reach of the entire world.

Under the veiled voice she felt the hidden warmth, under the hesitancies a hidden strength, under the fears a vaster dream more difficult to seize and to fulfill.

Alone, after an afternoon with him, she lay on her bed and while the bird he had carved gyrated lightly in the center of the room, tears came to her eyes so slowly she did not feel them at first until they slid down her cheeks.

Tears from this unbearable melting of her heart and body —a complete melting before the face of Paul, and the muted way his body spoke, the gentle way he was hungering, reaching, groping, like a prisoner escaping slowly and gradually, door by door, room by room, hallway by hallway, towards the light. The prison that had been built around him had been of darkness: darkness about himself, about his needs, about his true nature.

The solitary cell created by the parents.

He knew nothing, nothing about his true self. And such blindness was as good as binding him with chains. His parents and his teachers had merely imposed upon him a false self that seemed right to them.

This boy they did not know.

But this melting, it must not be. She turned her face away, to the right now, as if to turn away from the vision of his face, and murmured: "I must not love him, I must not love him."

The bell rang. Before she could sit up Paul had come in.

"Oh, Paul, this is dangerous for you!"

"I had to come."

As he stopped in his walking towards her his body sought to convey a message. What was his body saying? What were his eyes saying?

He was too near, she felt his eyes possessing her and she rushed away to make tea, to place a tray and food between them, like some very fragile wall made of sand, in games of childhood, which the sea could so easily wash away!

She talked, but he was not listening, nor was she listening

to her own words, for his smile penetrated her, and she wanted to run away from him.

"I would like to know . . ." he said, and the words remained suspended.

He sat too near. She felt the unbearable melting, the loss of herself, and she struggled to close some door against him. "I must not love him, I must not love him!"

She moved slightly away, but his hair was so near her hand that her fingers were drawn magnetically to touch it lightly, playfully.

"What do you want to know?"

Had he noticed her own trembling? He did not answer her. He leaned over swiftly and took her whole mouth in his, the whole man in him coming out in a direct thrust, firm, willful, hungry. With one kiss he appropriated her, asserted his possessiveness.

When he had taken her mouth and kissed her until they were both breathless they lay side by side and she felt his body strong and warm against hers, his passion inflexible.

He laid his hand over her with hesitations. Everything was new to him, a woman's neck, a shoulder, a woman's hooks and buttons.

Between the journeys of discovery he had flickering instants of uncertainties until the sparks of pleasure guided his hand.

Where he passed his hand no one else had ever passed his hand. New cells awakened under his delicate fingers never wakened before to say: this is yours.

A breast touched for the first time is a breast never touched before.

He looked at her with his long blue eyes which had never wept and her eyes were washed luminous and clear, her eyes forgot they had wept.

He touched her eyelashes with his eyelashes of which not one had fallen out and those of hers which had been washed away by tears were replaced.

His hair which had never been crushed between feverish

179

pillows, knotted by nightmares, mingled with hers and untangled it.

Where sadness had carved rich caverns he sank his youthful thrusts grasping endless sources of warmth.

Only before the last mystery of the body did he pause. He had thrust and entered and now he paused.

Did one lie still and at peace in the secret place of woman? In utter silence they lay.

Fever mounting in him, the sap rising, the bodies taut with a need of violence.

She made one undulatory movement, and this unlocked in him a whirlpool of desire, a dervish dance of all the silver knives of pleasure.

When they awakened from their trance, they smiled at each other, but he did not move. They lay merged, slimness to slimness, legs like twin legs, hip to hip.

The cotton of silence lay all around them, covering their bodies in quilted softness.

The big wave of fire which rolled them washed them ashore tenderly into small circles of foam.

On the table there was a huge vase filled with tulips. She moved towards them, seeking something to touch, to pour her joy into, out of the exaltation she felt.

Every part of her body that had been opened by his hands yearned to open the whole world in harmony with her mood.

She looked at the tulips so hermetically closed, like secret poems, like the secrets of the flesh. Her hands took each tulip, the ordinary tulip of everyday living and she slowly opened them, petal by petal, opened them tenderly.

They were changed from plain to exotic flowers, from closed secrets to open flowering.

180

Then she heard Paul say: "Don't do that!"
There was a great anxiety in his voice. He repeated: "Don't do that!"

She felt a great stab of anxiety. Why was he so disturbed? She looked at the flowers. She looked at Paul's face lying on the pillow, clouded with anxiety, and she was struck with fear. Too soon. She had opened him to love too soon. He was not ready.

Even with tenderness, even with delicate fingers, even with the greatest love, it had been too soon! She had forced time, as she had forced the flowers to change from the ordinary to the extraordinary. He was not ready!

Now she understood her own hesitations, her impulse to run away from him. Even though he had made the first gesture, she, knowing, should have saved him from anxiety.

(Paul was looking at the opened tulips and seeing in them something else, not himself but Djuna, the opening body of Djuna. Don't let her open the flowers as he had opened her. In the enormous wave of silence, the hypnosis of hands, skin, delight, he had heard a small moan, yet in her face he had seen joy. Could the thrust into her have hurt her? It was like stabbing someone, this desire.)

"I'm going to dress, now," she said lightly. She could not close the tulips again, but she could dress. She could close herself again and allow him to close again.

Watching her he felt a violent surge of strength again, stronger than his fears. "Don't dress yet."

Again he saw on her face a smile he had never seen there in her gayest moments, and then he accepted the mystery and abandoned himself to his own joy.

His heart beat wildly at her side, wildly in panic and joy together at the moment before taking her. This wildly beating heart at her side, beating against hers, and then the cadenced, undulating, blinding merging together, and no break between their bodies afterwards.

After the storm he lay absolutely still over her body, dreaming, quiet, as if this were the place of haven. He lay given, lost, entranced. She bore his weight with joy, though after a while it numbed and hurt her. She made a slight movement, and then he asked her: "Am I crushing you?"

"You're flattening me into a thin wafer," she said, smiling, and he smiled back, then laughed.

"The better to eat you, my dear."

He kissed her again as if he would eat her with delight.

Then he got up and made a somersault on the carpet, with light exultant gestures.

She lay back watching the copper bird gyrating in the center of the room.

His gaiety suddenly overflowed, and taking a joyous leap in the air, he came back to her and said:

"I will call up my father!"

She could not understand. He leaned over her body and keeping his hand over her breast he dialed his father's telephone number.

Then she could see on his face what he wanted to tell his father: call his father, tell him what could not be told, but which his entire new body wanted to tell him: I have taken a woman! I have a woman of my own. I am your equal, Father! I am a man!

When his father answered Paul could only say the ordinary words a son can say to his father, but he uttered these ordinary words with exultant arrogance, as if his father could see him with his hand on Djuna's body: "Father, I am here."

"Where are you?" answered the father severely. "We're expecting you home. You can continue to see your friends but you must come home to please your mother. Your mother has dinner all ready for you!"

Paul laughed, laughed as he had never laughed as a boy, with his hand over the mouth of the telephone.

On such a day they are expecting him for dinner!

They were blind to the miracle. Over the telephone his father should hear and see that he had a woman of his own:

182

she was lying there smiling.

How dare the father command now! Doesn't he hear the new voice of the new man in his son?

He hung up.

His hair was falling over his eager eyes. Djuna pulled at it. He stopped her. "You can't do that any more, oh no." And he sank his teeth into the softest part of her neck.

"You're sharpening your teeth to become a great lover," she said.

When desire overtook him he always had a moment of wildly beating heart, almost of distress, before the invading tide. Before closing his eyes to kiss her, before abandoning himself, he always carefully closed the shutters, windows and doors.

This was the secret act, and he feared the eyes of the world upon him. The world was full of eyes upon his acts, eyes watching with disapproval.

That was the secret fear left from his childhood: dreams, wishes, acts, pleasures which aroused condemnation in the parents' eyes. He could not remember one glance of approval, of love, of admiration, of consent. From far back he remembered being driven into secrecy because whatever he revealed seemed to arouse disapproval or punishment.

He had read the *Arabian Nights* in secret, he had smoked in secret, he had dreamed in secret.

His parents had questioned him only to accuse him later.

And so he closed the shutters, curtains, windows, and then went to her and both of them closed their eyes upon their caresses.

There was a knitted blanket over the couch which he particularly liked. He would sit under it as if it were a tent. Through the interstices of the knitting he could see her and the room as through an oriental trellis. With one hand out of the blanket he would seek her little finger with his little finger and hold it.

As in an opium dream, this touching and interlacing of two little fingers became an immense gesture, the very fragile bridge of their relationship. By this little finger so gently and so lightly pulling hers he took her whole self as no one else had.

He drew her under the blanket thus, in a dreamlike way, by a small gesture containing the greatest power, a greater power than violence.

Once there they both felt secure from all the world, and from all threats, from the father and the detective, and all the taboos erected to separate lovers all over the world.

Lawrence rushed over to warn them that Paul's father had been seen driving through the neighborhood.

Paul and Djuna were having dinner together and were going to the ballet.

Paul had painted a feather bird for Djuna's hair and she was pinning it on when Lawrence came with the warning.

Paul became a little pale, then smiled and said: "Wafer, in case my father comes, could you make yourself less pretty?"

Djuna went and washed her face of all make-up, and then she unpinned the airy feather bird from her hair, and they sat down together to wait for the father.

Djuna said: "I'm going to tell you the story of Caspar Hauser, which is said to have happened many years ago in Austria. Caspar Hauser was about seventeen years old when he appeared in the city, a wanderer, lost and bewildered. He had been imprisoned in a dark room since childhood. His real origin was unknown, and the cause for the imprisonment. It was believed to be a court intrigue, that he might have been put away to substitute another ruler, or that he might have been an illegitimate son of the Queen. His jailer died and the boy found himself free. In solitude he had grown into manhood with the spirit of a child. He had only one dream in his possession, which he looked upon as a memory. He had once lived in a castle. He had been led to a room to see his mother. His mother stood behind a door. But he had never reached her. Was it a dream or a memory? He wanted to find this castle again, and his mother. The people of the city adopted him as a curiosity. His honesty, his immediate, childlike instinct about people, both infuriated and interested them. They tampered with him. They wanted to impose their beliefs on him, teach him, possess him. But the boy could sense their falsities, their treacheries, their self-interest. He belonged to his dream. He gave his whole faith only to the man who promised to take him back to his home and to his mother. And this man betrayed him, delivered him to his enemies. Just before his death he had met a woman, who had not dared to love him because he was so young, who had stifled her feeling. If she had dared he might have escaped his fate."

"Why didn't she dare?" asked Paul.

"She saw only the obstacle," said Djuna. "Most people see only the obstacle, and are stopped by it."

(No harm can befall you now, Paul, no harm can befall you. You have been set free. You made a good beginning. You were loved by the first object of your desire. Your first desire was answered. I made such a bad beginning! I began with a closed door. This harmed me, but you at least began with fulfillment. You were not hurt. You were not denied. I am the only one in danger. For that is all I am allowed to give you, a good beginning, and then I must surrender you.)

They sat and waited for the father.

Lawrence left them. The suspense made him uneasy.

Paul was teaching Djuna how to eat rice with chopsticks. Then he carefully cleaned them and was holding them now as they talked as if they were puppets representing a Balinese shadow theater of the thoughts neither one dared to formulate.

They sat and waited for the father.

Paul was holding the chopsticks like impudent puppets, gesticulating, then he playfully unfastened the first button of her blouse with them, deftly, and they laughed together.

"It's time for the ballet," said Djuna. "Your father is evidently not coming, or he would be here already."

She saw the illumination of desire light his face.

"Wait, Djuna." He unfastened the second button, and the third.

Then he laid his head on her breast and said: "Let's not go anywhere tonight. Let's stay here."

Paul despised small and shallow waves. He was drawn to a vastness which corresponded to his boundless dreams. He must possess the world in some big way, rule a large kingdom, expand in some absolute leadership.

He felt himself king as a child feels king, over kingdoms uncharted by ordinary men. He would not have the ordinary, the known. Only the vast, the unknown could satisfy him.

Djuna was a woman with echoes plunging into an endless past he could never explore completely. When he tasted her he tasted a suffering which had borne a fragrance, a fragrance which made deeper grooves. It was enough that he sensed the dark forests of experience, the unnamed rivers, the enigmatic mountains, the rich mines under the ground, the overflowing caves of secret knowledges. A vast ground for an intrepid adventurer.

Above all she was his "ocean," as he wrote her. "When a man takes a woman to himself he possesses the sea."

The waves, the enormous waves of a woman's love!

She was a sea whose passions could rise sometimes into

larger waves than he felt capable of facing!

Much as he loved danger, the unknown, the vast, he felt too the need of taking flight, to put distance and space between himself and the ocean for fear of being submerged!

Flight: into silence, into a kind of invisibility by which he could be sitting there on the floor while yet creating an impression of absence, able to disappear into a book, a drawing, into the music he listened to.

She was gazing at his little finger and the extreme fragility and sensitiveness of it astonished her.

(He is the transparent child.)

Before this transparent finger so artfully carved, sensitively wrought, boned, which alighted on objects with a touch of air and magic, at the marvel of it, the ephemeral quality of it, a wave of passion would mount within her and exactly like the wave of the ocean intending merely to roll over, cover the swimmer with an explosion of foam, in a rhythm of encompassing, and withdrawing, without intent to drag him to the bottom.

But Paul, with the instinct of the new swimmer, felt that there were times when he could securely hurl himself into the concave heart of the wave and be lifted into ecstasy and be delivered back again on the shore safe and whole; but that there were other times when this great inward curve disguised an undertow, times when he measured his strength and found it insufficient to return to shore.

Then he took up again the lighter games of his recently surrendered childhood.

Djuna found him gravely bending over a drawing and it was not what he did which conveyed his remoteness, but his way of sitting hermetically closed like some secret Chinese box whose surface showed no possibility of opening.

He sat then as children do, immured in his particular lonely world then, having built a magnetic wall of detachment.

It was then that he practiced as deftly as older men the great objectivity, the long-range view by which men eluded all personal difficulties: he removed himself from the present and the personal by entering into the most abstruse intricacies of a chess game, by explaining to her what Darwin had written when comparing the eye to a microscope, by dissertating on the pleuronectidae or flat fish, so remarkable for their asymmetrical bodies.

And Djuna followed this safari into the worlds of science, chemistry, geology with an awkwardness which was not due to any laziness of mind, but to the fact that the large wave of passion which had been roused in her at the prolonged sight of Paul's little finger was so difficult to dam, because the feeling of wonder before this spectacle was to her as great as that of the explorers before a new mountain peak, of the scientists before a new discovery.

She knew what excitement enfevered men at such moments of their lives, but she did not see any difference between the beauty of a high flight above the clouds and the subtly colored and changing landscape of adolescence she traversed through the contemplation of Paul's little finger.

A study of anthropological excavations made in Peru was no more wonderful to her than the half-formed dreams unearthed with patience from Paul's vague words, dreams of which they were only catching the prologue; and no forest of precious woods could be more varied than the oscillations of his extreme vulnerability which forced him to take cover, to disguise his feelings, to swing so movingly between great courage and a secret fear of pain.

The birth of his awareness was to her no lesser miracle than the discoveries of chemistry, the variations in his temperature, the mysterious angers, the sudden serenities, no less valuable than the studies of remote climates.

But when in the face of too large a wave, whose dome seemed more than a mere ecstasy of foam raining over the marvelous shape of his hands, a wave whose concaveness seemed more than a temporary womb in which he could lie for the fraction of an instant, the duration of an orgasm, he sat like a Chinese secret box with a surface revealing no possible opening to the infiltrations of tenderness or the flood of passion, then her larger impulse fractured with a strange pain into a multitude of little waves capped with frivolous sunspangles, secretly ashamed of its wild disproportion to the young man who sat there offering whatever he possessed— his intermittent manliness, his vastest dreams and his fear of his own expansions, his maturity as well as his fear of this maturity which was leading him out of the gardens of childhood.

And when the larger wave had dispersed into smaller ones, and when Paul felt free of any danger of being dragged to the bottom, free of that fear of possession which is the secret of all adolescence, when he had gained strength within his retreat, then he returned to tease and stir her warmth into activity again, when he felt equal to plunging into it, to lose himself in it, feeling the intoxication of the man who had conquered the sea. . . .

Then he would write to her exultantly: you are the sea. . . .

But she could see the little waves in himself gathering power for the future, preparing for the moment when he would be the engulfing one.

Then he seemed no longer the slender adolescent with dreamy gestures but a passionate young man rehearsing his future scenes of domination.

He wore a white scarf through the gray streets of the city, a white scarf of immunity. His head resting on the folds was the head of the dreamer walking through the city selecting by a white magic to see and hear and gather only according to his inner needs, slowly and gradually building as each one does ultimately, his own world out of the material at hand from which he was allowed at least a freedom of selection.

The white scarf asserted the innumerable things which did not touch him: choked trees, broken windows, cripples, obscenities penciled on the walls, the lascivious speeches of the drunks, the miasmas and corrosions of the city.

He did not see or hear them.

After traversing deserted streets, immured in his inner dream, he would suddenly open his eyes upon an organ grinder and his monkey.

What he brought home again was always some object by which men sought to overcome mediocrity: a book, a painting, a piece of music to transform his vision of the world, to expand and deepen it.

The white scarf did not lie.

It was the appropriate flag of his voyages.

His head resting fittingly on its white folds was immune to stains. He could traverse sewers, hospitals, prisons, and none left their odor upon him. His coat, his breath, his hair, when he returned, still exhaled the odor of his dream.

This was the only virgin forest known to man: this purity of selection.

When Paul returned with his white scarf gleaming it was all that he rejected which shone in its folds.

He was always a little surprised at older people's interest in him.

He did not know himself to be the possessor of anything they might want, not knowing that in his presence they were violently carried back to their first dream.

Because he stood at the beginning of the labyrinth and not in the heart of it, he made everyone aware of the turn where they had lost themselves. With Paul standing at the entrance of the maze, they recaptured the beginning of their voyage, they remembered their first intent, their first image, their first desires.

They would don his white scarf and begin anew.

And yet today she felt there was another purity, a greater

purity which lay in the giving of one's self. She felt pure when she gave herself, and Paul felt pure when he withdrew himself.

The tears of his mother, the more restrained severity of his father, brought him home again.

His eighteenth birthday came and this was the one they could not spend together, this being his birthday in reality, the one visible to his parents. Whereas with Djuna he had spent so many birthdays which his parents could not have observed, with their limited knowledge of him.

They had not attended the birthday of his manhood, the birthday of his roguish humorous self, of his first drunkenness, his first success at a party; or the birthday of his eloquent self on the theme of poetry, painting or music. Or the birthday of his imagination, his fantasy, of his new knowledge of people, of his new assertions and his discoveries of unknown powers in himself.

This succession of birthdays that had taken place since he left home was the highest fiesta ever attended by Djuna, the spectacle of unpredictable blooms, of the shells breaking around his personality, the emergence of the man.

But his real birthday they could not spend together.

His mother made dinner for him, and he played chess with his father—they who loved him less and who had bound and stifled him with prohibitions, who had delayed his manhood.

His mother made a birthday cake iced and sprinkled with warnings against expansion, cautions against new friends, designed a border like those of formal gardens as if to outline all the proprieties with which to defeat adventure.

His father played chess with him silently, indicating in the carefully measured moves a judgment upon all the wayward dances of the heart, the caprices of the body, above all a judg-

191

ment upon such impulses as had contributed to Paul's very presence there, the act of conjunction from which had been formed the luminous boy eating at their table.

The cake they fed him was the cake of caution: to fear all human beings and doubt the motivations of all men and women not listed in the Social Directory.

The candles were not lit to celebrate his future freedom, but to say: only within the radius lighted by these birthday candles, only within the radius of father and mother are you truly safe.

A small circle. And outside of this circle, evil.

And so he ate of this birthday cake baked by his mother, containing all the philters against love, expansion and freedom known to white voodoo.

A cake to prevent and preserve the child from becoming man!

No more nights together, when to meet the dawn together was the only marriage ceremony accorded to lovers.

But he returned to her one day carrying the valise with his laundry. On his return home he had packed his laundry to have it washed at home. And his mother had said: "Take it back. I won't take care of laundry you soiled while living with strangers."

So quietly he brought it back to Djuna, to the greater love that would gladly take care of his belongings as long as they were the clothes he soiled in his experience with freedom.

The smallness of his shirts hurt her, like a sign of dangers for him which she could not avert. He was still slender enough, young enough to be subjected to tyranny.

They were both listening to César Franck's Symphony in D Minor.

192

And then the conflicting selves in Djuna fused into one mood as they do at such musical crossroads.

The theme of the symphony was gentleness.

She had first heard it at the age of sixteen one rainy afternoon and associated it with her first experience of love, of a love without climax which she had known with Michael. She had interwoven this music with her first concept of the nature of love as one of ultimate, infinite gentleness.

In César Franck's symphony there was immediate exaltation, dissolution in feeling and the evasion of violence. Over and over again in this musical ascension of emotion, the stairway of fever was climbed and deserted before one reached explosion.

An obsessional return to minor themes, creating an endless tranquillity, and at sixteen she had believed that the experience of love was utterly contained in this gently flowing drug, in the delicate spirals, cadences, and undulations of this music.

César Franck came bringing messages of softness and trust, accompanying Paul's gestures and attitudes, and for this she trusted him, a passion without the storms of destruction.

She had wanted such nebulous landscapes, such vertiginous spirals without explosions: the drug.

Listening to the symphony flowing and yet not flowing (for there was a static groove in which it remained imprisoned, so similar to the walled-in room of her house, containing a mystery of stillness), Djuna saw the Obelisk in the Place de la Concorde, the arrow of stone placed at the center of a gracefully turbulent square, summating gardens, fountains and rivers of automobiles. One pointed dart of stone to pierce the night, the fog, the rain, the sun, aiming faultlessly into the clouds.

And there was the small, crazy woman Matilda, whom everyone knew, who came every morning and sat on one of the benches near the river, and stayed there all day, watching the passers-by, eating sparingly and lightly of some mysterious food in crumbs out of a paper bag, like the pigeons. So familiar

193

to the policeman, to the tourists, and to the permanent in-
habitants of the Place de la Concorde, that not to see her there
would have been as noticeable, as disturbing, as to find the
Obelisk gone, and the square left without its searchlight into
the sky.

Matilda was known for her obstinacy in sitting there through
winter and summer, her indifference to climate, her vague
answers to those who sought her reasons for being there, her
tireless watchfulness, as if she were keeping a rendezvous with
eternity.

Only at sundown did she leave, sometimes gently incited
by the policeman.

Since there was not total deterioration in her clothes, or in
her health, everyone surmised she must have a home and no
one was ever concerned about her.

Djuna had once sat beside her and Matilda at first would
not speak, but addressed herself to the pigeons and to the
falling autumn leaves, murmuring, whispering, muttering by
turns. Then suddenly she said to Djuna very simply and clearly:
"My lover left me sitting here and said he would come back."

(The policeman had said: I have seen her sitting there for
twenty years.)

"How long have you been sitting here and waiting?" Djuna
asked.

"I don't know."

She ate of the same bread she was feeding the pigeons. Her
face was wrinkled but not aged, through the wrinkles shone
an expression which was not of age, which was the expression
of alert waiting, watchfulness, expectation of the young.

"He will come back," she said, for the first time a look of
defiance washing her face of its spectator's pallor, the pallor
of the recluse who lives without intimate relationship to stir
the rhythms of the blood, this glazed expression of those who
watch the crowd passing by and never recognize a face.

"Of course he will," said Djuna, unable to bear even the
shadow of anxiety on the woman's face.

194

Matilda's face recovered its placidity, its patience.

"He told me to sit here and wait."

A mortal blow had stopped the current of her life, but had not shattered her. It had merely paralyzed her sense of time, she would sit and wait for the lost lover and the years were obliterated by the anesthesia of the deadened cell of time: five minutes stretched to infinity and kept her alive, alive and ghostly, with the cell of time, the little clock of reality inside the brain forever damaged. A faceless clock pointing to anguish. And with time was linked pain, lodged in the same cell (neighbors and twins), time and pain in more or less intimate relationship.

And what was left was this shell of a woman immune to cold and heat, anesthetized by a great loss into immobility and timelessness.

Sitting there beside Matilda Djuna heard the echoes of the broken cell within the little psychic stage of her own heart, so well enacted, so neat, so clear, and wondered whether when her father left the house for good in one of his moods of violence as much damage had been done to her, and whether some part of her being had not been atrophied, preventing complete openness and complete development in living.

By his act of desertion he had destroyed a cell in Djuna's being, an act of treachery from a cruel world setting her against all fathers, while retaining the perilous hope of a father returning under the guise of the men who resembled him, to re-enact again the act of violence.

It was enough for a man to possess certain attributes of the father—any man possessed of power—and then her being came alive with fear as if the entire situation would be re-enacted inevitably: possession, love and desertion, replacing her on a bench like Matilda, awaiting a denouement.

Looking back, there had been a momentous break in the flow, a change of activity.

Every authoritarian step announced the return of the father and danger. For the father's last words had been: "I will come

195

back."

Matilda had been more seriously injured: the life flow had stopped. She had retained the first image, the consciousness that she must wait, and the last words spoken by the lover had been a command for eternity: wait until I come back.

As if these words had been uttered by a proficient hypnotist who had then cut off all her communications with the living, so that she was not permitted even this consolation allowed to other deserted human beings: the capacity to transfer this love to another, to cheat the order given, to resume life with others, to forget the first one.

Matilda had been mercifully arrested and suspended in time, and rendered unconscious of pain.

But not Djuna.

In Djuna the wound had remained alive, and whenever life touched upon this wound she mistook the pain she felt for being alive, and her pain warning her and guiding her to deflect from man the father to man the son.

She could see clearly all the cells of her being, like the rooms of her house which had blossomed, enriched, developed and stretched far and beyond all experiences, but she could see also the cell of her being like the walled-in room of her house in which was lodged violence as having been shut and condemned within her out of fear of disaster.

There was a little cell of her being in which she still existed as a child, which only activated with a subtle anger in the presence of the father, for in relation to him she lost her acquired power, her assurance, she was rendered small again and returned to her former state of helplessness and dependence.

And knowing the tragic outcome of this dependence she felt hostility and her route towards the man of power bristled with this hostility—an immediate need to shut out violence.

Paul and Djuna sat listening to César Franck's Symphony in D Minor, in this little room of gentleness and trust, barring violence from the world of love, seeking an opiate against

196

destruction and treachery.

So she had allied herself with the son against the father. He had been there to forbid and thus to strengthen the desire. He had been there, large and severe, to threaten the delicate, precarious bond, and thus to render it desperate and make each encounter a reprieve from death and loss.

The movements of the symphony and her movements had been always like Paul's, a ballet of oscillations, peripheral entrances and exits, figures designed to become invisible in moments of danger, pirouetting with all the winged knowledge of birds to avoid collision with violence and severity.

Together they had taken leaps into the air to avoid obstacles.

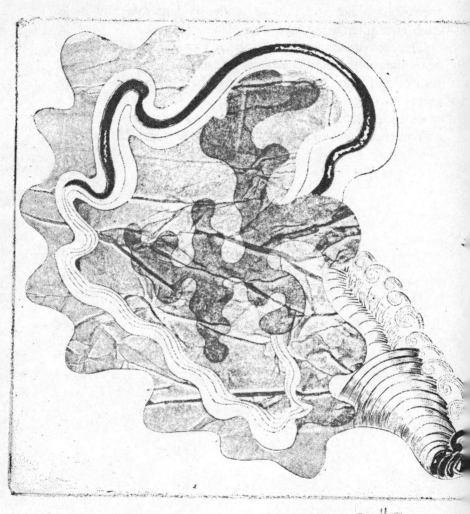

Hugo 1943

The Café

THE CAFÉS WERE THE WELLS of treasures, the caves of Ali
Baba.

The cafés were richer even than the oriental cities where
all living was plied openly under your eyes so that you were
offered all the activities of the world to touch and smell. You
saw your shoes being made from the skinning of the animal
to the polishing of the leather. You saw the weaving of cloth
and the dyeing in pails of multicolored liquids. You saw the
scribes writing letters for the illiterate, the philosopher meditating, the religious man chanting as he squatted and the lepers

199

disintegrating under your eyes, within the touch of your hand.

And so in the café, with one franc for a glass of wine and even less for coffee, you could hear stories from the Pampas, share in African voodoo secrets, read the pages of a book being written, listen to a poem, to the death rattles of an aristocrat, the life story of a revolutionary. You could hear the hummed theme of a symphony, watch the fingers of a jazz drummer drumming on the table, accept an invitation from a painter who would take you to the Zoo to watch the serpents eat their daily ration of white mice, consult a secretive Hindu on his explorations of occult streets, or meet an explorer who would take you on his sailboat around the world.

The chill of autumn was tempered by little coal stoves and glass partitions.

A soft rain covered the city with a muted lid, making it intimate like a room, shutting out sky and sun as if drawing curtains, lighting lamps early, kindling fires in the fireplaces, pushing human beings gently to live under the surface, inciting them to sprout words, sparkling colors out of their own flesh, to become light, fire, flowers and tropical fiestas.

The café was the hothouse, densely perfumed with all the banned oils, the censured musks, the richest blooms accelerated by enclosure, warmth, and crossgraftings from all races.

No sunsets, no dawns, but exhibits of paintings rivaling all in luxuriance. Rivers of words, forests of sculptures, huge pyramids of personalities. No need of gardens.

City and cafés became intimate like a room that was carpeted, quilted for the easy intermingling of man's inner landscapes, his multiple secret wishes vibrating from table to table as elbows and the *garçon* not only carried brimming glasses but endless messages and signals as the servants did in the old Arabian tales.

Day and night were colliding gently at twilight, throwing off erotic sparks.

Day and night met on the boulevards.

200

Sabina was always breaking the molds which life formed around her.

She was always trespassing boundaries, erasing identifications.

She could not bear to have a permanent address or to give her telephone number.

Her greatest pleasure consisted in being where no one knew she was, in an out-of-the-way café, a little-known hotel, if possible a room from which the number had been scratched off.

She changed her name as criminals efface their tracks.

She herself did not know what she was preserving from detection, what mystery she was defending.

She hated factual questions as to her activities. Above all she hated to be registered in any of the official books. She hated to give her birth hour, her genealogy, and all her dealings with passport authorities were blurred and complicated.

She lived entirely by a kind of opportunism, all her acts dictated by the demands of the present situation. She eluded tabulations only to place herself more completely at the disposal of anyone's fantasy about her.

She kept herself free of all identifications the better to obey some stranger's invention about her.

As soon as a man appeared the game began.

She must keep silent. She must let him look at her face and let his dream take form. She must allow time and silence for his invention to develop.

She let him build an image. She saw the image take form in his eyes. If she said what she wanted to say he might think her an ordinary woman!

This image of herself as a *not* ordinary woman, an image which was trembling now in his eyes, might suddenly disappear. Nothing more difficult to live up to than men's dreams. Nothing more tenuous, elusive to fulfill than men's dreams.

She might say the wrong phrase, make the wrong gesture, smile the wrong smile, and then see his eyes waver vulnerably

201

for one instant before turning to the glassy brilliance of disillusion.

She wanted desperately to answer man's most impossible wishes. If the man said: you seem perverse to me, then she would set about gathering together all her knowledge of perversity to become what he had called her.

It made life difficult. She lived the tense, strained life of an international spy. She moved among enemies set on exposing her pretenses. People felt the falseness at times and sought to uncover her.

She had such a fear of being discovered!

She could not bear the light of common, everyday simplicities! As other women blink at the sunlight, she blinked at the light of common everyday simplicities.

And so this race which must never stop. To run from the slanting eyes of one to the caressing hands of another to the sadness of the third.

As she collided with people they lost their identities also: they became objects of desire, objects to be consumed, fuel for the bonfire. Their quality was summarized as either inflammable or noninflammable. That was all that counted. She never distinguished age, nationality, class, fortune, status, occupation or vocation.

Her desire rushed instantaneously, without past or future. A point of fire in the present to which she attached no contracts, no continuity.

Her breasts were always heavy and full. She was like a messenger carrying off all she received from one to carry it to the other, carrying in her breasts the words said to her, the book given her, the land visited, the experience acquired, in the form of stories to be spun continuously.

Everything lived one hour before was a story to tell the following hour to the second companion. From room to room what was perpetuated was her pollen-carrying body.

When someone asked her: where are you going now? whom are you going to meet? she lied. She lied because this current

202

sweeping her onward seemed to cause others pain.

Crossing the street she nourished herself upon the gallant smile of the policeman who stopped the traffic for her. She culled the desire of the man who pushed the revolving door for her. She gathered the flash of adoration from the drugstore clerk: are you an actress? She picked the bouquet of the shoe salesman trying on her shoes: are you a dancer? As she sat in the bus she received the shafts of the sun as a personal intimate visit. She felt a humorous connivance with the truck driver who had to pull the brakes violently before her impulsive passages and who did so smiling.

Every moment this current established itself, this state of flow, of communication by seduction.

She always returned with her arms full of adventures, as other women return with packages. Her whole body rich with this which nourished her and from which she nourished others. The day finished always too early and she was not empty of restlessness.

Leaning out of the window at dawn, pressing her breasts upon the window sill, she still looked out of the window hoping to see what she had failed to grasp, to possess. She looked at the ending night and the passersby with the keen alertness of the voyager who can never reach terminations as ordinary people reach peaceful terminals at the end of each day, accepting pauses, deserts, rests, havens, as she could not accept them.

She believed only in fire. She wanted to be at every explosion of fire, every convergence of danger. She lived like a fireman, tense for all the emergencies of conflagrations. She was a menace to peaceful homes, tranquil streets.

She was the firebug who was never detected.

Because she believed that fire ladders led to love. This was the motive for her incendiary habits. But Sabina, with all her fire ladders, could not find love.

At dawn she would find herself among ashes again.

And so she could not rest or sleep.

As soon as the day dawned peaceful, uneventful, Sabina

slipped into her black satin dress, lacquered her nails the color of her mood, pulled her black cape around her and set out for the cafés.

At dawn Jay turned towards Lillian lying beside him and his first kiss reached her through the net of her hair.

Her eyes were closed, her nerves asleep, but under his hand her body slipped down a dune into warm waves lapping over each other, rippling her skin.

Jay's sensual thrusts wakened the dormant walls of flesh, and tongues of fire flicked towards his hard lashings piercing the kernel of mercury, disrupting a current of fire through the veins. The burning fluid of ecstacy eddying madly and breaking, loosening a river of pulsations.

The core of ecstacy bursting to the rhythmic pounding, until his hard thrusts spurted burning fluid against the walls of flesh, impulsion within the womb like a thunderbolt.

Lillian's panting decreased, and her body reverberated in the silence, filled with echoes . . . antennae which had drunk like the stems of plants.

He awakened free, and she did not.

His desire had reached a finality, like a clean saber cut which dealt pleasure, not death.

She felt impregnated.

She had greater difficulty in shifting, in separating, in turning away.

Her body was filled with retentions, residues, sediments.

He awakened and passed into other realms. The longer his stay in the enfolding whirls, the greater his energy to enter activity again. He awakened and he talked of painting, he awakened laughing, eyes closed with laughter, laughing on the edge of his cheeks, laughter in the corner of his mouth, the

204

laughter of great separateness.

She awakened unfree, as if laden with the seeds of his being, wondering at what moment he would pull his whole self away as one tears a plant out by the roots, leaving a crevice in the earth. Dreading the break because she felt him a master of this act, free to enter and free to emerge, whereas she felt dispossessed of her identity and freedom because Jay upon awakening did not turn about and contemplate her even for a moment as Lillian, a particular woman, but that when he took her, or looked at her he did so gaily, anonymously, as if any woman lying there would have been equally pleasant, natural, and not Lillian among all women.

He was already chuckling at some idea for a painting, already hungry for breakfast, ready to open his mail and embark on multiple relationships, curious about the day's climate, the changes in the street, the detailed news of the brawl of the night before which had taken place under their window.

Fast fast fast moving away, his mind already pursuing the wise sayings of Lao-tse, the theories of Picasso, already like a vast wheel at the fair starting on a wide circle which at no point whatever seemed to include her, because she was there like bread for him, a nonidentifiable bread which he ate of as he would eat any bread, not even troubling with the ordinary differentiations: today my bread is fresh and warm, and today it is a little dry, today it lacks salt, today it is lifeless, today it is golden and crisp.

She did not reach out to possess Jay, as he believed, but she reached out because so much of Jay had been deposited, sown, planted within her that she felt possessed, as if she were no longer able to move, breathe, live independently of him. She felt her dependence, lost to herself, given, invaded, and at his mercy, and the anxiety of this, the defenselessness caused a clinging which was the clinging of the drowning. . . .

As if she were bread, she would have liked Jay at least to notice all variations in moods and flavors. She would have liked Jay to say: you are my bread, a very unique and marvelous

205

bread, like none other. If you were not here I would die of instantaneous starvation.

Not at all. If he painted well, it was the spring day. If he were gay, it was the Pernod. If he were wise, it was the little book of Lao-tse's sayings. If he were elated, it was due to a worshipful letter in the mail.

And me, and me, said a small, anxious voice in Lillian's being, where am I?

She was not even the woman in his paintings.

He was painting Sabina. He painted her as a mandrake with fleshy roots, bearing a solitary purple flower in a purple bell-shaped corolla of narcotic flesh. He painted her born with red-gold eyes always burning as from caverns, from holes in the earth, from behind trees. Painted her as one of the luxuriant women, a tropical growth, excommunicated from the bread line as too rich a substance for everyday living, placing her there merely as a denizen of the world of fire, and was content with her intermittent, parabolic appearances.

So, if she was not in his paintings, Lillian thought, where was she? When he finished painting he drank. When he drank he exulted in his powers and palmed it all on the holy ghost inside of him, each time calling the spirit animating him by a different name that was not Lillian. Today it was the holy ghost, and the spring light and a dash of Pernod.

He did not say what Lillian wanted to hear: "You are the holy ghost inside of me. You make my spring."

She was not even sure of that—of being his holy ghost. At times it seemed to her that he was painting with Djuna's eyes. When Djuna was there he painted better. He did not paint her. He only felt strong and capable when he tackled huge masses, strong features, heavy bodies. Djuna's image was too tenuous for him.

But when she was there he painted better.

Silently she seemed to be participating, silently she seemed to be transmitting forces.

Where did her force come from? No one knew.

206

She merely sat there and the colors began to organize themselves, to deepen, as if he took the violet from her eyes when she was angry, the blue when she was at peace, the gray when she was detached, the gold when she was melted and warm, and painted with them. Using her eyes as a color chart.

In this way he passed from the eyes of Lillian which said: "I am here to warm you." Eyes of devotion.

To the eyes of Sabina which said: "I am here to consume you."

To the eyes of Djuna which said: "I am here to reflect your painter's dream, like a crystal ball."

Bread and fire and light, he needed them all. He could be nourished on Lillian's faith but it did not illumine his work. There were places into which Lillian could not follow him. When he was tormented by a half-formed image he went to Djuna, just as once walking through the streets with her he had seen a child bring her a tangled skein of string to unravel.

He would have liked the three women to love each other. It seemed to him that then he would be at peace. When they pulled against each other for supremacy it was as if different parts of his own body pulled against each other.

On days when Lillian accepted understanding through the eyes of Djuna, when each one was connected with her role and did not seek to usurp the other's place he was at peace and slept profoundly.

(If only, thought Lillian, lying in the disordered bed, when he moved away I could be quiet and complete and free. He seems bound to me and then so completely unbound. He changes. One day I look at him and there is warmth in him, and the next a kind of ruthlessness. There are times when he kisses me and I feel he is not kissing me but any woman, or all the women he has known. There are times when he seems made of wax, and I can see on him the imprint of all those he has seen during the day. I can hear their words. Last night he even fraternized with the man who was courting me. What does this mean? Even with Edgar who was trying to take me

207

away from him. He was in one of his moods of effusive display, when he loved everybody. He is promiscuous. I can't bear how near they come, they talk in his face, they breathe his breath. Anyone at all has this privilege. Anyone can talk to him, share his house, and even me. He gives away everything. Djuna says I lack faith. . . . Is that what it is? But how can I heal myself? I thought one could get healed by just living and loving.)

Lying in bed and listening to Jay whistling while he shaved in the bathroom, Lillian wondered why she felt simultaneously in bondage and yet unmarried, unappeased, and all her conversations with Djuna with whom she was able to talk even better than to monologue with herself once more recurred to her before she allowed herself to face the dominant impulse ruling her: to run away from Jay.

Passion gathered its momentum, its frenzy, from the effort to possess what was unpossessable in reality, because it sprang from an illusion, because it gained impetus from a secret knowledge of its unfulfillable quality, because it attacked romantic organisms, and incited to fever in place of a natural union by feelings. Passion between two people came from a feverish desire to fuse elements which were unfusable. The extreme heat to which human beings subjected themselves in this experiment, as if by intensity the unfusable elements could be melted into one—water with fire, fire with earth, rock and water. An effort doomed to defeat.

Lillian could not see all this, but felt it happening, and knew that this was why she had wept so bitterly at their first quarrel: not weeping over a trivial difference but because her instinct warned her senses that this small difference indicated a wider one, a difference of elements, by which the relationship would ultimately be destroyed.

In one of his cheerful, human moods Jay had said: "If my friends bother you so much, we shall put them all against a wall and shoot them."

But Lillian knew that if today Jay surrendered today's set

of friends, he would renew the same kind of relationships with a new set, for they reflected the part of him she did not feel close to, the part in fact she was at war with.

Lillian's disproportionate weeping had seemed childish to Jay who saw only the immediate difference, but Lillian was weeping blindly with a fear of death of the relationship, with her loss of faith sensing the first fissure as the first symbol of future dissolution, and knowing from that moment on that the passion between them would no longer be an affirmation of marriage but a struggle against death and separation.

(Djuna said: You can't bear to let this relationship die. But why must it die, Djuna? Do you believe all passion must die? Is there nothing I can do to avoid failure? Passion doesn't die of natural death. Everyone says passion dies, love dies, but it's we who kill it. Djuna believes this. Djuna said: You can fight all the symptoms of divorce when they first appear, you can be on your guard against distortions, against the way people wound each other and instill doubt, you can fight for the life and continuity of this passion, there *is* a knowledge which postpones the death of a relationship, death is not natural, but, Lillian, you cannot do it alone, there are seeds of death in his character. One cannot fight alone for a living relationship. It takes the effort of two. Effort, effort. The word most foreign to Jay. Jay would never make an effort. Djuna, Djuna, couldn't you talk to him? Djuna, will you talk to him? No, it's useless, he does not want anything that is difficult to reach. He does not like effort or struggles. He wants only his pleasure. It isn't possessiveness, Djuna, but I want to feel at the center so that I can allow him the maximum freedom without feeling each time that he betrays everything, destroys everything.)

She would run away.

When Jay saw her dressing, powdering her face, pulling up her stockings, combing her hair, he noticed no change in her gestures to alarm him, for did she not always comb her hair and powder and dress with the flurry of a runaway. Wasn't

209

she always so uneasy and overquick, as if she had been frightened?

He went to his studio and Lillian locked the door of the bedroom and sat at her piano, to seek in music that wholeness which she could not find in love. . . .

Just as the sea often carries bodies, wrecks, shells, lost objects carved by the sea itself in its own private studio of sculpture to unexpected places, led by irrational currents, just so did the current of music eject fragments of the self believed drowned and deposited them on the shore altered, recarved, rendered anonymous in shape. Each backwash, each cross-current, throwing up new material formed out of the old, from the ocean of memories.

Driftwood figures that had been patiently recarved by the sea with rhythms broken by anger, patiently remolding forms to the contours of knotted nightmares, woods stunted and distorted by torments of doubts.

She played until this flood of debris rose from the music to choke her, closed the piano with anger, and rose to plan her escape.

Escape. Escape.

Her first instinctive, blind gesture of escape was to don the black cape copied from Sabina's at the time of their relationship.

She wrapped Sabina's cape around her, and put two heavy bracelets around her wrist (one for each wrist, not wanting any more to be in bondage to one, never to one; she would split the desire in two, to rescue one half of herself from destruction).

And for the first time since her marriage to Jay, she climbed the worn stairs of a very old hotel in Montparnasse, experiencing the exaltation familiar to runaways.

The more she could see of the worn carpet and its bare skeleton, the more acrid the smell of poverty, the more bare the room, this which might have lowered the diapason of another's mood only increased the elation of hers, becoming trans-

210

figured by her conviction that she was making a voyage which would forever take her away from the prison of anxiety, the pain of dependence on a human being she could not trust. Her mood of liberation spangled and dappled shabbiness with light like an impressionist painting.

Her sense of familiarity with this scene did not touch her at first: a lover was waiting for her in one of the rooms of this hotel.

Could anyone help her to forget Jay for a moment? Could Edgar help her, Edgar with his astonished eyes saying to her: You are wonderful, you are wonderful! Drunkenly repeating you are wonderful! as they danced under Jay's very eyes not seeing, not seeing her dancing with Edgar in the luminous spotlight of a night club, but when her dress opened a little at the throat she could smell the mixed odor of herself and Jay.

She was taking revenge now for his effusive confessions as to the pleasures he had taken with other women.

She had been made woman by Jay, he alone held in his hands all the roots of her being, and when he had pulled them, in his own limitless motions outward and far, he had inflicted such torture that he had destroyed the roots all at once and sent her into space, sent her listening to Edgar's words gratefully, grateful for Edgar's hands on her pulling her away from Jay, grateful for his foolish gift of flowers in silver paper (because Jay gave her no gifts at all), and she would imagine Jay watching this scene, watching her go up the stairs to Edgar's room, wearing flowers in a silver paper. and she enjoyed imagining his pain, as he witnessed the shedding of her clothes, witnessed her lying down beside Edgar. (You are the man of the crowd, Jay, and so I lie here beside a stranger. What makes me lonely, Jay, are the cheap and gaudy people you are friendly with, and I lie here with a stranger who is only caressing you inside of me. He is complaining like a woman: you are not thinking of me, you are not filled with me.)

But no sooner had she shed her cape copied from Sabina's than she recognized the room, the man, the scene, and the feelings as not belonging to her, not having been selected by her, but as having been borrowed from Sabina's repertoire of stories of adventures.

Lillian was not free of Jay since she had invited him to witness the scene enacted solely to punish his unfaithfulness. She was not free, she was being Sabina, with the kind of man Sabina would have chosen. All the words and gestures prescribed by Sabina in her feverish descriptions, for thus was much experience transmitted by contagion, and Lillian, not yet free, had been more than others predisposed to the contagion by lowered resistance!

She was ashamed, not of the sensual meeting, but for having acted in disguise, and eluded responsibility.

When the stranger asked her for her name she did not say Lillian, but Sabina.

She returned home to shed her cape and her acts, pretending not to know this woman who had spent hours with a stranger.

To put the responsibility on Sabina.

Escape escape escape—into what? Into borrowing the self of Sabina for an hour. She had donned the recklessness of Sabina, borrowed her cape for a shy masquerade, pretending freedom.

The clothes had not fitted very well.

But after a while, would this cease to be a role and did the borrowing reveal Lillian's true desires?

The possibility of being this that she borrowed.

Blindly ashamed of what she termed unfaithfulness (when actually she was still so tied to Jay it was merely within the precincts of their relationship that she could act, with his presence, and therefore unsevered from him), she discarded all the elements of this charade, cape, bracelets, then bathed and dressed in her own Lillian costume and went to the café where she sat beside Sabina who had already accumulated several plates by which the waiter was able to add the number of drinks.

212

When Jay felt exhausted after hours of painting he went to see Djuna.

He always softened as he thought of Djuna. She was to him more than a woman. It had been difficult at first to see her simply as a woman. His first impression had been an association with Florentine painting, his feeling that no matter what her origin, her experiences, her resemblances to other women, she was for him like a canvas which had been covered first of all with a coating of gold paint, so that whatever one painted over it, this gold on which he had dissertated during one of his early visits to her, was present as it remained present in the Florentine paintings.

But even though his obsession for dispelling illusions, which made him pull at her eyelashes to see if they were real, which made him open jars and bottles in the bathroom to see what they contained, even though he always had the feeling that women resorted to tricks and contrived spells which man must watch out for, he still felt that she was more than a woman, and that given the right moment, she was willing to shed the veils, the elusiveness, and to be completely honest.

It was not her clarity either, which he called honesty. Her clarity he distrusted. She always made wonderful patterns—he admitted that. There was a kind of Grecian symmetry to her movements, her life, and her words. They looked convincingly harmonious, clear—too clear. And in the meanwhile where was she? Not on the clear orderly surface of her ideas any longer, but submerged, sunk in some obscure realm like a submarine. She had only appeared to give you all her thoughts. She had only seemed to empty herself in this clarity. She gave you a neat pattern and then slipped out of it herself and laughed at you. Or else she gave you a neat pattern and then slipped out of it herself and then the utterly tragic expression of her face testified to some other realm she had entered and not allowed one to follow her into, a realm of despair even, a realm of anguish, which was only betrayed by her eyes.

What was the mystery of woman? Only this obstinacy in concealing themselves—merely this persistence in creating mysteries, as if the exposure of her thoughts and feelings were gifts reserved for love and intimacy.

He suspected that some day an honest woman would clear all this away. He never suspected for a moment that this mystery was a part of themselves they did not know, could not see.

Djuna, he ruminated, was a more ornamented woman, but an honest one.

He had long ago found a way to neutralize the potencies of woman by a simplification all his own, which was to consider all women as sharing but one kind of hunger, a hunger situated between the two pale columns of the legs. Even the angels, said Jay, even the angels, and the mothers, and the sisters, were all made the same way, and he retained this focus upon them from the time when he was a very little boy playing on the floor of his mother's kitchen and an enormous German woman had come straight to them from the immigration landing, still wearing her voluminous peasant skirts, her native costume, and she had stood in the kitchen asking his mother to help her find work, using some broken jargon impossible to understand—everyone in the house dismayed by her foreignness, her braids, her speech. As if to prove her capabilities through some universal gesture, she had started to knead the dough expertly, kneading with fervor, while Jay's mother watched her with increasing interest.

Jay was playing on the floor with matches, unnoticed, and he found himself covered as by a huge and colorful tent by the perfoliate skirt of the German woman, his glance lost where two pale columns converged in a revelation which had given him forever this perspective of woman's being, this vantage point of insight, this observatory and infallible focus, which prevented him from losing his orientation in the vastest maze of costumes, classes, races, nationalities—no external variations able to deprive him of this intimate knowledge of woman's most secret architecture. . . .

Chuckling, he thought of Djuna's expression whenever she opened the door to receive him.

The dreamer wears fur and velvet blinkers.

Chuckling, Jay thought of himself entering the house, and of her face shining between these blinkers of her vision of him as a great painter, shutting out with royal indifference all other elements which might disturb this vision.

He could see on her face this little shrine built by the dreamer in which she placed him as a great painted. Won by her fervor, he would enter with her into her dream of him, and begin to listen raptly to her way of transmuting into gold everything he told her!

If he had stolen from the Zombie's pocketbook she said it was because the Zombie was provocatively miserly. If he complained that he was oversleeping when he should be working Djuna translated it that he was catching up on sleep lost during the period when he had only a moving-picture hall to sleep in.

She only heard and saw what she wanted to hear and see. (Damn women!) Her expression of expectancy, of faith, her perpetual absolution of his acts disconcerted him at times.

The more intently he believed all she believed while he was with her, the more precipitately he fell out of grace when he left her, because he felt she was the depository of his own dream, and that she would keep it while he turned his back on it.

One of the few women, chuckled Jay, who understood the artificial paradise of art, the language of man.

As he walked, the city took on the languid beauty of a woman, which was the beauty of Paris, especially at five o'clock, at twilight, when the fountains, the parks, the soft lighting, the humid streets like blue mirrors, all dissolved into a haze of pearl, extending their fripperies and coquetries.

At the same hour New York took on its masculine and aggressive beauty, with its brash lighting, its steel arrows and giant obelisks piercing the sky, an electric erectness, a rigid

215

city pitiless to lovers, sending detectives to hotel rooms to track them down, at the same hour that the French waiter said to the couples: do you wish a *cabinet particulier*—at the same hour that in New York all the energies were poured into steel structures, digging oil wells, harnessing electricity, for power.

Jay walked leisurely, like a ragpicker of good moments, walked through streets of joy, throwing off whatever disturbed him, gathering only what pleased him, noticing with delight that the washed and faded blue of the café awning matched the washed faded blue face of the clock in the church spire.

Then he saw the café table where Lillian sat talking with Sabina, and knowing his dream of becoming a great painter securely stored in the eyes of Djuna (damn women!) he decided to sin against it by sinking into the more shallow fantasies born of absinthe.

Djuna awakened from so deep a dream that opening her eyes was like pushing aside a heavy shroud of veils, a thousand layers of veils, and with a sensation similar to that of the trapezist who has been swinging in vast spaces, and suddenly feels again in his two hands the coarse touch of the swing cord.

She awakened fully to the painful knowledge that this was a day when she would be possessed by a mood which cut her off from fraternity.

It was also at those moments that she would have the clearest intuitions, sudden contacts with the deepest selves of others, divine the most hidden sorrow.

But if she spoke from this source, others would feel uneasy, not recognizing the truth of what she said. They always felt exposed and were quick to revenge themselves. They rushed to defend this exposure of the self they did not know, they were not familiar with, or did not like. They blamed her for excess of imagination, for exaggeration.

They persisted in living on familiar terms only with the surface of their personalities, and what she reached lay deeper where they could not see it. They felt at ease among their falsities, and the nakedness of her insight seemed like forcing open underworlds whose entrance was tacitly barred in everyday intercourse.

They would accuse her of living in a world of illusion while they lived in reality.

Their falsities had such an air of solidity, entirely supported by the palpable.

But she felt that on the contrary, she had contact with their secret desires, secret fears, secret intents. And she had faith in what she saw.

She attributed all her difficulties merely to the overquickness of her rhythm. Proofs would always follow later, too late to to be of value to her human life, but not too late to be added to this city of the interior she was constructing, to which none had access.

Yet she was never surprised when people betrayed the self she saw, which was the maximum rendition of themselves. This maximum she knew to be a torment, this knowledge of all one might achieve, become, was a threat to human joy and life. She felt in sympathy with those who turned their back on it. Yet she also knew that if they did, another torment awaited them: that of having fallen short of their own dream.

She would have liked to escape from her own demands upon herself.

But even if at times she was taken with a desire to become blind, to drift, to abandon her dreams, to slip into negation, destruction, she carried in herself something which altered the atmosphere she sought and which proved stronger than the place or people she had permitted to infect her with their disintegration, their betrayal of their original dream of themselves.

Even when she let herself be poisoned with all that was

human, defeat, jealousy, sickness, surrender, blindness, she carried an essence which was like a counter-poison and which reversed despair into hope, bitterness into faith, abortions into births, weight into lightness.

Everything in her hands changed substance, quality, form, intent.

Djuna could see it happen against her will, and did not know why it happened.

Was it because she began every day anew as children do, without memory of defeat, rancor, without memory of disaster? No matter what happened the day before, she always awakened with an expectation of a miracle. Her hands always appeared first from out of the sheets, hands without memories, wounds, weights, and these hands danced.

That was her awakening. A new day was a new life. Every morning was a beginning.

No sediments of pain, sadness yes, but no stagnating pools of accumulated bitterness.

Djuna believed one could begin anew as often as one dared.

The only acid she contained was one which dissolved the calluses formed by life around the sensibilities.

Every day she looked at people with the eyes of faith. Placing an unlimited supply of faith at their disposal. Since she did not accept the actual self as final, seeing only the possibilities of expansion, she established a climate of infinite possibilities.

She did not mind that by this expectation of a miracle, she exposed herself to immense disappointments. What she suffered as a human being when others betrayed themselves and her she counted as nothing—like the pains of childbirth.

She believed that the dream which human beings carry in themselves was man's greatest hunger. If statistics were taken there would be found more deaths by aborted dreams than from physical calamities, more deaths by dream abortions than child abortions, more deaths by infection from despair than from physical illness.

Carrying this ultimate knowledge she was often the victim

218

of strange revenges: people's revenge against the image of their unfulfilled dream. If they could annihilate her they might annihilate this haunting image of their completed selves and be done with it!

She only knew one person who might rescue her from this world, from this city of the interior lying below the level of identity.

She might learn from Jay to walk into a well-peopled world and abandon the intense selectivity of the dream (*this* personage fits into my dream and this one does not).

The dreamer rejects the ordinary.

Jay invited the ordinary. He was content with unformed fragments of people, incomplete ones: a minor doctor, a feeble painter, a mediocre writer, an average of any kind.

For Djuna it must always be: an extraordinary doctor, a unique writer, a summation of some kind, which could become a symbol by its completeness, by its greatness in its own realm.

Jay was the living proof that it was in this acceptance of the ordinary that pleasure lay. She would learn from him. She would learn to like daily bread. He gave her everything in its untransformed state: food, houses, streets, cafés, people. A way back to the simplicities.

Somewhere, in the labyrinth of her life, bread had been transformed on her tongue into a wafer, with the imponderability of symbols. Communion had been the actual way she experienced life—as communion, not as bread and wine. In place of bread, the wafer, in place of blood, the wine.

Jay would give her back a crowded world untransmuted. He had mocked her once saying he had found her portrait in one page of the dictionary under *Trans:* transmutations, transformation, transmitting, etc.

In the world of the dreamer there was solitude: all the exaltations and joys came in the moment of preparation for living. They took place in solitude. But with action came anxiety, and the sense of insuperable effort made to match the dream, and with it came weariness, discouragement, and

219

the flight into solitude again. And then in solitude, in the opium den of remembrance, the possibility of pleasure again.

What was she seeking to salvage from the daily current of living, what sudden revulsions drove her back into the solitary cell of the dream?

Let Jay lead her out of the cities of the interior.

She would work as usual, hours of dancing, then she would take her shoes to be repaired, then she would go to the café.

The shoemaker was working with his window open on the street. As often as Djuna passed there he would be sitting in his low chair, his head bowed over his work, a nail between his lips, a hammer in his hand.

She took all her shoes to him for repairing, because he had as great a love of unique shoes as she did. She brought him slippers from Montenegro whose tips were raised like the prows of galleys, slippers from Morocco embroidered in gold thread, sandals from Tibet.

His eyes traveled up from his work towards the package she carried as if she were bringing him a gift.

He took the fur boots from Lapland he had not seen before, and was moved by the simplicity of their sewing, the reindeer guts sewn by hand. He asked for their history.

Djuna did not have to explain to him that as she could not travel enough to satisfy the restlessness of her feet, she could at least wear shoes which came from the place she might never visit. She did not have to explain to him that when she looked at her feet in Lapland boots she felt herself walking through deserts of snow.

The shoes carried her everywhere, tireless shoes walking forever all over the world.

This shoemaker repaired them with all the curiosity of a great traveler. He respected the signs of wear and tear as if she were returning from all the voyages she had wanted to make. It was not alone the dust or mud of Paris he brushed off but of Egypt, Greece, India. Every shoe she brought him was his voyage too. He respected wear as a sign of distance,

220

broken straps as an indication of discoveries, torn heels as an accident happening only to explorers.

He was always sitting down. From his cellar room he looked up at the window where he could see only the feet of the passers-by.

"I love a foot that has elegance," he said. "Sometimes for days I see only ugly feet. And then perhaps one pair of beautiful feet. And that makes me happy."

As Djuna was leaving, for the first time he left his low working chair and moved forward to open the door for her, limping.

He had a club foot.

Once she had been found in the corner of a room by her very angry parents, all covered by a shawl. Their anxiety in not finding her for a long time turned to great anger.

"What are you doing there hiding, covered by a shawl?"

She answered: "Traveling. I am traveling."

The Rue de la Sante, the Rue Dolent, the Rue des Saint Pères became Bombay, Ladoma, Budapest, Lavinia.

The cities of the interior were like the city of Fez, intricate, endless, secret and unchartable.

Then she saw Jay sitting at the café table with Lillian, Donald, Michael, Sabina and Rango, and she joined them.

Faustin the Zombie, as everyone called him, awakened in a room he thought he had selected blindly but which gave the outward image of his inner self as accurately as if he had turned every element of himself into a carpet or a piece of furniture.

First of all it was not accessible to the door when it opened, but had to be reached by a dark and twisted corridor. Then he had contrived to cover the windows in such a manner with a glazed material that the objects, books and furniture appeared to be conserved in a storage room, to be at once dormant and veiled. The odor they emitted was the odor of hibernation.

One expected vast hoods to fall over the chairs and couch. Certain chairs were dismally isolated and had to be forcibly dragged to enter into relation with other chairs. There was an inertia in the pillows, an indifference in the wilted texture of the couch cover. The table in the center of the room blocked all passageways, the lamp shed a tired light. The walls absorbed the light without throwing it back.

His detachment affected the whole room. Objects need human warmth like human beings to bloom. A lamp sheds a meager or a prodigal light according to one's interior lighting. Even specks of dust are inhabited by the spirit of the master. There are rooms in which the dust is brilliant. There are rooms in which even carelessness is alive, as the disorder of someone rushing to more important matters. But here in Faustin's room there was not even the disorder caused by emotional draughts!

The walls of the rooming house were very thin, and he could hear all that took place in the other rooms.

This morning he awakened to a clear duet between a man and a woman.

Man: It's unbelievable, we've been together six years now, and I still have an illusion about you! I've never had this as long with any woman.

Woman: Six years!

Man: I'd like to know how often you have been unfaithful.

Woman: Well, I don't want to know how many times you were.

Man: Oh, me, only a few times. Whenever you went away and I'd get lonely and angry that you had left me. One summer at the beach . . . do you remember the model Colette?

Woman: I didn't ask you. I don't want to know.

Man: But I do. I know you went off with that singer. Why did you? A singer. I couldn't make love to a singer!

Woman: But you made love to a model.

Man: That's different. You know it's not important. You know you're the only one.

Woman: You'd think it was important if I had.

Man: It's different for a woman. Why? Why did you, what made you go with that singer, why, when I love you so much and desire you so often?

Silence.

Woman: I don't believe we should talk about this. I don't want to know about you. (Crying.) I never wanted to think about it and now you made me.

Man: You're crying! But it's nothing. I forgot it immediately. And in six years only a few times. Whereas you, I'm sure it was many times.

Woman: (still crying) I didn't ask you. Why did you have to tell me?

Man: I'm just more sincere than you are.

Woman: It isn't sincerity, it's revenge. You told me just to hurt me.

Man: I told you because I thought it would drive you into being honest with me.

Silence.

Man: How obstinate you are. Why are you crying?

Woman: Not over your unfaithfulness!

Man: Over your own then?

Woman: I'm crying over unfaithfulness in general—how people hurt each other.

Man: Unfaithfulness in general! What a fine way to evade the particular.

Silence.

Man: I'd like to know how you learned all you know about love-making. Who did you learn from? You know what very few women do.

Woman: I learned . . . from talking with other women. I also have a natural gift.

Man: I suppose it was Maurice who taught you the most. It enrages me to see how much you know.

Woman: I never asked you where you learned. Besides, it's always personal. Each couple invents their own way.

Man: Yes, that's true. Sometimes I made you cry with joy, didn't I?

Woman: (crying) Why do you use the past tense?

Man: Why did you go off with that singer?

Woman: If you insist so much I will tell you something.

Man: (in a very tense voice) About the singer?

Woman: No, someone else. Once I tried to be unfaithful. You were neglecting me. I took rather a fancy to someone. And all might have gone well except that he had the same habit you have of starting with: you have the softest skin in the world. And when he said this, just as you do, I remembered your saying that, and I left the man, I ran away. Nothing happened.

Man: But just the same he had time to note the quality of your skin.

Woman: I'm telling you the truth.

Man: You have nothing to cry about now. You have taken your revenge.

Woman: I'm crying about unfaithfulness in general, all the betrayals.
Man: I will never forgive you.
Woman: Once in six years!
Man: I'm sure it was that singer.

Faustin, lying down, smoking as he listened, felt the urgent need to comment. He knocked angrily on the wall. The man and the woman were silent.

"Listen," he said, in his loudest voice, "I heard your entire conversation. I would say in this case the man is very unjust and the woman right. She was more faithful than the man. She was faithful to a personal emotion, to a personal rite."

"Who are you?" said the man in the other room, angrily.

"No one in particular, just a neighbor."

There was a long silence. Then the sound of a door being closed violently. Faustin heard one person moving about with soft rustles. Judging from the steps, it was the man who had gone out.

Faustin lay down again, meditating on his own anxiety.

He felt at this moment like a puppet, but he became aware that all this had happened many times before to him, but never as clearly.

All living had taken place for him in the other room, and he had always been the witness. He had always been the commentator.

He felt a guilt for having listened, which was like the guilt he felt at other times for never being the one in action. He was always accompanying someone to a marriage, not his own, to a hospital, to a burial, to a celebration in which he played no part but that of the accompanist.

He was allowing them all to live for him, and then articulating a judgment. He was allowing Jay to paint for him, and then he was the one to write ironic articles on his exhibits. He was allowing Sabina to devastate others with her passion, and smiling at those who were consumed or rejected. Now at this moment he was ashamed not to be the one consumed or rejected. He allowed Djuna to speak, Michael to face the tragic

224

consequences of his deviations in love. He was allowing others to cry, to complain, to die.

And all he did was to speak across a protective wall, to knock with anger and say: you are right, and you are wrong.

Rendered uneasy by these meditations, he dressed himself and decided to go to the café.

He was called Uncle Philip by everyone, even by those who were not related to him.

He had the solicitous walk of an undertaker, the unctuous voice of a floorwalker.

His hands were always gloved, his heels properly resoled, his umbrella sheathed.

It was impossible to imagine him having been a child, or even an adolescent. It was admitted he possessed no photographs of that period, and that he had the taste never to talk about this obviously nonexistent facet of his personality. He had been born gray-haired, slender and genteel.

Attired in the most neutral suit, with the manners of someone about to announce a bereavement, Uncle Philip nevertheless did not fulfill such threats and was merely content to register and report minutely on the activity of the large, colorful, international family to which he was related.

No one could mention a country where Uncle Philip did not have a relative who . . .

No one could mention any world, social, political, artistic, financial, political, in which Uncle Philip did not possess a relative who . . .

No one ever thought of inquiring into his own vocation. One accepted him as a witness.

By an act of polite prestidigitation and punctuality, Uncle Philip managed to attend a ceremony in India where one of

225

the members of the family was decorated for high bravery. He could give all the details of the function with a precision of colors resembling scenes from the *National Geographic Magazine*.

And a few days later he was equally present at the wedding of another member in Belgium, from which he brought back observations on the tenacious smell of Catholic incense.

A few days later he was present as godfather of a newborn child in Hungary and then proceeded to attend in Paris the first concert of importance given by still another relative.

Amiable and courteous as he shared in the backstage celebrations, he remained immune to the contagion of colors, gaiety and fame. His grayness took no glow from the success, flowers, and handshakes. His pride in the event was historical, and shed no light on his private life.

He was the witness.

He felt neither honored nor disgraced (he also attended death by electric chair of a lesser member).

He appeared almost out of nowhere, as a family spirit must, and immediately after the ceremony, after he partook of the wine, food, rice, sermon or verdict, he vanished as he had come and no one remembered him.

He who had traveled a thousand miles to sustain this family tree, to solder the spreading and dissipated family unity, was instantly forgotten.

Of course it was simple enough to follow the careers of the more official members of the family, those who practiced orthodox marriages and divorces, or such classical habits as first nights, presentations at the Court of England, decorations from the Academie Francaise. All this was announced in the papers and all Uncle Philip had to do was to read the columns carefully every morning.

But his devotion to the family did not limit itself to obvious attendance upon the obvious incidents of the family tree. He was not content with appearing at cemeteries, churches, private homes, sanatoriums, hospitals.

He pursued with equal flair and accuracy the more mysterious developments. When one relative entered upon an irregular union Uncle Philip was the first to call, assuming that all was perfectly in order and insisting on all the amenities.

The true mystery lay in the contradiction that the brilliance of these happenings (for even the performance at the electric chair was not without its uniqueness, the electric power failing to achieve its duty) never imparted any radiation to Uncle Philip; that while he moved in a profusion of family-tree blossoms, yet each year he became a little more faded, a little more automatic, a little more starched—like a wooden figure representing irreparable ennui.

His face remained unvaryingly gray, his suits frayed evenly, his soles thinned smoothly, his gloves wore out not finger by finger but all at once, as they should.

He remained alert to his duties, however. His genius for detecting step by step the most wayward activities led him to his most brilliant feat of all.

One relative having wanted to travel across the Atlantic with a companion who was not her husband, deceived all her friends as to the date of her sailing and boarded a ship leaving a day earlier.

As she walked up and down the deck with her compromising escort, thinking regretfully of the flowers, fruit and books which would be delivered elsewhere and lost to her, she encountered Uncle Philip holding a small bouquet and saying in an appropriate voice: *"Bon voyage!* Give my regards to the family when you get to America!"

The only surprising fact was that Uncle Philip failed to greet them at their arrival on the other side.

"Am I aging?" asked Uncle Philip of himself as he awakened, picked up the newspaper at his door, the breakfast tray, and went back to his bed.

He was losing his interest in genealogical trees.

He thought of the café and of all the people he had seen there, watched, listened to. From their talk they seemed to have been born without parents, without relatives. They had all run away, forgotten, or separated from the past. None of them acknowledged parents, or even nationalities.

When he questioned them they were irritated with him, or fled from him.

He thought they were rootless, and yet he felt they were bound to each other, and related to each other as if they had founded new ties, a new kind of family, a new country.

He was the lonely one, he the *esprit de famille*.

The sap that ran through the family tree had not bloomed in him as the sap that ran through these people as they sat together.

He wanted to get up and dress and sit with them. He remembered a painting he had seen in a book of mythology. All in coral and gold, a vast tree, and sitting at each tip of a branch, a mythological personage, man, woman, child, priest or poet, scribe, lyre player, dancer, goddess, god, all sitting in the same tree with a mysterious complacency of unity.

When Donald had been ejected from his apartment because he had not been able to pay his rent, all of them had come in the night and formed a chain and helped him to move his belongings out of the window, and the only danger had been one of discovery due to their irrepressible laughter.

When Jay sold a painting he came to the café to celebrate and that night everyone ate abundantly.

When Lillian gave a concert they all went together forming a compact block of sympathy with effusive applause.

When Stella was invited by some titled person or other to stay at a mansion in the south of France, she invited them all.

When the ballet master fell ill with asthma and could no longer teach dancing, he was fed by all of them.

There was another kind of family, and Uncle Philip wished he could discover the secret of their genealogy.

With this curiosity he dressed and went off to the café.

228

Michael liked to awaken first and look upon the face of Donald asleep on the pillows, as if he could extract from the reality of Donald's face asleep on a pillow within reach of his hand, a certitude which might quiet his anxiety, a certitude which, once awake, Donald would proceed to destroy gradually all through the day and evening.

At no time when he was awake could Donald dispense the word Michael needed, dispense the glance, the smallest act to prove his love.

Michael's feelings at that moment exactly resembled Lillian's feelings in regard to Jay.

Like Lillian he longed for some trivial gift that would prove Donald had wanted to make him a gift. Like Lillian he longed for a word he could enclose within his being that would place him at the center. Like Lillian he longed for some moment of passionate intensity that would be like those vast fires in the iron factory from which the iron emerged incandescent, welded, complete.

He had to be content with Donald asleep upon his pillow.

With Donald's presence.

But no sooner would his eyes open than Donald would proceed to weave a world as inaccessible to Michael as the protean, fluid world of Jay became inaccessible to Lillian.

This weaving began always with Donald's little songs of nonsense with which he established the mood of the day on a pitch too light for Michael to seize, and which he sang not to please himself, but with a note of defiance, of provocation to Michael:

> Nothing is lost but it changes
> into the new string old string
> into the new bag old bag . . .

"Michael," said Donald, "today I would like to go to the zoo and see the new weasel who cried so desperately when she was left alone."

Michael thought: "How human of him to feel sympathy for the weasel crying in solitude in its cage." And Donald's

229

sympathy for the weasel encouraged him to say tenderly: "Would you cry like that if you were left alone?"

"Not at all," said Donald, "I wouldn't mind at all. I like to be alone."

"You wouldn't mind if I left you?"

Donald shrugged his shoulders and sang:

> in the new pan old tin
> in the new shoe old leather
> in the new silk old hair
> in the new hat old straw . . .

"Anyhow," said Donald, "what I like best in the zoo is not the weasel, it's the rhinoceros with his wonderful tough hide." Michael felt inexplicably angry that Donald should like the rhinoceros and not the weasel. That he should admire the toughness of the rhinoceros skin, as if he were betraying him, expressing the wish that Michael should be less vulnerable.

How how how could Michael achieve invulnerability when every gesture Donald made was in a different rhythm from his own, when he remained uncapturable even at the moments when he gave himself.

Donald was singing:

> in the new man the child
> and the new not new
> the new not new
> the new not new

Then he sat down to write a letter and the way he wrote his letter was so much in the manner of a schoolboy, with the attentiveness born of awkwardness, an unfamiliarity with concentration, an impatience to have the task over and done with that the little phrase in his song which Michael had not allowed to become audible to his heart now became louder and more ominous: in the new man the child.

As Donald sat biting the tip of his pen, Michael could see him preparing to trip, skip, prance, laugh, but always within a circle in which he admitted no partner.

To avoid the assertion of a difference which would be emphasized in a visit to the zoo, Michael tempted Donald with a visit to the Flea Market, knowing this to be one of Donald's favorite rambles.

There, exposed in the street, on the sidewalk, lay all the objects the imagination could produce and summon.

All the objects of the world with the added patina of having been possessed already, loved and hated, worn and discarded.

But there, as Michael moved and searched deliberately he discovered a rare book on astronomy, and Donald found the mechanism of a music box without the box, just a skeleton of fine wires that played delicately in the palm of his hand. Donald placed it to his ear to listen and then said: "Michael, buy me this music box. I love it."

In the open air it was scarcely audible, but Donald did not offer it to Michael's ear, as if he were listening to a music not made for him.

Michael bought it for him as one buys a toy for a child, a toy one is not expected to share. And for himself he bought the book on astronomy which Donald did not even glance at.

Donald walked with the music box playing inside of his pocket, and then he wanted reindeer horns, and he wanted a Louis Fifteenth costume, and he wanted an opium pipe.

Michael studied old prints, and all his gestures were slow and lagging with a kind of sadness which Donald refused to see, which was meant to say: "Take me by the hand and let me share your games."

Could he not see, in Michael's bearing, a child imprisoned wishing to keep pace with Donald, wishing to keep pace with his prancing, wishing to hear the music of the music box?

Finally they came upon the balloon woman, holding a floating· bouquet of emerald-green balloons, and Donald wanted them all.

"All?" said Michael in dismay.

"Maybe they will carry me up in the air. I'm so much lighter than the old woman," said Donald.

But when he had taken the entire bunch from the woman,

and held them and was not lifted off the ground as he expected, he let them fly off and watched their ascension with delight, as if part of himself were attached to them and were now swinging in space.

Now it seemed to Michael that this divorce which happened every day would stretch intolerably during the rest of their time together, and he was wishing for the night, for darkness.

A blind couple passed them, leaning on each other. Michael envied them. (How I envy the blind who can love in the dark. Never to see the eye of the lover without reflection or remembrance. Black moment of desire knowing nothing of the being one is holding but the fiery point in darkness at which they could touch and spark. Blind lovers throwing themselves in the void of desire lying together for a night without dawn. Never to see the day upon the body that was taken. Could love go further in the darkness? Further and deeper without awakening to the sorrows of lucidity? Touch only warm flesh and listen only to the warmth of a voice!)

There was no darkness dark enough to prevent Michael from seeing the eyes of the lover turning away, empty of remembrance, never dark enough not to see the death of a love, the defect of a love, the end of the night of desire.

No love blind enough for him to escape the sorrows of lucidity.

"And now," said Donald, his arms full of presents, "let's go to the café."

Elbows touching, toes overlapping, breaths mingling, they sat in circles in the café while the passers-by flowed down the boulevard, the flower vendors plied their bouquets, the newsboys sang their street songs, and the evening achieved the marriage of day and night called twilight.

An organ grinder was playing at the corner like a fountain of mechanical birds singing wildly Carmen's provocations in this artificial paradise of etiolated trees, while the monkey rattled his chains and the pennies fell in the tin cup.

They sat rotating around each other like nearsighted planets, they sat mutating, exchanging personalities.

Jay seemed the one nearest to the earth, for there was the dew of pleasure upon his lips, there was this roseate bloom of content on his cheeks because he was nearest to the earth. He could possess the world physically whenever he wished, he could bite into it, eat it, digest it without difficulty. He had an ample appetite, he was not discriminating, he had a good digestion. So his face shone with the solid colors of Dutch paintings, with the blood tones of a well-nourished man, in a world never far from his teeth, never made invisible or insubstantial, for he carried no inner chamber in which the present scene must repeat itself for the commentator.

He carried no inner chamber in which this scene must be stored in order to be possessed. He carried no echo and no retentions. No snail roof around his body, no veils, no insulators.

His entrances and exits were as fluid, mobile, facile, as his drinking and its consequences. For him there was no sense of space between human beings, no distance to traverse, no obstacles to overcome to reach one another, no effort to make.

Because of his confidence in the natural movements of the planets, a pattern all arranged beforehand by some humorous astrologer, he always showed a smiling face in this lantern slide of life in Paris, and felt no strings of bondage, of restraint, and no tightrope walking as the others did.

From the first moment when he had cut utterly the umbilical cord between himself and his mother by running away from home at the age of fourteen and never once returning, he had known this absence of spools, lassos, webs, safety nets. He had eluded them all.

Thus in the sky of the café tables rotating, the others circled around him to drink of his gaiety, hoping to catch his secret formula.

Was it because he had accepted that such an indifference to effort led men to the edge of the river, to sleep under bridges, was it because he had decided that he did not mind sleeping under bridges, drinking from the fountain, smoking cigarette butts, eating soup from the soup line of the Hospital de la Santé?

Was this his secret? To relinquish, to dispossess one's self of all wishes, to renounce, to be attached to no one, to hold no dream, to live in a state of anarchy?

Actually he never reached the last stage. He always met someone who assumed the responsibility of his existence.

But he could sense whoever unwound from the center of a spool and rewound himself back into it again at night, or the one who sought to lasso the loved one into an indissoluble spiral, or the one who flung himself from heights intent on catching the swing midway and fearful of a fatal slip into abysms.

This always incited him to grasp giant scissors and cut through all the patterns.

He began to open people before the café table as he opened bottles, not delicately, not gradually, but uncorking them, hurling direct questions at them like javelins, assaulting them with naked curiosity.

A secret, an evasion, a shrinking, drove him to repeat his thrusts like one hard of hearing: what did you say?

No secrets! No mystifications allowed! Spill open! Give yourself publicly like those fanatics who confess to the community.

He hated withdrawals, shells, veils. They aroused the barbarian in him, the violator of cities, the sacker and invader.

Dive from any place whatever!

But dive!

With large savage scissors he cut off all the moorings. Cut off responsibilities, families, shelters. He sent every one of

234

them towards the open sea, into chaos, into poverty, into solitude, into storms.

At first they bounced safely on the buoyant mattress of his enthusiasms. Jay became gayer and gayer as his timid passengers embarked on unfamiliar and tumultous seas.

Some felt relieved to have been violated. There was no other way to open their beings. They were glad to have been done violence to as secrets have a way of corroding their containers. Others felt ravaged like invaded countries, felt hopelessly exhibited and ashamed of this lesser aspect of themselves.

As soon as Jay had emptied the person, and the bottle, of all it contained, down to the sediments, he was satiated.

Come, said Jay, display the worst in yourself. To laugh it is necessary to present a charade of our diminished states. To face the natural man, and the charm of his defects. Come, said Jay, let us share our flaws together. I do not believe in heroes. I believe in the natural man.

(I now know the secret of Jay's well-being, thought Lillian. *He does not care.* That is his secret. He does not care! And I shall never learn this from him. I will never be able to feel as he does. I must run away from him. I will return to New York.)

And at this thought, the cord she had imagined tying her and Jay together for eternity, the cord of marriage, taut with incertitude, worn with anxiety, snapped, and she felt unmoored.

While he unmoored others, by cutting through the knots of responsibilities, he had inadvertently cut the binding, choking cord between them. From the moment she decided to sail away from him she felt elated.

All these tangled cords, from the first to the last, from the mother to the husband, to the children, and to Jay, all dissolved at once, and Jay was surprised to hear Lillian laugh in a different tone, for most times her laughter had a rusty quality which brought it closer to a sob, as if she had never determined which she intended to do.

At the same hour at the tip of the Observatory astronomers were tabulating mileage between planets, and just as Djuna had learned to measure such mileage by the oscillations of her heart (he is warm and near, he is remote and cool) from her first experience with Michael, past master in the art of creating distance between human beings, Michael himself arrived with Donald and she could see instantly that he was suffering from his full awareness of the impenetrable distance between himself and Donald, between himself and the world of adolescence he wanted to remain in forever and from which his lack of playfulness and recklessness barred him.

As soon as Michael saw Djuna's eyes he had the feeling of being restored to visibility, as if by gazing into the clear mirrors of her compassion he were reincarnated, for the relentless work accomplished by Donald's exclusion of him from his boyish world deprived him of his very existence.

Djuna needed only to say: Hello, Michael! for him to feel he was no longer a kindly protective ghost necessary to Donald's existence. For Djuna saw him handsome, gifted in astronomy and mathematics, rich with many knowledges, eloquent when properly warmed.

Hello, Michael! Djuna said, and the 1000000000000000 00000000000 miles between himself and human beings became like a small pencil addition on a note paper and not a state of being. They were laid aside like a student's abstractions, and now he was sitting in a café and Donald at his right was merely a very beautiful boy of which there were so many, cut out like a clay pigeon at the fair, with only a façade, and that is what Djuna had called him from the very beginning (the first time she had said it he had been angry and brooded on the insufferable jealousy of woman). Hello, Michael! How is your clay pigeon today?

Such fine threads passed between Michael and Djuna. He could always seize the intermediary color of her mood. That was his charm, his quality, this fine incision from his knowledge of woman, this capacity for dealing in essences.

This love without possibility of incarnation which took place between Djuna and all the descendants of Michael, the lineage

236

of these carriers of subtleties known only to men of his race.

They had found a territory which existed beyond sensual countries, and by a communion of swift words could charm each other actively in spite of the knowledge that this enchantment would have no ordinary culmination.

"Djuna," said Michael, "I see all your thoughts running in all directions, like minnows."

Then immediately he knew this in her was a symptom of anxiety, and he avoided the question which would have wounded her: "Has Paul's father sent him to India?"

For in the way she sat there he knew she was awaiting a mortal blow.

At this moment there appeared on the marble-topped tables the stains of drink, the sediments and dregs of false beatitudes.

At this moment the organ grinder changed his tune, and ceased to shower the profligacies of *Carmen*.

The laughter of Pagliacci bleached by city fumes, wailed like a loon out of the organ, so that the monkey cornered by a joviality which had neither a sound of man or monkey rattled his chains in greater desperation and saluted with his red Turkish hat every stranger who might deliver him from this loud-speaker tree to which he had been tied.

He danced a pleading dance to be delivered from this tree from which the twisting of a handle brought forth black birds of corrugated melodies.

But as the pennies fell he remembered his responsibilities, his prayer for silent trees vanished from his eyes as he attempted a gesture of gratitude with his red Turkish hat.

Djuna walked back again into her labyrinthian cities of the interior.

Where music bears no titles flowing like a subterranean

237

river carrying all the moods, sensations and impressions into dissolutions forming and reforming a world in terms of flow ...

where houses wear but façades exposed to easy entrances and exits

where streets do not bear a name because they are the streets of secret sorrows

where the birds who sing are the birds of peace, the birds of paradise, the colored birds of desire which appear in our dreams

there are those who feared to be lost in this voyage without compass, barometers, steering wheel or encyclopedias

but Djuna knew that at this surrender of the self began a sinking into deeper layers of awareness deeper and deeper starting at the topsoil of gaiety and descending through the geological stairways carrying only the delicate weighing machine of the heart to weigh the imponderable

through these streets of secret sorrows in which the music was anonymous and people lost their identities to better be carried and swept back and forth through the years to find only the points of ecstasy ...

registering only the dates and titles of emotion which alone enter the flesh and lodge themselves against the flux and loss of memory

that only the important dates of deep feeling may recur again and again each time anew through the wells, fountains and rivers of music. ...